RISE
OF THE
ELITES

REIGN OF THE WHITE PHOENIX

USA TODAY BESTSELLING AUTHOR
JESSICA CAGE

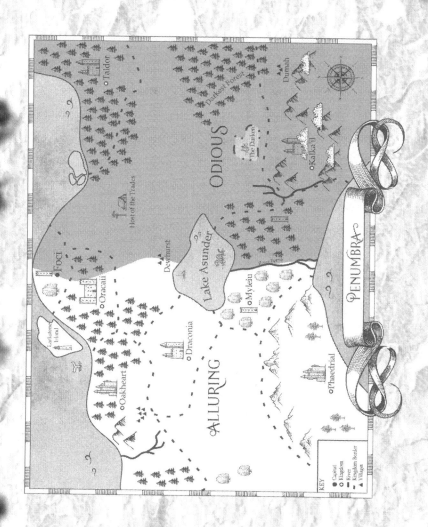

Reign of the White Phoenix

Copyright © 2021 by Jessica Cage

Publisher: Caged Fantasies Publications, LLC

Formatted by: Jennifer Laslie

ISBN: 978-1-7364885-1-5

ACKNOWLEDGEMENTS

I'd like to thank the authors who joined me on this journey. It's been an exciting ride and I'm looking forward to doing this again.

Also, Jeremy for being my sounding board and an extremely thorough Beta Reader!

PROLOGUE

First, They Must Fall

THE SUN SET ON THE HORIZON AS THE SYLO BIRDS BEGAN their song. Everyone in Penumbra, a magical world parallel to the human realm, knew what that somber yet melodic tune meant. It was time for the leaders of Penumbra, known as the Elites, to gather at the temple Foci. This gathering marked the beginning of a new season and the long-anticipated shift in power.

In Penumbra, a realm filled with and protected by magic, only two seasons existed. The first season was the Rising, when the dark powers quieted, and the light blossomed. Light powers gave way to dark energy in the second season of Falling. The Elites' arrival set the stage for the time of the Rising.

Chosen by the High Spirit, the Elites were charged with keeping watch over the supernatural world and maintaining the balance between Light and Dark magic, both in their magical homeland and in the human realm. It gave each side it's time to rule with the constraint that neither would shift the balance too far in their favor while at power.

It's a delicate balance that often teetered, and if not for the meeting at Foci and the changing of seasons to keep matters in check, the opposing powers of Penumbra would have long ago gone to war and annihilated one another.

Inside the colosseum, structured from the earth itself, the Elites took their place. Those who pledged to the dark took to one side while the light took to the other. The Elites, along with their council and guards, settled in as the ceremony began. Typically, they would elect a member of each side to recount the season, noting anything of key importance before proceeding with the shift of power. This time was different. The Dark had tilted the hands of balance further than they should have during their rule, and the air was tense.

Just as the time came for the council to call their representatives, the hearts of every being in the room stopped. The twelve deathly chimes rang for the first time in over two hundred years. One chime for each of the Original Elites. And as the first one split the air, the room grew cold, and silence descended on all those present. It was the moment every elite dreaded. The chimes were the signal that an Elite's rule would end. Anxiously, they waited for the twelfth and final chime, and as the eerie proclamation finished its terrifying song, an altar appeared in the center of the room.

A hooded being emerged from the altar, cloaked in

shadows. The Prophet. She was the High Spirit's messenger and her arrival confirmed that one elite would never return home.

"Five. Five to fall, Five to rise, to right the wrong. Balance must be restored."

Whispers of shock spread through Foci. Five Elites would fall. This was the last call when their lives would end, and their life energy would return to the High Spirit. Every pair of eyes widened and darted around, wondering which of them it would be. Some fell to prayer, while others stood tall, accepting the fate that was to come.

Five chimes rang out and again they waited. The Prophet held her hand out, and a scroll appeared. She read the names of those who would fall.

The first to be called came from the side of the dark, the Shifter Elite, Cyrus Ostara. The six-foot-two blond-haired wolf shifter stood from his seat as his council members stared in disbelief. He turned to his guard, Thomas, and nodded. As he climbed down from his seat, Mae Ching, the female Jaguar shifter and council member, stood to watch him. Cyrus approached the Prophet and, as he did, he shifted to his wolf. He let out one last howl as his form vanished along with the sacred moonstone. The sound of his howl echoed throughout Foci for a moment longer.

The second called brought some relief to the dark, as it was a name from the light, the Orc Elite, Ryza the Black. This was not a punishment for their transgression, it was an equal playing field. Ryza was one of the largest Elites outside of the giants. Built for battle, he stood over

3

seven feet tall. Like those before him, he made no protest. He turned to his clan members, bowed, and headed for the Prophet.

On the side of the light, those he passed bowed their heads, a show of respect and gratitude for his service and his sacrifice. When he made it to the Prophet, the Orc stood tall, as it claimed his spirit, and his form vanished. A silver warrior's collar hung in the air. The blood-red knowledge stone at its core gleamed under the light. It disappeared like its master and would appear again on the neck of the chosen.

The third to be called was a name that brought pause. The Dark Elite was the Irin, Anael. Five Irin had attended the Foci, including Anael and his triplet brothers, Remiel and Zerachiel. Their cedar-colored skin, stark-white brows, and bare-chested armor made them imposing figures. Born in the second generation of Angel rulers, Anael was one of the longest standing Elites and the only one who hadn't appeared worried, until his name was called.

With a tightened jaw, the eight-foot-tall Irin stood, along with his brothers. Suddenly, two sets of crimson wings spread from within him, sparks of energy glittering as they moved. He took to the sky as if he would try to escape his fate, but a moment later he landed with a force so hard it cracked the floor of Foci. He turned, looking only at his people, as the crimson color faded from his wings and he, too, disappeared.

The fourth to be called was the Dragon Elite, Horace, once known as the devourer. He stood from his position on the side of the Light, turned to the other members of the House of the Blue Flame, and allowed his honey brown skin to partially shift to reveal the sea blue scales of his dragon. He plucked one scale from his arm and handed it to the council members.

This was his gift to she who would replace him. In a vibrant show, he turned to descend the steps of the colosseum while allowing his Blue Flame to dance across his skin. When he reached the altar, he shifted into the massive beauty that was his dragon, shot one blue streak of fire into the sky, and by the time the light had faded, the dragon was gone.

The sixth to be called was the Phoenix Elite, Paereon. The bird of fire sat perched on the highest level of the Foci looking down on his fellow Lights. When his name was called, his full lips lifted in a sad smile, and his mint green eyes glistened before shifting to a golden hue. Hanging around his neck was the Obsidian stone. Worn by each of the Phoenix Elites, it was a symbol of their strength.

Accepting his fate, Paereon removed the stone and handed it to Olise, his trusted guard. She would ensure its safe handling until the new Elite was chosen. Allowing his flamed wings to blaze once more, he glided from his perch to the Prophet's altar. Before his feet could touch the ground, the Phoenix turned to ash, never to rise again.

With no more names to call, the Prophet's scroll disappeared from her hands and the hollow voice spoke once more. "Five. Five have fallen, five will rise, to right the wrong. Balance must be restored."

CHAPTER 1

THEY SELL FANTASIES TO THE WEAK MINDED IN EXCHANGE for obedience.

I'd spent my entire life being a dutiful student at the Kai Temple. Sitting at the top of Pikes Peak at Sheep Mountain in Colorado, it was the safest place Zodiac could think of take me when it was time to flee our true home. Not only was it cloaked by ancient magic, very few people knew it existed.

When you're trying to hide someone who many people would seek to kill, great measures had to be taken. While Phaedrial, the home of the Phoenix people, stood proudly in Penumbra, the birthplace of magic, my handlers raised me far from it. So far that you had to cross realms to get to it. Penumbra wasn't just a place, it was a world and Kai Temple was in a parallel realm on Earth.

They carved the ancient structure directly into the mountain itself. It took the monks centuries to bring the temple to what it was. The architecture respected nature while allowing new life to blossom. Throughout the grounds were the markings of the magic of Penumbra, the symbols of balance and power meant the magic of that realm protected Kai Temple.

I spent my life there learning the histories of both Earth and Penumbra. As a wingless phoenix, I had no choice but to accept the temple as my home. I'd tried many times to escape, but the unforgiving mountain side and the magic of the temple made it impossible for me to leave. There was a silver lining, though.

Soon I would reach maturity, which meant freedom for this couped up bird. When a phoenix matured, not only did they get their wings, but they got to leave the nest. The moment I got mine, I planned to fly as far away as I could from my hidden home in the sky.

My fantasies of freedom had to be put on hold yet again because this day was like many before it. After morning lessons about the history of Phaedrial, they scheduled me for combat training. Six days out of seven, he made me to train. It was necessary that I learn to defend myself. Life outside of Kai Temple would leave me unprotected. I would need to take care of myself because my handlers wouldn't be there to do it.

Though my gear was bulky, my body was strong and ready to put in the work. You don't spend your entire life training with the best fighters in the world and come out of it without the strength to back up what you learned. I took my time getting dressed, exchanging the red and gold robes I wore to my morning lessons for black and white base gear. The material was thick enough to help cushion the blows I would undoubtable take.

As always, I looked in the mirror that stood in my bedroom's corner and gave myself a pep talk.

"You can do this." I said as I pulled my long auburn hair up into a tight bun. "There's only a few more training sessions. Then you'll get your wings and get to travel this realm and the next."

The hair tie I used snapped, and I cursed the air. It was hard enough getting the right kind. It would be nice if my thick hair would just behave. I looked closer at my hair as I tried once again to tame it and noticed another silver streak traveling up the back of my head.

"Dammit," I sighed. Wasn't it enough that those strange markings covered my body? Did they have to mess with my hair, too? How was I ever going to blend in with regular people?

Sure, I could say the intricate webbing of white spirals that covered me from head to toe, clashing with my brown skin, were a style choice, a tattoo if you will. Or I could walk around with makeup every day. But how was I to explain the streaks of white that even the best hair dye wouldn't cover?

I stood in the large training room with vaulted ceiling, and red walls trimmed in gold. Above my head, the clouds moved over the glass ceiling and cast their strange shadows on the floor. Poised for the next fight, I took a deep breath as the cool breeze moved around me. The combat space had one open wall, easier for a fire bird to come and go, though there weren't many who ever visited the temple.

Combat was a dance. It was muscle straining choreography learned in parts only strung together in a different sequence every time you did it. Learning the steps was easy, but too many fighters fell into comfort zones. The moment your dance became more routine than intuition was the moment you lost the battle.

One of the earliest lessons Zodiac taught me was to never be predictable. As we entered the second hour of our training for the day, I realized his own teachings had escaped him. Dressed in battle gear of his own, his movements were stiff and repetitive.

My dedicated trainer's mind was somewhere far from the combat space that sat at the back of Kai Temple. It was unlike Zodiac to become distracted during battle, but he might as well have been with the birds who flew through the clouds behind us.

As a cool breeze pushed through the room again, he lunged forward with his sword, repeating a move he'd done two times prior. This time, I was ready. I swung my weight and the weight of my armor out of the way just in time to avoid the hit.

Avoidance wasn't enough, though. I spun and within two steps was behind him. I slammed the palm of my hand into his back, just beneath his neck. He stumbled forward from the force before recovering his balance. When he turned to face me, sword limp at his side, the tip of my own blade pressed into his chest and he froze.

"Very good," Zodiac pulled the helmet from his head and that aged smile stretched across his face. "You've come a long way, Elsfaer." He stepped back from the tip of my sword and wipe the sweat from his brow with the towel that hung from his belt.

"Just imagine how good I'd be if my armor wasn't two sizes too big." I tugged at the ill-fitting chest plate that hung from my body like an old housecoat. "You might get a run for your money."

I couldn't count the number of times he'd wiped the floor with me. Each time I had to stand, dust off my bruises and pretend like it didn't hurt my entire soul. It felt good for once to not be the one licking my wounds.

"Yes, I know, and as I've told you every day for the past month, it is in route." He shook his head.

"How could they make a mistake with the fitting?" I dropped my sword and headed to the sideline where the cool offering of water waited. "They only made me stand there for thirty-seven hours while they took countless measurements! I thought these people were the best in their field!"

"The material is very finicky. One false placement of a stitch and it would throw off the entire product," Zodiac spoke about the armor he'd commissioned with more pride than he had the tales of his own days in battle.

A former Elitesman, the guards that protected the Phoenix Elite, he'd proven himself worthy to the Grand Court, where they awarded him the Silver Flame. It was the highest honor any Elitesman could receive. Not long after being honored, he retired from the field and traded a life on the battlefield for a life at Kai Temple, caring for me.

Often I looked at him, this man who stood over six feet tall with the build of a warrior, and wondered why he left it all behind. I also wondered why he didn't have anyone in his life outside of the people he ordered around. He was handsome, with dark brown skin, silver hair, and a goatee. Zodiac could have any eligible phoenix woman he wanted, and yet he lived his life like a monk.

"Right, special material." I shrugged. "I'd be happy with anything that fit!"

"Yes, designed to be lightweight and allow you fluidity of your movement. You're agile on your own, and your armor shouldn't take away from that." He explained yet again why the suit he designed was so specific.

"You mean how this old clunker does?" I pounded my fist against my chest and winked.

"Hey, you still beat me in that old clunker." He laughed, grabbed the collar of my armor, and shook me around like a rag doll.

"Hey! Let go!" I smacked his hand away. "I barely beat you, and only because your head wasn't in the fight, which is unlike you."

Free from his hold, I grabbed a cup of water and took a long sip as I watched him do anything to avoid my comment. When it was clear he wouldn't address what I said, I poked the bear a little more.

"What's got your mind so preoccupied, Zodiac?"

"Nothing, I'm not sure what you mean?" Zodiac was skilled in many areas, but I could always tell when he kept something from me.

"There is no way you would make such an amateur move. You stepped right into my sword." I lifted my weapon again and pointed it at his chest. "Any other time, you would have continued through the fall and countered my attack."

"Very observant of you to notice that." He nodded with a small grin that wrinkled the corners of his mouth.

"Complimenting me won't stop my questioning you."

"I can't imagine it would." He picked up the second glass to sip the water. "You never were one to give up on something you were sure of."

"So, are you going to tell me?" I took another sip of water and waited.

"I suppose I will, of course, when the time is right." He winked over the glass as he took another long sip.

"Let me guess… the time isn't right?" I rolled my eyes. I don't know why I expected anything else from him.

"No, not quite." He laughed. "Patience, Elsfaer."

"Of course not." I finished my drink and unstrapped the bulky armor. Because it was so big, I needed to wear three additional layers of clothing beneath to keep it from falling off my body. It was like fighting while wrapped in a sauna bag. I'd melt down to nothing and by the time my custom suit arrived, they would have to do the fitting all over again.

"What are you doing?" Zodiac frowned as he watched me struggle with one of the buckles.

"Taking this thing off." I huffed as I fought with the left shoulder strap, which always jammed. "I'm burning up in this thing."

"We're not done here." He put down his glass. "Again."

"Fine!" That's what I got for calling out his lie.

Zodiac tacked on another brutal hour of training on what they scheduled to be my short day.

It was hard enough trying to keep up with Zodiac, my guardian and resident ass kicker. But now he wanted me to train in bulky, ill-fitting armor. Why? Because though the custom gear was delayed by over a month and there was no way Zodiac would let me get off the training plan.

So, for the next twenty-seven days, I had to battle the man nearly twice my size in armor that slowed me down. No, I couldn't just wear the same stuff I'd been wearing for years prior. He thought the challenge would be good for me. Something about how it would push me to adapt. Yeah, whatever.

I went into the next sparring with far too much confidence. And why wouldn't I? I had just beat him. Unfortunately, I'd also told him why I beat him, which meant I prepared him for his own victory. Zodiac was sharp. He countered every attack, and any offense he launched blindsided me.

Duck, sidestep, swing the arm, make contact. Dodge the sword and hope like hell that my hair, which had fallen out of the tie, and now hung expose out the back of my helmet, didn't get chopped off. Steady breathing, focus my fire, dip and kick. As I tried to keep the battle gear from sliding from my waist, the stubborn left strap decided it was ready to release. I missed the gut shot he tossed, and it landed hard. I fell to the ground, clutching my side.

"You must stay focused, Elsfaer!" he barked at me. The peaceful exchange we'd just had was forgotten.

"I'm trying!" I coughed as I climbed back to my feet. "It's difficult to do that with armor meant for someone twice as wide and with the ass of a horse! How do you expect me to function in this for the next month?"

"Like I've said before," he started with an almost evil grin, "training with this armor will be good for you."

"How is having my armor slow me down good for me?" I barked, struggling to get up from the ground.

"It forces you to think and act in a way that is unnatural for you. If you want to win, you'll have to get creative and learn everything about your opponent. Just as you did before." He pointed out my previous win. "You realized something distracted me, noted a weakness, and took advantage of it. The armor acts as a handicap, so you're going to put a lot more effort in to claim a victory."

"It's official. You've lost your mind." I threw the sparring sword to the ground. "You're insane."

"I am concerned for you." He pointed to the discarded weapon and waited for me to retrieve it. "A change is coming soon. You know that. Things are going to be different."

"You keep saying that but have yet to explain what these supposed differences are." I picked up the sword and wipe the blade against my pants leg. "Change is constant Zodiac, nothing to be worried about."

"This is something I cannot speak about." Zodiac avoided.

"Because you don't know what it is," I challenged him as I struggled to unstrap the heavy armor that hung from my shoulders.

"If that is what you wish to believe."

"Then what is it? Because I'm tired of the secrecy. And if I'm honest, I'm not sure I believe much of what you have to say anymore." The sound of the armor falling to the ground echoed in the training space. "I'm thinking that you and everyone else here came up with this conspiracy to keep me in check."

"Keep you in check, huh?" he chuckled as if my theory was so convoluted it deserved to be mocked. "Conspiracy."

"Yes, as long as I believe in this thing, that you won't explain to me, I won't be bold enough to venture off without your permission." I pointed to the opening that led outside, as if I could fly right out of it if I wanted to. "It's how you all keep me under your thumb. Well, at least until I'm old enough to bust out of here, regardless of what you all have to say about it."

"That's right, you will come of age soon." he nodded with a somber expression.

"And when I do," I continued, unfazed by his mood change. "When my wings light up and carry me out of here, there will be nothing any of you can do about it."

"That reminds me, there is something we need to discuss." Zodiac sighed. "I've wanted to tell you for a while, but it was never the right time."

"Are you going to tell me you found out my armor is coming sooner?" I joked because that's what I did whenever I felt uncomfortable and the way Zodiac looked made my stomach seize.

"No, not that. It's about your wings."

"What about them?" I frowned. How could Zodiac have anything to tell me about my wings? I didn't even have them yet. What could he know that I didn't?

"You need to prepare yourself in case they don't meet your expectations."

"Lose the mystery talk and just tell me what you mean, please." I wasn't in the mood to solve any riddles. Especially when it was about my wings.

"Elsfaer, you know you're special. That is no secret. It's why we raised you here at Kai Temple, by yourself, your entire life."

"I do." I removed the glove from my hand to reveal my flesh. Though my skin tone was an even shade of tawny brown, there was still that special quality I was born with. Primeval tattoos of light etched into my skin. The markings stretched across my entire body, marking even my face.

"The markings on your body, they've spread each day since your birth and even more now that we are near your coming of age. I can only wonder what you must feel now. We've tested the energy that radiates from you, and it's like nothing we've ever seen before."

"Okay?" I hadn't considered how my life, the things I felt, differed from the other people in my life. Yes, I felt energy, power, but I was a phoenix nearing maturity and as far as I was told, that's what we all felt.

"That difference in you may be something that your wings reflect." Zodiac touched the spot on my back where my wings would one day break through. "We only suspect this, but like most things about you, we do not know how this will work."

"Will they work?" I looked over my shoulders as if the wings had appeared during our conversation.

"What do you mean?" He frowned. "Work?"

"Do you think my wings won't work?" I clarified. "Will I be able to use them? What if I won't be able to fly?"

"No, they should function just fine." He laughed, waving off the panic he inspired. "That's not what I meant."

"Okay," I shrugged, because that was all I cared about. "What's the issue?"

"They may not look the same as other phoenix wings. As if your markings aren't enough to make you stick out in a crowd, your wings will put a certain spotlight on you." He finally said the quiet part out loud. "They will make you stand out to the others and some people will see the differences as a bad thing. They will see your existence as something to be afraid of."

"Zodiac!" Kenya, a phoenix who'd already gained her wings, called as she ran into the training space.

She wore red robes that stood in bright comparison to her dark skin and flowed around her body as she moved. Her waist length braids, adorned with wooden beads, sounded an applause with every step she took.

"Yes?" he answered her. "Kenya, is everything alright?"

"It's happening," she said, out of breath as she pushed her long braids out of her face, revealing those almond eyes with light brown irises.

"What?" Zodiac stepped forward. "Are you sure?"

"The Prophet has arrived." She nodded. "At Foci."

"This is too soon." Zodiac looked at me with worried eyes, then back to Kenya. "When did this happen? How do we know for sure?"

"I cannot speak about the timing of events. I only report the arrival." She took a deep breath. "Jamila sent me here to find you. They need you in the council chambers."

"Take Elsfaer to her room, please." Zodiac grabbed my shoulder and pushed me towards my elected chaperone.

"What's going on?" I asked. "Since when do I need an escort to get to my room?"

"Its nothing, just a precaution." he paused. "On second thought, take her to the sanctuary. I'll meet you both there shortly."

"The Sanctuary? Precaution?" I turned to look him in the eye. "Be honest with me for once. What is going on, Zodiac?"

"I'll explain it later." He returned his sword to the waiting slot along the wall. "It won't be long."

Zodiac rushed out of the room and left me standing beside Kenya, who waited for me to snap out of my thoughts. What was I supposed to think? My guardian was clearly panicked about something, yet he wanted me to pretend everything was okay. Sure, he would tell me about it later, just like all the other secrets he kept from me.

"We must go," she urged.

"Yeah, yeah, that's fine." I put my sword away and kicked the chest plate that lay by my feet. "I'm coming."

CHAPTER 2

I CONSIDERED DOING WHAT I WAS TOLD. KENYA LED THE way down the hall from the combat room to the sanctuary, and I told myself to follow her. Going against Zodiac would be bad for me, yes, but experience taught me it would be worse for Kenya, who Zodiac would reprimand for letting me out of her sight. He had a way of misdirecting his anger when it came to me. Sometimes I wondered if he was afraid of what would happen if he lashed out at me.

Despite her being a mere four years older than me, she was in charge of my day-to-day life. With Zodiac's approval, Kenya dictated everything from when I ate breakfast to when I went to bed at night. Yes, she was just doing her job, but that didn't mean I couldn't hate her for it.

Besides, how could I just follow her without question, as if something major wasn't happening? From Zodiac's reaction to Kenya's news, it had something to do with me and I deserved to know about it. It was also unlike Kenya to give Zodiac any alarming news in front of me.

"You sure you can't tell me what Zodiac is upset about?" I asked her as we walked. "I can keep a secret."

"We both know that you cannot, and no, I can't tell you." Kenya gave me a side eye. "Zodiac will tell you what you need to know, when you need to know it."

"Right." I scoffed. "I'm sure I know everything I need to know. They're not keep any secrets from me. Everyone is one hundred percent honest with me."

"You can cut the sarcasm, Elsfaer." Kenya sighed as two monks dressed in brown robes approached, both carrying gold boxes in their hands. "Give me a minute. I need to speak with them."

I nodded and stepped aside. Of course, I didn't believe her. If something juicy ever happened, I found out about it long after it was over and typically after I felt I should have known. There were times my life had been in danger and no one told me. Zodiac made sure of it. I found out about it through eavesdropping.

This was the same, I could feel it. Easier to keep me in line without inciting panic over the unexpected arrival of a prophet. A prophet's appearance was a rare occurrence and usually meant a change in power. They were the messengers of the High Spirit, which meant that things were about to change in Penumbra.

It was rare that I heard anything current about the supernatural realm. I'd learned the history, because Zodiac felt it was important, but events that my textbooks hadn't already captured were unknown to me. That alone piqued my interest in Zodiac's secret.

Here I was with a prime opportunity and I had to take it. Whatever was going on, Zodiac would make sure they kept it from me. Hell, even when I called him out on being distracted in training, he dodged my questions, then scolded me about being clumsy in the gear he knew didn't fit me.

Kenya walked ahead of me with the monks, whispering more secrets. I slowly fell back, allowing them to get further ahead of me until the trio rounded the corner and was out of sight, which meant I could change course without being noticed. I headed straight for the council chambers. It wouldn't take her long to realize I wasn't behind her and she'd know exactly where I'd gone.

Kai Temple was a stone maze that I knew like the back of my hand. Spend over two decades in a place and you learn every shortcut there was to know. Lucky for me, Kenya hadn't spent her spare time researching the secret passages the monks had built into the structure.

A few minutes later, I was standing outside the chamber doors, struggling to hear what was being said within. The door was ajar, just enough that I could see the shadows of the people moving inside. Despite the risk of being caught, I pressed my ear against the opening and listened.

Zodiac's deep and familiar voice echoed as he addressed the room. "What does this mean?"

"This is not unexpected," Acai, the elder monk who'd taught me to play chess, spoke. Her voice was unmistakable. Aged with wisdom and tinged with boredom. "We've done the preparations and are ready."

"Are we? As I remember it, the predictions gave

another thirty years. We aren't ready," Zodiac disagreed with Acai. "She isn't ready!"

"And whose fault is that?" a voice of a man I didn't recognize questioned Zodiac. "You've had plenty of time to prepare the girl and yet you have her taking history lessons and playing around in clunky armor. As if she would ever need it."

"As I remember correctly, it was a collective decision to wait until after her maturity to introduce all this to her." Zodiac's response confirmed my own suspicions. They were talking about me. "Her training is important. Special or not, she needs to know her history, and she needs to defend herself."

"Well, we have about two hours to do it now," the unfamiliar voice snipped. "Anyone have a PowerPoint presentation cued up for the info dump?"

"Two hours?" Another woman whose voice I'd never heard before spoke. "Why do you say that?"

"The Prophet has arrived in penumbra," Jamila, Zodiac's second hand, joined the conversation. Her voice was powerful but soft and reminded me of the actress Angela Bassett. "We all know that a prophet's arrival during a meeting at Foci means one thing and one thing only. A new elite will be called to rise."

"We're getting ahead of ourselves," Acai spoke. "Just because the High Spirit may choose a new elite, doesn't mean it will be a phoenix."

"Right, because why else would she be moving into the next phase of her life at the exact moment that the High Spirit shakes things up? It all lines up too perfectly. The universe is petty and would never allow such a grand opportunity to pass by." The sarcastic male pointed out the timing of events.

"He's right." Jamila sounded defeated. "We need to be ready."

"I know," Zodiac's voice deflated. "I asked Kenya to take Elsfaer to the sanctuary, just in case." Zodiac slammed his fist into the table. "I can't believe this is happening. She is not ready to handle this. There is so much more we needed to do."

"Don't underestimate her, Zodiac," Acai offered him reassurance. "You've taught her well these years."

"True, but she should know so much more than she does." He spoke with regret. "We need to buy more time. Even if it's true."

"Hey, this is mostly speculation. We don't know exactly how any of this is going to work out," Jamila spoke again.

"Whatever happens, it's on my head. She entrusted me with her life," Zodiac's voice turned dark. "It was my job to prepare her for this possibility."

"Again, you've done a good job." Acai spoke as her feet shuffled across the floor. The woman once told me she was too old to lift her feet to walk. If the shuffling bothered anyone, they could suck a toad's eye. "This is a hurdle, an obstacle in the path that you will help her conquer."

"How do I even begin?" Zodiac asked, and a moment later, the room erupted with commentary I could no longer decipher.

"You could start by telling me the truth." I pushed the door open, and the room fell silent from the opinions of

23

those who thought they had the right to decide my life for me.

"Elsfaer, what are you doing here?" Zodiac's sorrowful eyes met my angry ones.

"Apparently learning that there is some big secret you've been keeping from me my entire life. Care to share that with me now?"

"I—" He started, but stopped when I held my hand up to his face.

I gathered my thoughts, and they watched me like a ticking time bomb. There, in a room with arched doorways and gold painted floors, sat my counsel. Men and women who I hoped wanted the best for me. I drew my eyes around the oval table that sat in the heart of the space and noted the papers laid out in front of each person.

"Spare me the excuses or the deflections." I looked around the room at faces that were both familiar and not. "So, these are the ones who decide for me? I can tell there is something major happening and you keeping it from me is no longer an option. I heard you speaking of the Elites and the Prophet, so just spill it already."

"Okay, you're right." Zodiac nodded as he stepped away from the table. "You deserve to know the truth."

"Yes, I do."

"The Prophet has arrived in Foci. As you know, this is the sign that a new elite will rise." He looked back over his shoulder at Acai, who nodded for him to continue. "We're concerned, for good reason, that it may be time for the rise of a new Phoenix Elite."

"Okay." I took a deep breath and when every set of

eyes in the chamber turned to me, a tight knot formed in my gut. "Wait, you think it's me?"

"Yes, it is the prophecy." Acai nodded slowly.

"What prophecy?" I looked at Zodiac because, despite his obvious omissions, he was the one I trusted. "What is she talking about?"

"The one born with the mark of the white flame will rise to the highest power," Acai recited and the skin beneath her chin shook, same as it always did when she spoke.

"White flame." I looked down at my bare arms covered in the white tattoos. "Are you talking about my markings?"

"Yea, they grow more prominent each day," Zodiac commented. "The closer you get to maturity, the more pronounced they become."

"This doesn't make any sense." I shook my head.

"This isn't news to you. You've had the markings your entire life," the unfamiliar man, who I could now see sported a scar just above his full lips, spoke. His golden eyes glistened, and I knew he wasn't human, like Acai.

"Yes, I know about the markings." I rolled my eyes. "They were supposed to only mean that I was special. I thought they were a mutation. No one ever said that this could mean that I would be the next elite!"

"Oh?" He shrugged, unconcerned with the mental breakdown I was on the verge of having. "It seems an obvious thing that you would be chosen for some monumental task. That goes with the supernatural territory girl."

"I mean, surely there are people who are much more

qualified for this position than I am." I looked at the faces of people who agreed with me but offered no alternative. "Why would the High Spirit choose someone who has yet to reach maturity to be the Elite? I don't even live in that world."

"And that's exactly why you've been chosen to lead it," Jamila answered the question that had stumped everyone else.

"Excuse me?" I stepped closer to where she sat. "How could that make me a better choice?"

"You're unbiased and have taken no sides in the internal struggles of our people. You can learn and make decisions that are best for the whole, not just for one part. That has been the issue our people have faced for quite some time." Jamila reported. "Each Elite has had their own selfish reasons for wanting the position and their own agendas to satisfy. That has caused a great divide among the Phoenix people."

"And you expect me to fix that?" I scoffed. "I'll remind you I'm a woman in her twenties. This is exactly the time of my life that I'm supposed to be selfish! My plan is the travel the world, flirt with men, and make new friends. Not lead a species of people who have no reason to believe in me besides some strange birthmarks on my body."

"Yes. That's exactly what we expect." Acai nodded. "It's the prophecy and your destiny."

"Okay, stop with the prophecy crap." I stomped across the room to Zodiac. "Why didn't you tell me any of this? Why didn't you prepare me? Aren't you the one always talking about not going into battle unprepared, and yet you intend to send me out into the world with a huge handicap?"

"Elsfaer," again I cut Zodiac off as I continued my rant.

"I know nothing about the world that you expect me to lead outside of the incomplete history in the books you've allowed me to read. Oh, and let's not forget the fact that has been drilled into my head. The phoenix people won't accept me because of how different I am."

"I thought this was best. Focus on getting you strong and once you were mature, you could learn about the rest." Zodiac squared his shoulders as he explained his decisioning. "I didn't want the pressure of this to serve as a distraction."

"How do you know it wouldn't have motivated me more?" I pointed at him and waited for him to answer, but he didn't. "Why did you not allow me to make that decision?"

"In hindsight, I see where my mistake was. I should have handled this differently." Zodiac sighed. "There is nothing I can do about that now."

"You should have, yes, but you didn't. And now I'm screwed." The room spun about as fast as my thoughts and I felt like I would fall over, but I stood there. I wouldn't walk away from this conversation. They could no longer decide my fate for me.

"Calm down, Elsfaer," Jamila spoke. "We don't know for sure that this is happening. At this point, this is all speculation. Nothing is saying that the current Phoenix Elite will fall or that the High Spirit will call on you to rise."

"Right, we're meeting solely as a precaution. I—" Zodiac stopped and stared at me. "Are you okay?"

"I'm fine, pissed, but I'm fine." I waved off his concern, but the floor waved beneath my feet and my vision blurred.

"No, I think something is wrong." Zodiac voice sounded deeper than usual.

"What?" I frowned because there was an unnatural echo in my ear. "What did you say?"

Jamila walked over to me and placed her hand on my forehead. "She's burning up," she said, looking back at Zodiac. "We need to get her to the sanctuary. Now!"

CHAPTER 3

"I'M SORRY! I DON'T KNOW HOW SHE GOT AWAY FROM ME!" Kenya panicked as they rushed my crumpled body into the sanctuary. She continued with more hushed apologies, but my increasing pain made it impossible for me to have any concern about her unnecessary remorse.

"Get her to the table." Acai pointed to the long stone table that sat at the head of the sanctuary. "We need to secure her before it begins."

"What?" They ushered me toward the table that had been the home for ceremonies of all sorts, but it looked different this time. The last time I saw it, it was a clean slate, but now there were familiar symbols of the Phoenix people etched into the surface.

I climbed onto the table with their help. "What is happening?"

"Paereon has fallen, Elsfaer." Zodiac grabbed my hand and peered into my eyes. "The time is now for the next Elite to rise."

"Me?" I looked around at all the people frantically working to prepare for what came next.

"Yes," he nodded.

"What if I'm not ready for this?" I question. "Hell, I know I'm not ready for this."

"Time to get ready," Jamila commented.

"We need to strap her down." Acai tossed the stack of leather straps to Jamila. "There isn't much time left."

"Strap me down?" Before I could get my question out, they were already grabbing my arms and legs and pulling me into position. I struggled against them but lost the fight as they secured the leather straps to the legs of the table. "Is this necessary?"

"Trust me," Acai answered, rubbing my forehead with a funky paste. "What you are about to experience is going to be intense. This is as much for our safety as it is for yours."

"It's real fucking hard to trust you right now," I snapped, and pulled my head away from her hand.

"I understand," she responded with forced calmness.

"How much time do we have?" Zodiac asked as she approached the table.

"A few minutes perhaps," Jamila answered.

"Elsfaer," Zodiac spoke to me. "I promise I will tell you everything as soon as this is over. I'm sorry."

Before I could tell him where to shove his apology, the glass ceiling above the sanctuary shattered. Sharp pieces of colored glass fell around us, and those who weren't strapped to a stone table like an open target ran for cover. With the shower of glass came a blinding, feverish light that poured into the space and wrapped around me.

At first, fear gripped my soul like the bindings of a prisoner. The touch of the light was like fire across my skin. After a few moments, it changed, or I did. It became more of an unyielding hug, like being tucked into the bed as a child. As soon as I calmed down, it shifted again. The hug became more of a vice grip that focused on my heart and mind.

Voices inside of my head that didn't belong to me rejoiced as a new fire spread across my body. Their celebration felt like mockery of the pain that gripped every part of me. My struggle against the straps was pointless as I tried to escape the burning in my chest and mind. The blood rushed in my ears as my heart pounded, fighting against the surge of power.

I cried out for help, but not one person who swore they would protect me answered my cry. My body seized beneath the grips of the light and my mind struggled to remain conscious. Through the shattered ceiling above me, I saw a shadowy figure looking down at me. No matter how hard I tried, I couldn't bring it into focus. As the figure descended, my mind lost its battle, and everything went dark.

Whenever my eyes closed to sleep, my subconscious would concoct vivid imaginings that left my heart and soul full. It was the coping mechanism for an orphaned child. This dream, this escape from reality, was nothing like that. My mind lingered in a dark void as my head filled with echoes of pain and confusion.

This void left me feeling disconnected from my body. I searched around the darkness, hoping to find some sign that I hadn't completely lost myself. Just when I'd given up on the hope of finding myself again, I felt something new. Echoing pulses of energy, and because it was the only thing that felt real, I moved towards it.

Soon I saw something, wrapped in light and bound at the arms and legs. It was me. My hair flowed around my head in loose auburn curls. I usually straightened my hair, so it'd been a while since I saw it in its natural state. My face looked fuller, and so did my hips. I'd always been straight up and down, but now it looked like I'd had a subtle BBL. The kind that doesn't make you look like an ant. Everything else was the same. It was still me.

I pushed my consciousness back toward my body. As I got closer, I realized I was not in control of the movement. There was a gravitational force that took the choice away. Like a vacuum, something pulled me into myself and I couldn't do anything to stop it.

Pain accompanied the reconnection to my physical self. Every agonizing spark was a new geographical mark on my body. The sharper the jolt, the closer it was to my brain. The numb nudges were my feet and ankles, while the sharp hits were my chest, neck, and shoulders.

When the experience is mental, when you're trapped inside your own mind, all you can do is wait for it to be over and beg for the ending to come. I knew I had no control. All I could do was hope that I'd survive whatever happened to me.

When the assault ended, it settled me in my body. My mind merged with my physical form and the breath that filled and exited my chest was real again. The suffocating effect lifted, and I waited for the rest of my body to connect, allowing me the use of my extremities. I wiggled my toes and fingers, checking for signs of trauma before opening my eyes.

My first breath was a deep, controlled intake of air. As my lungs filled, I conducted a mental survey of my body, checking for any pain points. It was what I did after a tough training. I asked myself where the pain was, and I expected the answer to be everywhere, but it was nowhere at all. With each consecutive pull of air, the tightness eased. After a few more moments of caution, I worked up the nerve to open my eyes.

When I did, the familiar environment brought relief. I wasn't still inside the sanctuary strapped to the cold table. Nor was I floating in a void, waiting for insanity. The sights and smells were home. When I breathed again, I recognized the light scent of rosemary that lingered in the air. I was safe.

I no longer wore the sweat soaked training gear. No doubt a service of Kenya. Zodiac wouldn't have done it, neither would he have allowed any of the others to. She dressed me in a nightgown she could never get me to wear because of how sheer the fabric was. It felt like one strong breeze would dissolve the damn thing.

I sat up in the bed and looked at my arms and legs. After taking a deep breath, I touched my stomach. I was okay, I'd survived. For a moment, I felt relaxed, then I remembered something. How I looked wrapped in the light. Was my body still different? My hair? Was there anything else that changed that I hadn't noticed before? The corner mirror beckoned me to come find out.

It was an unsettling thing to think about how I might not recognize my own reflection. After what I'd just experienced, the person who sat in my bed wasn't the one who'd woken up there the morning before. I'd existed in this body for twenty-five years before that moment, but I didn't know if I was the same person.

"Suck it up!" I mumbled to myself and climbed from the plush comfort. "Gotta do it eventually."

It was easier to start at the feet. So, I focused there. Feet the same, ankles, legs. Hips and ass were more defined, but definitely were not on the butt life level. Everything checked out. My markings were more prominent. Instead of shadowed etches, the branding was much deeper. This was something I'd been expecting with my maturity. Each year of my life, the markings became more prominent. When my eyes reached my chest, though, where the locket lay, I froze.

I couldn't force my eyes to climb further. I knew it would be a change. How could there not be? For a moment, I focused on the locket. The only thing I had of my mother. A small brass thing that no longer opened. Zodiac had given me the memento of the woman I never knew on my fifteenth birthday. I cried for three days afterwards.

She would want me to be strong. She'd want me to face whatever stood ahead of me. Including my own reflection. "Get it over with!" I huffed and looked up to find my face. "What the hell?"

The eyes reflected in the mirror weren't my own.

For a moment, they belonged to someone else. A stranger stared back at me, and she possessed a terrifying power. I shuddered and sweat formed on my forehead as my temperature rose. This woman had a hold on me and as much as I wanted to look away, she wouldn't allow it.

The voices returned. This time, their celebration came in a cacophony of noise. I covered my ears with my hands, hoping for it to stop, but it didn't. "Please, stop!" I screamed and finally found the strength to look away from my reflection.

Eyes tightly closed; I shook my head like a madwoman. It was the rhythmic tapping on the bedroom door that pulled me from my manic state. The familiar sound reconnected me to the version of myself I was afraid of losing. Over the years, it had become a secret code between us.

"Come in, Zodiac," I spoke through a tightened jaw as I still struggled to clear my head of the lingering voices.

"You're awake finally." He entered with an upbeat mood until he spotted me. "Oh god, are you okay? What's wrong? What happened?"

"My eyes, there's something wrong with my eyes." The moment I looked away from my reflection, my eyes slammed shut and I couldn't open them again. The harder I tried, the tighter the seal became.

"Open your eyes, Elsfaer." His hands gripped my wrists, and he tried pulling my hands from the side of my face. "I need to see."

"I can't." Tears fought to spill, but my eyes were too tightly closed. "It hurts."

"You have to," he spoke calmly. "Breathe, just relax, it's going to be alright. I'm here."

"I can't."

"You can do this. Focus on me, feel my breaths, let them guide your own." He inhaled deeply and slowly exhaled, repeating the action until I was following along.

Steady breaths were a struggle to accomplish. It only transferred the tightness of my eyes to my chest, but in time, listening to him and matching my breaths with his, the tension eased. Slowly, I opened my eyes to find his face in front of me, and the panic inside my head quieted.

"You're okay," Zodiac assured me, and he examined my face. "I see nothing wrong."

"What?" I stared at him. "But, my eyes, they were different."

"They look the same as they always have. Green with white flecks of light."

"How?" I turned to look at the mirror, again met with the reflection of my face, eyes now back to normal. "They were... different before."

"Are you sure you're okay? You were out for a while. That may have had an adverse effect on you." Zodiac stepped away from me.

"How long has it been?" I blinked slowly, staring deeper into my own reflection, expecting the change to happen again.

"You've been asleep for four days." He reported like it was no big deal.

"Days? What do you mean, four days?" I whipped around to see him again. "How is that possible?"

"The Rising is a painful experience, eons of knowledge

and power pool into your body all at once. The fire of the Elites who came before you battle the fire that already exists within you. It's why we had to strap you down during the rising. We had to contain you. Even with the restraints, you nearly burned down the temple."

"Oh, my god!" Images of the shattered glass ceiling flashed through my mind. "Is everyone okay? Did I hurt anyone?"

"Um," he hesitated, clearly keeping the information back.

"Who? Tell me."

"Kenya, she got too close to you. One of your restraints broke, and she tried to secure your leg." Zodiac recounted the events. "I told her to stand back, but she didn't listen. She got burned."

"What?" I headed for the door, but Zodiac stopped me. "Is she okay?"

"She is fine. Just a small scar, but she is healing."

"A scar? But she is a phoenix. How did I scar her?" A phoenix rarely bore scars from another's flame. An accidental injury shouldn't have left a scar. While Kenya was meek in her demeanor, she was a powerful phoenix with a strong flame of her own. It was why Zodiac trusted her with controlling my life.

"Yes, but Elsfaer, you need to understand, your flame is like nothing that we have ever seen before. It's a thing of myth. Now that you are the Elite, your flame is much more lethal. This has been our concern since you were a child. You are already unique because of the differences you were born with. That would no doubt affect your flame in maturity."

"So, I'm really the new Elite?" I returned to the mirror to review my reflection again. Maybe Zodiac couldn't see it, but I was different. Even with my eyes back to normal, I could see the change.

"I'm sure you can feel it, Elsfaer. That is the change you see in yourself. The High Spirit chose you to lead our people." His voice inflated with pride.

"Our people?" I laughed, abandoning my reflection again. "What the hell are you talking about? You want me to lead a group of people I've never even met? I know what, ten phoenixes and only three of you ever stick around for more than small talk."

A part of becoming a new elite must have been extreme mood swings, because I went from being concerned about the changes in my body and the people I might have harmed to being angered by the responsibility being thrust on me.

"I know this is a lot to take in."

"A lot?" I paced the floor. "You think this is a lot? Talk about a damn understatement. I've never even seen Penumbra. I've been nowhere near Phaedrial, the supposed home of the people you want me to lead. And now you expect me to go there and rule. And god forbid someone challenges me. How do I defend myself? Who would be on my side?"

"Elsfaer, you need to calm down." Zodiac lifted his palms to me.

"Excuse me?" The greater my anger became, the hotter I felt. "How dare you tell me to calm down! Would you be calm right now? Oh, wait, maybe you would be, because you know every damn thing they kept from me. All the secrets are yours. Secrets that you didn't think I was deserving or mature enough to know. My entire life, everything I had the audacity to plan for myself, just blew up in my face. So, until I know more than the mice that creep around your bedroom, don't tell me to calm down."

"I agree. You have every right to be upset right now." Zodiac spoke in an even tone. "I only say that because if you don't gather yourself, you'll burn this entire place down."

"What the hell are you talking about?"

He pointed to the mirror and once again I looked to find my reflection. Only this time, I had to step back to see what he saw.

Spread around me, like flames of the sun were my wings! My initial reaction was pure elation. This was a moment a young phoenix waited their entire life for. Then it hit me. My flame was different. Every phoenix's flame was red or blue, with the blue being the rarer showing. Mine were neither.

My wings, the beautiful things that sprouted from my back, the connection to my soul, were white. White flames moved with every breath I took. Not only that, but the markings on my body glowed with fiery energy and spiraling flames danced up and down my arms.

"Zodiac." I spoke his name, but continued to examine my reflection.

"Yes?" he answered.

"What is this?" I turned slightly to see him. "Why are they... white? And why aren't the flames isolated to my wings? Have you ever seen anything like this before?"

"Elsfaer, just breathe."

"I am," I shook my head. "I'm breathing fine."

"No, you aren't. Take deep breaths to center yourself. Calm your spirit and your wings will retract."

My mind was racing, but I didn't want to harm anyone else, especially not Zodiac. Of course, I was still angry with him. I didn't understand his decision to keep so many secrets from me, but I knew in my heart that he was only doing what he thought was best for me. It took seven deep breaths to calm my mind and another two before the white flames cooled and, with a final breath, my wings retracted.

"There, that was easy." He said proudly. "How do you feel?"

"Yeah, sure. I'm fine." I turned my back to the mirror and looked over my shoulder to see the burn marks on the nightgown I wore. "Red or blue, that's what all the books say. That's what I've always been told. Every phoenix's wings are red or blue. I have to admit I hoped for blue, to be one of the rare birds, but white? Nothing I ever read said white was an option."

"That's because it never was, at least not until you." he answered and took a seat in the chair next to my desk. "Like I said before, tales of the white phoenix were only myths and legends. Until you were born, we put little stock in it."

"Me?" I sighed. "Why me?"

"Yes, Elsfaer, you are different. You're powerful. You know that. It's why I brought you to the temple and raised you away from the others. We had to keep you safe."

"And now I have to go there," I sighed. "Suddenly, my safety is of no concern."

"Yes, you do." He shook his head. "Your safety will always be the most important thing to me. You have a duty to perform now."

"I'm not ready to do that."

"We'll get you ready." He assured me. "There is still time."

"Good, because there is a lot I want to do." I headed for the closet to find something to replace the singed nightgown.

"Like what?"

"I want to travel the world. See all the places I've never been able to." I pulled the red shirt from the hanger. "There is so much I have to see and do, Zodiac."

"Elsfaer."

"I also wanted to visit Penumbra. And I want to see Dragonia. I know it's risky, but I've been dreaming of that place since I was a girl." I rambled on. "The dragons will love me, don't you think? Since I'm not like the other phoenixes."

"There won't be time for all of that, not right away." Zodiac dismissed my dreams of travel.

"What?"

"We have to get you ready for the Rising."

"I thought I already did that."

"No, well, you were selected, but the process takes thirty days. At which point you will need to be in Phaedrial. There isn't any time to waste."

"I've waited all my life for this and now you're telling me I have to go from one prison to another?"

41

"It isn't a prison." He rejected the thought. "Phaedrial is our home."

"Home? You know, I've done everything you said my entire life. I've played the game by your rules. This is my chance to live the life I want to, and now you're taking that away."

"I do not intend to take anything away from you. There are rules to this. You're the Elite."

"So, you keep telling me." I rolled my eyes. "Being the Elite means giving up everything that matters to me?"

"I promise it will not always be this way."

"Yeah, right."

The light knocks at the door called our attention. Zodiac stepped out into the hall briefly before returning. "We must go."

"What?"

"There is a problem and you're—"

"The Elite, right?"

"Elsfaer—" Zodiac started, but stopped speaking when I lifted my hand.

"Does the Elite have the right to change into clean clothes or do I have to meet with the masses in my torn nightgown?" I pointed to the clothes still in my hand.

"Right, I'm sorry. I'll give you time to change." Zodiac left me sitting alone in the room.

I sat on the bed, avoiding my reflection and dreams I felt slipping from me yet again. I shrugged, thinking I could be free when my job as elite was done, then sobbed when I realized the only way out of the job was in death.

CHAPTER 4

"WHAT SEEMS TO BE THE PROBLEM?" I ENTERED THE council room, this time with an open invitation. The same faces sat around the table, only this time they looked at me less like a child they had to monitor and more like a bomb they hoped wouldn't explode.

"Elsfaer," Zodiac addressed me and held his hand out to the empty chair. "Please sit."

As directed, I took the seat at the head of the table. "You said there was something I just *had* to deal with. What is it?"

Jamila cleared her throat while throwing Zodiac a questioning gaze. "Well, we have some concerns back at Phaedrial. There are factions that are rising against the Elite."

"Against me?" I scoffed. "Already?"

"Not you specifically, considering no one knows who you are." She tried and failed to soften the blow.

"What do they want?" I scanned the twelve faces at the

table. Seven were the monks who stood as council for Zodiac. Jamila sat next to the man with the scar and two other who I still did not know. Members I assumed came from Penumbra for the occasion, and of course there was Zodiac.

"They want to know your identity," Jamila answered me.

"So, tell them who I am. Now, that wasn't so hard, was it?" I pushed back in the chair to get up, but the large hand on my wrist stopped me.

"There's more," Zodiac spoke before removing his hand. "There are those who refuse to accept an outsider as their leader. Considering it's been four days and your identity is still unknown, they have decided that you aren't trustworthy."

"You're telling me I'm already enemy number one without ever having a chance to prove myself?" I laughed. Every time they told me something new, it was worse than before. I was the untrusted outsider meant to lead a species of fire birds who didn't want me. Great.

"That's how these things work out sometimes," Jamila shrugged. "We roll with the punches and get through it."

"Great. Just how things work out. Thank you for being so helpful in this most difficult time."

"There is more," Acai announced. "Zodiac, tell the girl."

"What is she talking about?"

Acai had a habit of limiting her voice and only using it in situations where it was called. As a monk, it was her place to offer guidance only when asked of her. Kai Temple was her responsibility, but in matters of our people, she was purely an observer, a historian collecting facts.

"There is a high probability that someone will challenge you." Zodiac answered.

"Challenge?" I questioned. "What does that mean?"

"Those who don't want you in power have the option of challenging you for the right to be the Elite." he explained.

"Great, so let them. I'll gladly hand it over." I laughed. "It's not like I asked for this!"

"It's not that simple," Jamila added.

"What does she mean?" I looked at my guardian again for answers.

"What Jamila means is this is a life-or-death situation," Zodiac carefully clarified. "If someone issues a challenge, and you fail, you will die."

"Are you fucking kidding me?" My anger grew and with each passing moment, it became harder to breathe. "You're telling me I could lose my life for something I never wanted to begin with?"

"You need to calm down." He urged. "Don't let the fire consume you."

"You no longer have the right to tell me to calm down!" I snapped at him and the markings on my skin glowed. "I cannot believe this!"

"I understand your frustrations."

"How can you possibly understand what I am going through right now?" I looked around again at the guilt riddled faces that avoided me. "Either way it goes, in twenty-six days, my life changes forever. I have to become the leader of a race of people who don't want me and to give up my life to protect theirs. And at any moment, one of them can decide that not only should I not be their leader, but I should also lose my life. I could die, Zodiac!"

"Maybe I can't understand your position entirely. You're correct, I haven't dealt with this specific set of problems. There has been no decision in my life that amounts to what you are facing." Zodiac paused for a moment and ran his hand across that silver goatee. "What I can say is that I am here for you, Elsfaer, as I have always been. You know this. I will be by your side every step of the way. You are not alone in this."

"I need time to think." I stood from my seat and tried to keep my voice from shaking as I spoke. "This is too much. I really wish that you had prepared me for this. I wish you had allowed me the chance to live a life outside these walls, knowing that there would be a day that I would no longer have that option. There is so much now that I will never see, so much that I may never experience. As much as I love you Zodiac, as much as I care about you, I don't know that I'll ever be able to forgive you for that."

This time, when I turned to leave the room, no one stopped me. I left them in the wake of my admission. The sun had already set on my fourth day as the Elite and a new internal clock sounded in my mind. I needed to go somewhere that would bring me peace.

I found that peace in the courtyard. After nightfall, there was little movement in the gardens that surrounded the temple. The monks settled into their quarters and the

Phoenixes, if any had visited, had already returned to Penumbra.

The courtyard presented a maze of bushes that bloom year-round with Red Phoenix flowers. As a child, I would spend hours running through the passageways, imagining my life was full of adventure. I'd done it so many times that taking the path was second nature. Three lefts, two rights, one left, three rights, and there I was in the center of the maze where the fire stone rested.

The orange stone had black markings that traveled the length of its oval shape. In the sunlight, they looked like flickers of flames. At night, they looked like the scars those flames left behind. The stone possessed no power. It stood as a symbol that Kai Temple was a safe space for any phoenix in need of help, though in all my years, I'd never seen one come who Zodiac didn't know about in advance.

I ran my fingers up the side of the metal post that held the stone and wondered again about the fire birds who had the freedom to roam. I longed for adventure. Even one that ended with me searching for refuge at Kai Temple. Anything that said I had lived.

It was hard not to mourn the life that I'd planned. Zodiac claimed that there would be time, but that was a lie. All that would happen was a transfer. They would transfer my life in solitude at Kai Temple to a life under the microscope in the Elite's chair. That's if no one challenged me and tried to end my life.

The more I thought of everything that I would give up, the hotter I became until I could no longer contain the fire. I smiled because for the first time, I could actually relieve that pressure the way any phoenix should.

Before unleashing my wings, I chose the spot that would cause the least amount of damage. I didn't want to harm the flowers, or the fire stone, should anyone ever be looking for it. I closed my eyes and breathed deeply, centering my thoughts and emotions.

The first few times you called your wings, you had to be careful. I'd read enough material to know that an unsure phoenix could mean a destroyed temple. With patience, I allowed my phoenix spirit to emerge.

Unlike in my bedroom, when my emotions blinded my senses, I felt my wings as they spread from me. Tingles stretched across my back and I smiled as tears fell from my eyes. This night would be for me. Tomorrow Zodiac would tell me what the rest of my life looked like. Tonight, I would fly without worry of that.

They protected though Kai with magic, but that barrier allowed passage to those mature phoenixes whose flames carried them through the sky. My wings afforded me a freedom I had never had before. I couldn't waste a single moment.

The books said to think about using your wings like any other appendage. When you walked, you didn't think of each step, you just decided that there was a destination you wanted to reach. Flying was the same. Think of the destination, breathe, and lift. I thought of the sky and the clouds and willed myself to join them.

Yes, it was just that simple, except that when I lifted, I nearly flew right into the post that held the fire stone and then crashed right back to the ground. Happy that no one was around to see my failure, I dusted myself off and tried again, this time thinking less about the sky and more about two feet above the ground. When I accomplished that without hurting myself, I pushed a little further until I was far above the temple.

The feeling of flying was everything I dreamed it would be and more. I lifted further above the temple and into the clouds until I could no longer see the red painted rooftops. The cool air brushed against my body and cooled my core from the fire. Once in the clouds, I hovered, looking down at the place that was my home, my prison.

"How does it feel?" Kenya's voice interrupted my thoughts of flying away from the temple and never returning.

"It's amazing!" I turned to see her there, Red Flames blazing and carrying her through the clouds. When she came closer, I could see the fresh scar that stretched from the bottom of her left chin to the top of her right eye. "Oh my god, I did that to you?"

"No, you didn't." she held her hands up to brush off my concern. "Before you blame yourself, this was my fault. I was told to stay back, but I didn't."

"I'm so sorry," I apologized anyway.

"Thank you, but again, you have no reason to be." She looked down at the temple. "How do you feel right now?"

"Honestly?" I looked up at the moon and listened to the rhythmic movement of my wings. The flapped in a steady pace to keep me lifted from the ground.

"Yes." Kenya smiled. "There's no need to pretend with me. You know that."

"I feel lost, afraid, powerful, and yet weak all at the same time. How does that even make sense? I feel like I'm losing myself. The strange part about that is I've never felt more whole than I do now."

"You're the Elite, the only one in our history that hadn't been around for a century before being named." Kenya reminded me of another reason to be upset about the hand they dealt me. "That's a daunting thing."

"God, I hadn't even thought of that." I sighed. How was it fair that everyone before me lived a long life before the High Spirit deemed them worthy of the role? "How am I supposed to do this?"

"I wish I could give you the answer." She looked at me as if trying to read my mind. "You're thinking of leaving, aren't you?"

"What?" I frowned. I hadn't been thinking about it, but maybe I should have. There was nothing stopping me.

"It's okay. It's only natural that you would be." She shrugged. "What are you going to do?"

"Zodiac says I have to go to Penumbra. I need to establish myself there even though most of them have already decided I'm not fit for the job."

"I'm sorry." She placed her hand on my shoulder.

"What are you apologizing for?" I shrugged. "You had nothing to do with this. It's not your fault the High Spirit chose me."

"Well, no, I had nothing to do with that, but we should have told you everything."

"You knew, too?"

"Of course, I had to." She nodded. "Everyone here had to know how important it was that we keep you safe."

"I don't know what I'm going to do. I don't even know what I'm walking into. Part of me is ready to go there and do whatever it takes to prove myself. A bigger part is freaking out because I do not know what it means to be a leader. How the hell am I supposed to convince them I will be any good at it? Those people don't know me. They won't accept me."

"You don't know how they're going to respond to you. And I know that is a scary thought, but it's something that you're going to have to face, eventually." She sighed and looked at the moon before continuing. "He is going to kill me for telling you this, but I know Zodiac wanted to tell you everything. And I probably shouldn't be saying this right now, but don't let him fool you into thinking that this was his decision. He made a promise to keep you safe and to let you live a life without fear. Maybe he did it the wrong way, but he did the best he could."

"Who could he possibly have made that promise to?" I questioned her. This was the most I'd ever heard about Zodiac and his reasoning for lying to me. I wanted to know everything.

She hesitated. "I don't know if I should tell you that."

"I deserve to know Kenya. It's my life."

"I'm going to get so much heat for telling you this." She paused, taking my hands in hers. "He made the promise to your mother."

"My mother?" I had to have heard her wrong. There was no way she said what I thought she did.

"Yes." she said calmly.

"How is this possible?" I asked, then tossed my hands up in frustration. "You know what? No. I'll ask him that."

Kenya called out after me as I dove for the ground. She'd want to talk me out of the angered fit, but there was no use. I decided I had to confront him. I landed and in a breath, my wings folded back into my back and disappeared.

As I tore through the halls to his room, I thought of every lie I'd uncovered in the past few days. There was so much he kept from me. Most of it I'd been trying to forgive him for. However, this was different. How could he lie to me about my mother? What harm would it have done for him to tell me the truth?

When I slammed my palm against the oak door, I expected to startle the man inside. I didn't expect for it to fly off its hinges and land on the floor inside. I stared into the room I'd never seen the inside of and watched Zodiac jump from his seat at the desk next to the window.

"How many lies have you kept from me, Zodiac?" It was hard to remain calm when all I wanted to do was yell and shoot fire at his head. "How much about my life have you decided I didn't have the right to know?"

"Elsfaer, what are you doing here?" He stepped over the shattered door. "What is this about?"

"Let me stop you before you spit out any more of your lies. You hid something from me my entire life. Something I would have done anything to know. Why?"

"What are you talking about?" he grabbed the robe that hung by the door and put it on, covering his bare chest.

"You knew my mother all this time. Every time I asked, you told me you didn't know who she was. You said she was someone who you met for a moment, that you never spoke to her and that the next day they gave me to you and told you to take care of me. Was that the truth?" I pointed my finger in his face.

"I—"

"You know what?" I held my hand up to stop him. "Don't even start. I trusted you. All this time, I've trusted you with my life. I've believed everything you've told me. I've spent my entire life locked away here, restricted by magic you said protected me. And now I get to find out from someone else that not only did you know these things about my life and what my future would look like as an elite, but you knew my mother.

You more than knew her, Zodiac! You made a promise to her to keep me hidden here. No, stolen from the life that I should have had. All this time I trusted you, Zodiac. I trusted you with my life. I don't even know who you are through all of your lies."

"Elsfaer, understand my position," he spoke. "I had a duty to perform."

"Your position and your duty were to keep me safe. Your duty was to prepare me for the shit storm that my life is becoming. Where in that does it say lie to me? Where in that does it say to tell me that my mother was a ghost who left me in the night? I keep trying to forgive you for keeping the prophecy from me, but this is something that I can't forgive." I took a step back from him, feeling unstable in my anger. "If I never see your face again, it would be too soon."

I turned and walked away from the man who'd been my only family. He called after me, but he didn't follow. He knew I didn't want to see him and knowing Zodiac, he would think it best to give me time alone. In his mind, I would cool off overnight and in the morning, we could speak about things with level heads.

In most instances, Zodiac would be correct, but in this one, he couldn't be more wrong. I had no plan on being there in the morning.

CHAPTER 5

I WISH I COULD HAVE BEEN THERE TO SEE HIS FACE. IT'S A cruel thing to think, but to witness the panic creep over him as he realized I was no longer in the temple, no longer under his control, would have been so satisfying. It would have been amazing. Instead, I had to settle for the feeling of knowing that I'd done the right thing for myself. I had twenty-five days left of my life, twenty-five days that I could still call my own, and I wouldn't spend that time taking orders from Zodiac.

Before I left, I had to make sure I covered my markings. This was not a new practice. Often, we would get visitors at Kai Temple, and I had to make sure that no one saw the strange designs imbedded in my flesh. Even if they didn't invite me to the meetings, Kenya would go through hiding every visible mark under a layer of specialized concealer. She applied the stuff to any part of my body that my clothing didn't cover.

After applying the makeup to my skin, I grabbed the

fireproof gear that Kenya had stuffed my closet with to prepare for my maturity. Unlike the nightgown that was now in the trash, they made the new clothes from kamular. It was a natural material from our homelands that could withstand the hottest phoenix burn. It was the same material that my armor was made of, the armor I'd likely never get to wear.

I grabbed one of the wing proof bags and filled it with only the stuff that would prove essential to my survival. It fit like a sports bra, with a singular strap that went down the center of the back. The pockets set at the lower back and along the hips, safe from emerging wings.

If only my armor had arrived on time. I wasn't taking that clunky old stuff I trained in. Odds are I wouldn't need it, anyway. It wasn't my plan to look for trouble. I wanted to lie low and figure out things on my own. Still, I grabbed my pair of Cinquedea daggers and secured them at my waist beneath the long overcoat. They were my weapon of choice and had never let me down.

I waited in my room until the temple quieted. There were the night owls like Acai, who I wanted to avoid. If anyone saw me leave, they would waste no time in telling Zodiac. Under the cloudy night sky, I called my wings to return and left Kai Temple behind.

————

To get to Penumbra, I needed a gateway. They were access points shielded by magic and skillfully hidden all over the world. I'd memorized maps of places I'd never been to. Finding an opening wouldn't be too difficult.

The flight took me from the top of the Sheep mountain, down to the Hurricane Canyon Natural Area.

My desire to roam the world and see all the places I'd studied made it difficult not to take to the sky and never come back down. But there were things I needed to do. Penumbra was my destination.

An hour from the temple was a gateway to Penumbra. One that Zodiac never used. Often, spies would follow him across the barriers he and would need to ditch the tail. If he came across the barrier that was close to the temple, he could risk leading them right to me.

From the sky above, under the cover of the clouds, I looked for the markings. They were magic symbols that phoenix eyes could only see, like the fire stone at Kai Temple. The markings relayed you were not only on safe lands, or near a gateway, but they also told what side of Penumbra the gateway opened to. It wasn't uncommon for the destination to change.

The first one I found was on the side of a large stone. The gateway wasn't far from there. I only had to keep moving north. Though my lessons had prepared me for the initial exhaustion of flying, I still believed I could travel the world in one night. But after only a half hour, my back and chest were burning. I couldn't stop though, not until I crossed the barrier. Once I was in Penumbra, I would be safe to rest. I could get lost in the world. It'd be hard for Zodiac to find me.

Two more markings led me to a pair of old trees. To any passerby, the twin pines would look like nothing more than a prime spot for a photo op. They were so much more. The trees radiated with magic and power derived from Penumbra. The energy moved from the tree roots, through the ground, and into my body as I stood and examined the site.

The power told of the world that waited on the other side. My phoenix spirit danced inside of me, excited about the opportunity to explore. Just as I stepped forward to cite the spell to open the portal, the deep growl of a beast rumbled behind me.

My eyes locked with the yellow eyes of a massive gray wolf. Zodiac had brought wolf cubs to the temple, as he did with other animals. It was his way of enhancing my lesson plans. Those wolves were nothing like the one that stood in front of me. They were smaller and cuter variations of the adult animals and meant to show the power of the wolf, but this one was full grown, and it looked hungry. I back away from it slowly, reaching for my cinquedea as I did.

Drool dripped from its mouth as it continued to growl at me. This thing would not back down. As careful as I was to unsheathe the dagger, the tip of the blade tapped the end of the covering and the sound set the wolf off. Teeth bared and eyes wide, intending to kill, it pounced.

Adrenaline motivated my instincts to kick in. I fell to the ground, and the mass of fur flew over my head. A hard kick sent me flipping forward and away from the beast. I held out my blade, a visual warning to the animal, but it came for me again.

I jumped out of the way, but it caught my leg with its claw, leaving a nasty cut along my calf. I screamed out in pain as I fell and scooted away from the animal. It circled, growled, and charged again. Despite the pain I felt, I pushed myself to move. After dodging it three more times, I tried another tactic. I would tire out long before it did, especially with the cut on my leg. It was healing, but slowly, and the continued struggle wasn't helping.

Instead of dodging the attack when it ran for me, I leaned into it. And when the wolf neared me, I jumped over its head, caught it by the neck, wrapped my legs around its torso, and tumbled with it. I had to move fast. The weight alone was enough to crush me. I drew my blade across its neck. The warmth of its blood spilled across my arm as it emitted a short, painful howl and then fell limp. I struggled to push the heavy body off me.

I apologized to the beast; I didn't intend to kill it, but it was my life or his. If I had more time, I would have given it a proper burial, but wolves often ran in packs. The blood that spilled from its neck would have them on me in no time. I wiped the blood from my blade and returned it to its cover.

The trees waited, the power pulsing and welcoming me home. I stood at the center of their connection and recited the spell that would give me access to Penumbra.

"Into the shadows out of the light hide no more from human sight."

Electricity charged the air, and the area rippled with power as the magic worked. The branches of the trees reached across the space between them, and as they connected, the gateway appeared. I'd always thought the gate would be iron and rigid, but this was an intricate design of blended branches that never settled. It was like watching two lovers embrace. After they completed their formation, they parted, giving me access to the realm of magic.

The world of Penumbra opened to me, and I lost every breath I had hoped to catch. On the other side of the two trees was a full forest, lush with shrubs, plants, flowers, and animals that called out to me.

I looked back at my home in the mountain, at the guardian I had left in the night. For a moment, I considered going back. I could confront him with my concerns and handle things like an adult, but that moment was fleeting. There was no way I could turn away from adventure when I was so close to tasting it. I stepped across the barrier to Penumbra. The passage closed behind me as the wolves, no doubt realizing their pack mate had died, howled in the background.

CHAPTER
6

I'd dreamt of Penumbra my entire life. In my dreams, I'd traveled to and from the magical world countless times, and every time was better than the one before. The thing about dreaming of a place is that it can look however you imagine it. The structure of the landscapes, what the animals look like, and where the rivers run, were all up to you to decide.

Yes, there were books, but books like anything else did the place no justice. It gave you a loose structure, leaving your mind to fill in the blanks. I was excited to compare my imaginings to the real thing.

I landed in the middle of the Darkest Forest, a troublesome place that most of the sane citizens of Penumbra avoided. Of course, this is where the closest doorway to Kai would land. It was the best way of making sure no one stumbled across it. Hidden away in the deceptive place.

Crossing over the barrier left me with an unsettled

feeling. My feet felt too heavy, and my wings tingled, begging to be let free. Flying would have been the simple thing to do, but my wings would call too much attention. The goal was to make it hard for Zodiac to find me.

I made sure I secured my bag on my back. The struggle with the wolf loosened the straps. I also doubled checked the cinquedea and tucked it safely out of sight before I started my journey. It took a bit to get used to walking. I was used to walking in the high altitudes of the mountain. Being on the ground was difficult enough but Penumbra's atmosphere made the change more difficult. Eventually my limbs adjusted, and I walked less like a newborn calf.

Two hours into my trek, I heard them. Voices of men who called out, teasing me from the bushes. The best thing to do was ignore them, so I did. They would be there regardless. I had to keep moving. Unless they engaged, I would not.

"Oh, look at her, walk steady girl," a deep voice laughed.

"You think she'll turn and show us that beautiful face?" a smaller voice hissed like a snake.

"She might be a dog under that hood," the deeper voice returned. "We might not want to see her face at all. Would ruin the fun!"

"Oh now, come on, don't count her out just yet." A goofy laugh echoed around me before others joined it.

While I didn't stop moving, I kept my ears trained on their voices. There were four. From the reckless footfalls I counted, three mid-sized men and one larger. Nothing to worry about. Just needed to keep my breathing steady and my mind clear. They quickened their pace as they pursued me. It wouldn't be long before they were on top of me.

I still had my blade at the ready. I could use it to defend myself. My surroundings would also benefit me. The tight spacing of the trees, the uneven ground, and the low-hanging branches would all prove to make maneuvering difficult for the stalkers, who I could already tell were less than graceful.

"Oh, she's going to keep ignoring us boys," the big voice commented.

"Guess that means we have to make her pay attention!" the snake-like tone hissed again.

They quieted, but I could hear them move. Two ahead now, two behind. They surrounded me. For years, I'd trained for scenarios like this. I could hear Zodiac's voice in my mind guiding my actions. Deep breath, steady, listen to the sounds. My vision was limited, and my sense of smell also proved unreliable. Thanks to the surrounding nature. It was all unfamiliar to me, which made it more difficult to discern nature from my stalkers. Sound was my winner. I kept walking as if unaware of their new positions.

They didn't play their taunting game for too much longer. The smallest of the bunch, who positioned behind me and to the right, was the first to try his luck. He ran for me, arms poised to wrap around my chest. I ducked and used my right arm to flip him over my head. Before his back slammed into the ground, stalker two was in motion.

From the left, he came barreling in, screaming like a

madman, and stumbled before he ever reached me. I used his own momentum against him and simply side stepped to dodge his weight. Once he passed me, I kicked him in the ass, and sent him flying to the ground where he landed beside his friend.

The two lay there in their ragged clothing covered in dirt that was there long before I ever knocked them down. Were they simply looking for money, something to get them provisions? Regardless of their intentions, they were attacking me, and I would defend myself.

"You guys really gonna let this girl kick your asses like that?" a third voice called from the trees. He hadn't spoken before. His voice had more mystery to it, more caution.

"All that talking you're doing. Why don't you try taking her down?" the smallest one coughed as he tried to pull himself up from the ground only to have his chunky friend stumble and knock them both back down.

"Don't worry, I got this." The biggest one of the quad stepped into view.

I steadied myself, placing my hand on the still hidden blade and waited for his charge. He looked imposing, but I could tell he was used to his using his size as a point of intimidation.

Though he was clearly still a novice in battle, he was better than his friends. He charged from one direction but quickly shifted his weight, almost catching me off guard. If it weren't for the years of training, I might have ended up on my ass. Instead of embarrassing myself, I adjusted my own footing and narrowly missed both the ground and his second attack.

He returned, ready for a battle. Instead of pulling my dagger, I met him with my fists. The big guy dodges the first two punches, but my third landed square on his jaw. He stumbled back and cursed before he charged again. This time, I connected every blow of the combo. Right hook to his jaw, left jab to his chest, knee to his stomach to end with a powerful right uppercut that landed my attacker on his back.

"Damn it, man, you just gonna stand there?" he spit more blood from his mouth and wiped his lips on his arm as he yelled at the fourth guy still covered in mystery. "Get your ass over here, man, and do something about this!"

"You guys are worthless." the man stepped forward with dark hair wild, framing the strong jawline and high cheekbones. "I have to do everything myself." Unlike the others, who wore tattered rags, his clothes were well intact. He wore black leather pants and a loose-fitting V-neck shirt with gold decorative threading along the collar. A light sheen of sweat covered his amber skin. Judging from his appearance and his proud posture, he had to be their leader.

This new man was more calculating than his companions. He sized me up before he made a move. He positioned himself for the attack, informing me almost instantly that he was prepared to do a lot more than yell and charge in like a toddler drunk on milk.

"Alright, let's see what you got." He winked before engaging.

We went hand to hand, blow for blow, for a few minutes while his buddies watched. As long as it looked like their leader had a fair shot at winning, they stayed out of it. The second my elbow connected with his temple, causing him to stumble back, and blood to drip from his nose, things changed.

They were on top of me in waves. One after the other, taking cheap shots. Still, I kept my blade hidden, until the little one revealed his own.

"I'm sick of this shit!" he proclaimed as a small switchblade appeared in both hands.

"Excellent," I responded, pulling my twin daggers from hiding.

"Aw shit!" the biggest one retorted. "She has a few tricks up her sleeve."

"Let's make her work for it, fellas!" the leader called out, and they closed in on me.

Her wailing was louder than the horrible shrieks of my nightmares. The small frame of a woman clothed in black fell from the treetops onto the back of the leader of the unruly group. He stumbled and fell forward as her fingertips dug into his eye sockets, temporarily blinding him.

"Damn it, man, there are more of them. I'm not sticking around here to get my ass kicked by some girls." The smallest of the quad turned to run away, but the largest caught him by the collar before he could.

"Oh, shut up, Axel. It's just one little girl. We can take her." He flashed an enormous grin full of yellowed teeth. "More to take home with us. The others will celebrate us."

"Bring it on, big boy," the hooded woman commented, and she beckoned him forward.

They took her invitation, and not one but two jumped

her. As the leader locked his eyes on me again, I had to do something. It wasn't just my ass on the line now, but the stranger's as well.

While the girl occupied the others, I called my flame, a small display that wrapped around my hand as I punched the leader again. He jumped back, yelling and putting out the small fire that caught on his shirt, ruining the fabric.

"What the hell?" He looked at me with fear in his eyes before calling off his goons. "Yo, let's get out of here."

"What? You can't be serious!" the big one huffed. "There's no way—"

"Look, I'm in charge here and I said it's time to go!" the leader repeated his order and this time they obeyed him.

Their leader paused his own escape, looking back at me with suspicious eyes. He squinted a little, as if trying to see something that wasn't there, then turned and ran after his ego hurt friends.

"Thanks for jumping in there." I nodded to the small woman as I placed the daggers back in safe hiding.

"No problem. It looked like you had it covered, though. I just hate those rogue boys." She dropped the hood from her head, revealing long blonde braids that flowed past her shoulders and contrasted against her dark skin. Her wide eyes locked on me as she pulled the braids up into a bun.

"Rogue boys?" I frowned.

"Yeah, a band of misfits and rejects. They walk around like they're saving the day when really they're the ones terrorizing most people."

"Oh," I looked over my shoulder in the direction the

guys fled. *Were they really there to do more than rob me?* "Is there anything I can do to thank you?"

"No, you don't need to thank me." She paused as her eyes sized me up. "Actually, you could let me join you. There's a lot of dangerous stuff out there. I could watch your back."

"You want to join me?" I chuckled. "Do you think that's safe? You know nothing about me."

"I know you're a badass fighter and you don't back down. That's all I need to know. Besides, you're walking through the Darkest Forest, all alone, with no one to watch your back. I'd think you would want me on your side." She held her arms out, putting the forest on display. "I know this place like the back of my hand. I can get you where you need to be."

"Is that right?" before she could speak again, the wails of a creature echoed around us. The things sounded massive and too close for comfort.

"Well, unless you want to face the Kynuski on your own, I suggest we team up." She shrugged.

"What's a Kynuski?" I asked.

"The Kynuski? It's just one of the many monsters that dwell in the Darkest Forest. And it would have no problem with having you as a meal." She pasted an ominous grin on her face.

The Kynuski wailed again, and I was forced to concede. I knew nothing of the monster or what it could do to me. Penumbra was much more of a mystery than I thought it was.

CHAPTER 7

THIRTY MINUTES INTO OUR WALK, WITH THE SUN FINALLY rising, my new companion was trying her best to hold on to the questions that filled her mind. Though the light from the sun barely made it through the thick of the trees, I could see the struggle to contain the intruding thoughts consuming her.

"One," I gave in. The girl looked like she would pass out.

"What?" She looked at me with her brown eyes wide with intrigue.

"You get one question." I took my eyes off the path ahead, which was overgrown with vines and a total tripping hazard. "Maybe then you won't look like you're going to collapse."

"You're the new Elite, aren't you?" She asked eagerly.

There it was, spit out into the world. It just hung there between us. So much for trying to stay hidden. I thought she would be silly and ask something simple like my name, wasting her once chance, but no. She went straight to the heavy hitter.

"What?" It took me too long to respond. Any hope I had of changing her mind had flown away like the birds from the treetops.

"You don't have to say it. I know it's true." Her walk was now more of a bounce as she became filled with pride over her discovery. "Besides, I saw what you did to that guy back there. Or at least I saw the smoke from his shirt burning. Which means at the very least, you're a power phoenix with a controlled flame. Epic."

"What are you going to do?" I stopped walking. I had to know her intention before I could continue traveling with her.

"Nothing. Why would I do anything?" She shrugged. "Just happy I was right."

"Being the Elite is supposed to put a target on my head." I studied her.

"Well, I'm not the type to shoot for targets. I know I was all badass back there, but really, that's not my thing." She looked behind us as if she could see it all replaying in the forest. "Besides, if the High Spirit chose you, it's for a reason. Who am I to question that?"

"If only everyone thought about things the way you do." I sighed. "From what I told, there are plenty of people who would like nothing more than to remove my head and take my place."

"I can't speak for everyone else, but I think the Phoenix people could use a bit of change. All this Red Flames versus Blue Flames stuff is tearing our people apart. The dumbest part about it is that most of the ones fighting don't even have their wings."

"They don't?" There are moments when memory fails you. This was not one of them. There were phoenixes that didn't get their wings, but from my lessons, this was far and few in between. She spoke as if it was a far greater disparity than they had taught me.

"Yeah, you know, not everyone gets them. It's been that way for a while. The numbers keep rising." She shook her head. "My mother used to say that one day there wouldn't be any more phoenix people. No fire at all. Then we'd be one again."

"Do you have yours?" I asked intrusively, and without thinking how personal of a question it was.

"Um," she looked away.

"Oh, I'm sorry." How insensitive could I get? Life in the temple didn't afford me much time with strangers. I would have to work on my people skills if I wanted to make it through this without more people realizing who I was.

"No, it's okay. Three years and counting, so I'm fine with it. I can still create fire." She held her hand out and small Blue Flames danced across her fingertips. "It's better than most people who don't get their wings. They have no connection to their fire spirit at all. It's really sad to see."

"Your flame is blue." I smiled longingly. The Blue Flame always seemed so enticing to me.

"Yeah." Her face lit up. "What about you?"

"My flame?" I hesitated, looking back over my shoulder to verify my wings were out of sight.

"Yes, are you blue or red?" She called the flames to dance across her fingers again. "It would be so cool if we were both blue!"

"Um." How could I tell her the truth about my wings without freaking her out? How could I trust she wouldn't turn on me the moment she found out?

"You don't have to answer." she sighed. "Your wings must be spectacular to see!"

"Yea, I guess so." I hurried to change the subject. "You know, I thought you would have asked my name."

"Oh crap, you're right." She smacked her forehead with her palm. "Is it too late to ask?"

"No, not at all." I considered lying to her, telling her a fake name, but it would make no difference. No one in Penumbra knew I existed and if Zodiac got close enough to ask questions, a fake name wouldn't be enough to keep him from catching me. "Elsfaer. My name is Elsfaer."

"Oh, even your name is wonderful!" she beamed. "Mine's Ali."

"Ali, it's nice to meet you." I held my hand out to her, and she eagerly shook it.

"So, have you figured out where you're going?" She turned her head in the direction we'd been walking. "I can tell you not much is out that way. You're walking to things far more dangerous than those rogues."

"Honestly, no." I shook my head. I hadn't really thought of a plan. I had no idea where I was going, only that I didn't want to be where I was before.

"Would you like to go to Phaedrial?" Ali's eyes grew wider as she spoke of our people's home.

"I'd like to avoid that for as long as possible." Phaedrial was the very first place Zodiac would look to find me.

"Not ready to face the music?" She frowned.

"Hell, I don't even know the tune." I stopped walking. "There's so much I don't know about this place. I've never been to Penumbra. I just wanted to take time to explore before I'm locked down again."

"I understand. I can't imagine the pressure you're under right now. Wherever we're headed, I got your back." She pointed in the direction east of our current path. "Might I suggest we go that way, though?"

"You know nothing about me, and you still want to stay by my side." The forest stood around us and nature, both good and bad, called out to us. "I mean, this could be dangerous. You could put your life at risk if people think that you're on my side."

"Yeah, I mean, we defeated those idiots back there. Doing something like that kinda means we're bonded now. Best friends for life."

"Great." I smiled. "I've never really had a friend before." The confession just fell out of my mouth.

"Really? Someone as amazing as you?" She looked at me like I had to be lying to her, but I wasn't.

"I have advisors, counselors, and Zodiac, but no one I would ever consider being a friend. Let alone a best friend. Most days, the people I grew up around treated me like nothing more than another item on their lists of responsibilities." I mimed holding a pen and checking a box on a pad of paper. That's exactly how I felt.

"That sounds horrible." She shook her head. "Was there no one to show you love?"

"I try to be grateful, happy that they took me in and protected me, but it was hard to live like that. It's hard to look people in the eye every day and wonder if they would still be a part of your life if someone hadn't decided you were special."

"I'm sorry." She adjusted her hood. "That had to be difficult. I mean, life hasn't always been the best for me, but at least I always knew the people in my life were there because they wanted to be."

"I didn't mean to dump that on you like that. I guess it's just nice to have someone to speak to and not feel like they will report every word back to my handler." We needed to change the topic and bring the smile back to her face. "What about you? Any friends?"

"No, not really." She shrugged. "I mean, I used to have a ton, but then they all got their wings, and I didn't. It was like overnight, all those people, people who meant the world to me, turned their backs on me. Suddenly I was lesser than them. They look down on me."

"Because you have no wings? You still have your fire."

"You don't get it. There are four factors now with the Phoenix people." Ali explained the piece I'd misunderstood. "Blue flames are like the chosen ones. They are rare and beautiful and so people treat them like royalty. I guess it helps that our last elite was a Blue Flame. Red flames come next. Powerful but more common. Then there's my group, made of just under a thousand people. The Wingless. No wings, but we have our fire. And on the lowest rung, the Flameless. Those who hit maturity but never gained their wings and have no connection to their fire spirit. They treat them like dirt."

"How did the people become so divided?" I questioned. "The Elite allowed this to happen?"

"People like to feel like they are special, like you are. They want to have something to lord over others." She kicked the dirt and huffed. "Special people get special treatment. You may not like it, but others crave it."

"It's easy to want something when you've never experienced it." I scanned the sky above us, wishing I could fly. "While they want special treatment, I just want a chance at a normal life. Instead, I have to go from one restricted lifestyle to another and honestly, I'm not okay with it."

"Well, we can pretend while we travel that we're just two normal girls on a normal trek across magical lands." Ali waved her hands in front of my face and made a goofy face at me.

"Until—" I started, but Ali cut me off.

"No, no until. That's where you mess up. We will not concern ourselves with the 'until'. Live in the now. Now we walk, and we need to get out of the woods soon. We aren't far from the forest's edge. The Darkest Forest isn't a safe space to linger." She walked away from me, prompting me to follow her. "I'm surprised you lasted this long without me."

"Who wouldn't want a friend like you?" I paced behind her, continuing the conversation. "I mean, you risked your own safety to help someone you didn't even know. Surely I would be dead now if it weren't for you."

"I don't know. I think you could have handled yourself out there without me." She laughed, easily noting my sarcasm. "I tried to keep a straight face, but could you imagine if those guys knew who they were really messing with?"

"It was my plan to keep that under wraps." I stated, just in case she didn't understand my intentions. "I don't want to bring any unwanted attention my way. The longer no one knows who I am, the better."

"You could have taken them without ever revealing your true self, huh? I mean, you were doing pretty well before I showed up. All I really did was blind one asshole, and the others ran." She laughed. "They probably thought there were hundreds more bad ass babes coming to kick their asses."

"I think I would have fared okay, but I'm glad you showed up." I chuckled. "That big one might have sat on me and there was no way I was getting out of that!"

"Aw, thanks! Now, can we stop being mushy? It makes me itch." She laughed, then gagged. "Imagine the smell under all that ass!"

"Oh, no!" Laughter echoed around us as we continued to walk.

We walked through the day, stopping only to eat and drink before continuing. Just as Ali predicted, we made it near the edge of the forest just as the sun fell from the sky. We could have pushed on and made it out of the Darkest Forest, but Ali thought it best to stay under the cover of the trees. The real danger was deeper within.

We made our campsite and prepared to rest. We would decide where our journey would take us the next morning. Ali went on and on about wanting to visit Lake Asunder. Apparently, there was a curious beast that dwelled within it.

"My mom said if the monster shows itself to you, it's good luck." She propped her feet up on a log. "I guess that's why I spent three years trying to find the damn thing. Never did though."

"Good luck to see a monster?" I sipped the lukewarm water from the canteen she handed me.

"Yep, I think we could both use a bit of good luck, don't you?"

As if cued by her question, the whistling of an incoming projectile called out just moments before the ball of flames ripped through the trees. We jumped from our campground only moments before they set our cozy, little hideout ablaze.

CHAPTER 8

"Move!" I heard someone call out to just before the attack landed.

Pummeling balls of fire sounded like thunder as they reached us. The flaming projectiles smacked the ground around us and set anything they touched on fire.

"What the hell is that?" I called out to Ali as she jumped behind a large tree that barely withstood the impact of the blast.

"Run!" Ali yelled, as if I weren't already trying my best to avoid death at all costs. "We have to get out of here. They won't stop coming."

"Who are they?" I huffed as I joined her behind the massive tree trunk. "What do they want?"

"The Flameless." She handed me my backpack. I hadn't seen her grab it, but was grateful she had.

"The what?" I secured the bag on my back as another flaming ball landed just a few feet away from us. "Looks like they have plenty of firepower to work with."

"They're the Phoenix people who never got their wings. They've been moving out of the inner city and living in the Odious. I had no idea they'd come to the Darkest Forest." She ran for another hiding spot away from the fire and I followed her. "I try to keep up with their movements and stay as far away from them as possible. The good thing is, if we're running into them, we're close to safe grounds. Bad thing is that they'll likely kill us before we get there."

"Why would they want to kill us?" I asked, still running under the cover of the trees.

"Remember how you were so worried about you being the dangerous one to be around here? Well, I'm a bit dangerous myself." She shrugged and made another dive for better cover.

You need to keep moving! The mysterious voice reached me again and as I searched for it, the Flameless launched another attack.

"Did you hear that?" I ducked behind another tree, catching up with Ali.

"Hear what?" She called back as she peeked around a bush to track our attackers.

"I thought I heard—"

"Go!" Ali called and again we ran, narrowly missing another hit.

The closer the fireballs got, the further we ran. When I caught back up to her, she was panting like a dog locked outside in the summer heat.

"You mean to tell me that this is happening because of you?" I looked over my shoulder. There was a pause in the attack, but something told me not to get too comfortable.

"Yes, I'm technically Flameless, too. I don't have my wings, but as you know, I still have my fire." She wiped her forehead with the back of her hand. "They wanted me to join them, but I declined."

"Why?" I caught my breath. "Why wouldn't you want to join them? At least you wouldn't be alone out here."

"Because I don't want to go around hurting people," she admitted. "That's what they do. They pick and choose who is fit to be a part of their little club. And those who they deem unworthy, they take care of. As far as I'm concerned, they're no better than the rogues."

"What are we going to do?" Again, I checked over my shoulder, looking for more incoming fire, but found nothing but the trees, which were still burning. "We can't keep running from them. They'll burn the entire forest down."

"The forest would fight back long before that happened. But you're right." She held her hands up, stood from her crouched position, and stepped out into the line of fire.

"What are you doing?" I reached for her, but she pulled away. "You just said they want to kill you! You're going to jump right in their path?"

"Trust me," she winked before walking out of my line of sight.

There were three more explosions that left me frozen in fear. *What if they got her?* There was no sign of life from Ali, not even the sound of her footfalls. I was moments from running out to find her when she spoke.

"Kaden, I know you're out there. I know you're hiding

and waiting for me. Stop setting fire to the forest and come out so we can talk." Ali called out into the darkness, but no one answered her. "Look, attacking me with fire will not make me join you. We both know you don't want to kill me or my friend here. We're both like you. So, save us some time and a few more trees and come out so we can talk things through."

"How do I know you won't trick me and run off like you did the last time?" The deep voice boomed from the shadows. I wanted so badly to find the source of the voice, but I stayed in my position.

"Something tells me it's more than just you here with the amount of fire you've been throwing around. Even if I tried to run, how far would I really get?" she reasoned with the man.

"Alright, I'll hear you out," he answered. The forest fell silent again. The only sound was the cautious footfalls of an approaching man.

"Ah, look at you. Healthy, I see," Ali complimented him, *a great strategy.*

"Save it, Ali. Are you joining us or not?" He wasn't one to be swayed by sweet words.

"That depends," she teased him, ready to issue her ultimatum.

"On what?" He asked, again with cautious consideration.

"If you'll accept my friend as well." She dropped the bombshell on both the mystery man and me. When did I ever sign up to be a part of this group? With resignation, I trusted her for the moment. If we survived the night, I would ask her why the hell she put me on the chopping block too.

"Why should we?" he asked, skeptical of the proposal.

"We're a packaged deal here," she answered him. "You get both of us, or neither of us."

"Is that so?" The deep laugh rumbled in his chest.

"Yes, so if you want me to join you, you're going to have to welcome my friend. I'm not coming without her."

"Who is she?" he questioned. "Why should we accept her among our ranks?"

"Your ranks?" Ali laughed. "Come off it, Kaden. She's another firebird with no red or Blue Flame to call her own. Since when do you have any other qualifiers to join your group of outcasts?"

"What use would we have for her?"

"Why don't you ask her? E!" Ali called out to me to join and when I did, she spoke for me. "She's a fighter, strong, too. When I met her, she was taking on four rogue boys all on her own. I mean, I jumped in at the end, but I know she could have handled them with no help from me."

"You would vouch for her?" Kaden questioned again, still hidden in the shadows of the trees. I struggled to see him, but he was too far from us. Clearly, he didn't trust Ali as much as I did.

"Isn't that what I'm doing now?" Ali once again made fun of the man who threatened our lives. "You'd be foolish not to accept her into your *ranks,* as you put it."

"How well do you know this woman?" Kaden was unconvinced of my worthiness. I had to appreciate that about him. He had a healthy sense of paranoia.

"Well, enough to stake my life on it. If she turns out to be not trustworthy, that's the price, right? That's how you operate." She confronted him. "I would put my life on the line. Is that good enough for you?"

"It's good that you understand the risk you're taking here." Kaden lifted his finger and more shadowed figures appeared behind him. This was only a show of his power. If he wanted to take us out, he would have no problem doing so. Or so he thought. I might have wanted to stay undercover, but I wouldn't lie down and die at the hands of him or anyone else.

"I do." She looked at me, then back at him. "Well, are we in or not? If you don't want us, we can go on our merry way."

"Yes, fine." He placed his finger and thumb between his lips, blowing to emit a high pitch whistle. "Let's go."

"Go where?" I asked Ali. Kaden hadn't even spoken to me and yet here we were, walking into the darkness, following him to an undisclosed location.

"Time to be initiated in the Flameless."

"Is this wise?" I whispered to Ali as we followed Kaden from a safe distance.

"Of course. Why wouldn't it be?" She shook her head. "Kaden is all talk. Trust me, if he really wanted to hurt us with those fireballs, he would have. Kaden has damn near perfect aim. He missed us on purpose."

"Outside the fact that I know nothing about these people, I'm not—"

"Hey—" she cut me off. "I know you're not sure of this. It can be daunting joining a new group, but we're outcasts in this world and we need a place to call home. Why not make it with them where it's at least safer? I'm good on my own, but with you, we need more. You're keeping your secret. Just focus on doing that."

"Yeah, okay, maybe you're right." I yielded. What's the worst that could happen?

I expected to be led out of the dangerous forest, but Kaden and his shadowed crew led us further into the darkness. Ali explained that this was one of the safest places for outcasts. And like the rogue boys, that's exactly what the Flameless were. They were the ones who our people had turned their backs on and because they refused to be treated lesser than they deserved. This left them with no other option but to leave Phaedrial.

They gave the Flameless the worst jobs, and they lived in the grimiest areas. They were paid far below the living wage and forced to work multiple jobs to make ends meet. It seemed some inequities of Earth had found their way to Penumbra. How was I expected to fix so much damage? The more Ali explained to me, the more I wanted to run away from it all.

Their hideout was in a prime location, as they explained it. Deep enough within the forest where no one would risk trying to find them, but not so deep that things like the Kynuski, a fifteen-foot monster with twelve tentacles, would reach them. I couldn't imagine that being the best place for the group.

After an hour of walking, viewing only the back of Kaden's head where long dreadlocks hung to reach the middle of his back, we reached the thickest line of trees I'd seen since I landed in Penumbra. They were so compact that it didn't appear that we could get through. Still, the group walked forward, and as they did, the line of trees shimmered and they disappeared.

"What the hell?" I stopped walking and grabbed Ali by the arm to keep her from leaving me. "What was that?"

"Wow, they really didn't tell you much, did they?" She laughed as she tapped my arm. "It's simple illusion magic. This is a barrier, meant to keep any unwanted company out."

"They taught me about magic, but it's all figurative." I explained my shock. "It's a lot different seeing this stuff in person."

"It'll be okay, trust me."

"I do," I shook my head. "It's odd. I mean, I just met you, so I don't really understand why, but I do trust you. Maybe I'm just that desperate for friendship."

"I think that's a compliment. So, I'll take it, shall we?" she pointed at the line of trees where Kaden stood watching us. "He might think we're planning to ditch them."

I held my breath as we walked through the magical barrier. What was I supposed to expect? There was no physical sensation that came with the visual representation of the wall bending around us as we passed through. The moment we made it to the other side of the magical barrier, Kaden had us ushered off to our bunkers.

"You'll stay in the guest quarters." Our escort, a thin male with a sleeveless top, pointed to the huts in the opposite direction of where Kaden and the others headed.

"Guest?" Ali scoffed. "You're telling me you have people over for entertainment?"

"Yes, absolutely," he rolled his eyes. "We like to make sure everyone feels welcomed here."

"Right," she nodded. "No place else I'd rather be."

"This is temporary," he looked over his shoulder at the few who passed in the distance. One man shot us a questioning gaze but kept moving. "The group has to accept you first. If that happens, we'll give you a better space to bunk."

"Excellent. We have to prove ourselves worthy, huh?" Ali shook her head and her braid fell loose from the bun. "Bad enough I didn't want to be here. Kaden came after me, remember?"

"Hey, I don't make the rules. I just enforce them." He laughed and left us standing outside of the hut with the crooked door. "I'll be back for you in one hour!"

"I didn't want to mention this before, but you may want to touch up your makeup." Ali closed the door after making sure we were alone.

"What?" Her comment caught me off guard. "What do you mean?"

"The marks on your face. I assumed you hid them with makeup. But it's been a long, hot day and well." She pointed to the broken mirror that hung on the wall to the left of her.

"Crap." My reflection revealed spots on my face where the foundation failed. The etchings I was born with bled through the layers of the makeup. "I forgot to reapply it. There has been so much going on."

"Don't worry about it. I don't think anyone else saw it. It's not that noticeable yet."

"How am I going to do this?" I scrambled for my bag and said a silent prayer that Ali had been thoughtful enough to save it from the fires. I dug the makeup from the inside pocket.

"What do you mean?" Ali sat on the cot closest to me as I reapplied the makeup to my face.

"Be a part of this world and stay hidden. I mean, there is so much that I want to do, so much to experience. None of that will be possible." I sighed. "It's not like I have an endless supply of this stuff. If people see what I really look like, it's over for me."

"Why do you say that? Once you're... you know... Once you take your place, you can do whatever you want." Ali suggested as if it were obvious. "It comes with the territory."

"If that happens." I muttered, and focused on the spot closest to my lip. It was always the worst for me.

"What?" She sighed. "You're really a downer, you know that."

"Yeah, I know. Sorry about that." I took a deep breath to calm my growing nerves. "I'm just trying to be realistic here. Odds are, someone is going to challenge me. Most people here don't know who I am and the longer I remain a mystery—"

"The more likely it is that someone will challenge your position." She finished my thought.

"Exactly." It was all I could think about. There was someone out there, counting the days, just waiting to take me out. I was strong, yes, a skilled fighter, too. But what if they were stronger? What if they were older and had people who would support them in the fight? I had none of that.

"That's heavy."

"Tell me about it." Finished with my makeup, I put the case back into my bag and paused, lost in my own thoughts. There was so much I didn't know. For a moment, I wondered if I made the wrong move, leaving the way I did. Yes, I wanted freedom, but at what cost?

"What are you going to do?" Ali interrupted my introspection.

"I don't know. It's not like I want to die. I just started living. But I'm not sure I can win a fight. Regardless of all that, all I can think about is how in a few weeks, my life is no longer mine. I go from being this mysterious outsider to either a dead woman or the leader of our people. Those are the only options and it sucks like hell."

"Well, let's say we make this an adventure." She jumped from the cot and spread her arms wide like she was prepared to hug me. "Whatever happens, we live and have fun and when we get to Phaedrial, because we have to go there eventually, then you can face whatever comes next. Is that fair enough?"

"Yeah, I think so." I relaxed my shoulders and stared at the girl whose head barely reached my shoulder.

"Good. Now, wipe away the worry so we can get moving." She clapped. "There are people waiting to meet their new combat master!"

CHAPTER 9

JUST AS I SHOOK AWAY THE REST OF MY STRESS, THE GUARD knock on the door, notifying us it was time to head in for judgment. When Ali opened the door, he stood there with a smug grin crookedly painted on his face. This man did not expect us to do well with what was coming next.

He led us from the bunks on the outskirts of their chosen territory. There were two borders to the circular home. The first was the magical wall that we'd passed through when we first arrived. The second was a brick construction, built at least twenty feet high.

As we entered through the opening in the wall, we saw hundreds of people, all flameless, going about their lives. It was like stepping back in time. The women carried baskets on their heads loaded with goods. Dirt and grime covered the men, telling of the work they'd put in all day. They had no advanced technology, only that which they could produce with their hands and limited resources.

Every person we passed worked towards a common goal, building a sustainable home. The structures, their houses, were small and shaped with the materials the forest provided. They put together huts with branches, leaves, vines, whatever they could use.

The guard who spoke the bare minimum led us through the makeshift town to the area where the Flameless met to commune. The closer we got, the more people we saw, and they were all headed to the same spot. He wasn't joking when he said everyone had to accept us into the fold.

"Ah, they've graced us with their presence," Kaden announced as we entered the communal space behind our assigned escort. "Thank you, newcomers."

That was the first I got a clear view of him. His dreadlocks fell free around his face, where the crooked grin met us. He had a low-cut beard, the and the coarse hair blended into his skin, which was as dark as the sky above us. If not for his presence, the strength of him that filled the surrounding space, I wouldn't think he was any different from the others. He wore the same clothing as them, thrifted materials fashioned into functional attire.

Hanging from a leather rope around his neck was a metal carving of a wing that rested on his chest. Around his waist was a small holster where a short dagger rested on his hip. His fingers tapped the hilt of the dagger as he looked at me.

"What is this?" Though I felt nervous standing in a sea of eyes, all locked on us, my tone didn't betray me by revealing my concern. I squared my shoulders and focused on the host of the event.

"Your welcome ceremony, of course. You didn't think that we wouldn't celebrate this event, did you?" Suddenly, he wasn't the brooding man we met in the forest under fire. He was a showman, and this was his greatest act. "Let's get this started."

"Oh, a party in our honor?" Ali plastered on a sarcastic smile. "How thoughtful of you!"

"Fellow Flameless," Kaden called out, silencing the murmurs of the crowd. "It has been quite some time since we accepted new members into our ranks. Today I present to you two candidates and, as is our standard policy, you will decide if they stay or if they'll have to take their chances with the Kynuski!"

"Wait, what?" my eyes bulged as the crowd cheered. "Ali, you didn't say anything about facing that monster."

"I'm sure it's just for show," she whispered back. Her words reassured me, but the unsure expression on her face revealed she had no idea what she was talking about.

"It better be," I mumbled as Kaden continued addressing his people.

"Now, it's time to show us what you're made of." Kaden's words lingered before they registered with us.

"What?" We turned to him and questioned simultaneously.

"A display of your power." He clarified. "Our people need to see what you're made of. We need to know that you will bring some value here."

"I—" I struggled to respond. There was no way I could put my fire on display like that.

"Well, my friend here has no fire but I," Ali covered for me and held up her hand and on command, her fire danced across her flesh, "have a lovely connection to the Blue Flame."

"Excellent," Kaden nodded, though he already knew about Ali's fire. This wasn't a trial for her. It was for me. "What does she bring to us? What skill?"

"Is it not enough that she is flameless?" Ali asked. "I thought this was a safe space for all of us."

"She must carry her weight!" a woman called out, and the crowd agreed with her.

"She is a fighter." Ali announced over their cheers.

"Prove it!" a man twice my size stepped to the center of the room where we stood. "If she's such a great fighter, let her show us what she's capable of."

"You want me to fight?" I looked from Ali back at the man whose biceps were the size of my waist.

"Yes, unless Ali is lying to us about your abilities." Kaden nodded.

"I suppose that's fair." I reached back to pull my hair up from the hanging ponytail into a tight bun.

"Oh, she's gotta get herself pretty first," the ogre of a man laughed. And the men behind him joined in on the crude response.

Instead of engaging in pointless banter, I centered myself. The years of lessons with Zodiac had prepared me for opponents like him. Both his size and his ego would work against him. I lifted my hand palm to the sky and beckoned him forward.

If he was the best fighter they offered, they were in a lot of trouble. His footfalls were unsteady as he lumbered forward. His struggled movements made it easy to side-step him and land the elbow on the back of his neck. The massive man stumbled and fell to the ground with a thunderous smack. While he recovered from the fall, even that could have been done better.

I gave him the time to steady himself, hoping for a better approach. He lunged again instead of allowing me to make the next move, and again I dodged him and sent him flying to the ground. This unsteady choreography went on until he was breathless and struggling to get back to his feet.

"You call that fighting?" he huffed. "You're not even trying."

"Yes, I call it letting your opponent beat themself." I crossed my arms as he struggled to breathe. "If you need more time, I can wait."

"Okay, you're good with that." Kaden stepped forward, holding two swords in his hand. "What about an actual fight?"

He tossed one sword to me, which I caught, and the next fight was on. Kaden was a better opponent than the sweaty ogre. His form and technique was that of someone with training. He wielded his sword with confidence and challenged my abilities.

If I hadn't known better, I'd think Zodiac trained him. Unlike his friend, he didn't rush to fight. He considered my skill before engaging. While I was assessing his stance, strength, training, he was doing the same with me.

Still, he took the first move. Our blades met time and time again, echoed by the sharp breaths of anticipation from the watching crowd. Twice his blade came just inches from my face, but both times I deflected and retreated.

Our fight became more of a dance. With each movement we breathed each other in and exhaled an unfamiliar tension, one that filled the air and threatened to cloud my judgement. Just as the scent of his flesh consumed me with that rising musk, I spotted his weak spot.

Kaden had a stuttering step. His left foot always moved twice before he found his balance. It was subtle, but it was enough. The plans for his defeat replaced thoughts of his aroma. I swept around him, coming up from the right. My attack timed just perfectly. I dropped and swept my leg beneath him before he could make the second step for balance.

He fell to his back, his sword slipped from his hand, and he froze. The blade of my sword pressed against his throat, and I smiled. Kaden lifted his hands in defeat.

"You are good," he conceded.

"Thanks." I backed away, removed my blade from his throat and picked up his lost weapon from the ground.

"Perhaps we will have use of you after all." He held his hands out for the return of the weapons and smirked when I hesitated. "I'm a man of my honor, Elsfaer. You won, this time."

"What use do you have for me?" I handed him the swords and reclaimed my position next to Ali.

"Well, as you can see, our people aren't exactly combat ready," he announced as the crowd went back to their usual agendas, our acceptance into the fold complete. "I've planned to train them, but not all skilled fighters can teach others."

"Do you need them to be combat ready?" We followed

him closely, leaving the room. "Are you planning to fight?"

"Change is coming. The new elite is out there, and we don't know what they will do when they take the seat. We need to be ready for anything," Kaden spoke as we entered a private hut fit with five seats and a small round table.

"What makes you think the new elite would want to do any harm against you?" I asked, careful not to reveal anything more about myself than I wanted.

"It's not uncommon. The last elite is the reason the Flameless are treated so poorly now. It's his fault that there is such a great divide between our people." He scoffed. "He spoke about this glorious future for the phoenix people. One tied with deafening technology and the erasure of our history and practices. And that divide grows larger each day. I can't see the next doing much to improve that. I bet they'll make things worse, especially if they're a Red Flame."

"Why do you think that?" Ali asked as she took a seat and bit down on a piece of bread I didn't see her take.

"The Blue Flames are the top tier; the Red Flames want nothing more than to further themselves from us more than they already have." Kaden explained. "How do you think they will do that? They'll target us to make themselves look better. Too bad they don't see that once we're gone, they're next on the chopping block."

"I think it would be good to keep an open mind about the new elite. You never know what they might do," I offered with a side eye to Ali, who looked like a deer caught in headlights. I would not give up my identity, but I could passively defend myself.

"Yeah, I'll keep that in mind, but until then, we need to prepare." Kaden put away the swords and took a seat, leaving me standing alone. "Will you help with training them or not?"

I looked at Ali, who nodded. She wanted me to do this. With a moment of hesitation, I sat in the empty seat next to her. "Of course, I will. I'm part of the team now, aren't I?"

"Good, well, there is plenty of food out there. Eat and rest up." Kaden suggested. "We start first thing in the morning!"

CHAPTER 10

"ARE YOU READY FOR THIS?" ALI BOUNCED BESIDE ME AS WE headed to the shared space again. The sun hadn't yet risen, though we wouldn't be able to see it even if it had thanks to the thick canopy that hung over the campsite. At night, the Flameless lifted the covering as a precaution. Anyone flying overhead would see nothing below but impenetrable treetops.

"No," I felt like I was headed to my judgment for the second time since arriving there. They pushed the communal seating aside to allow for us ample room for combat training. "This isn't exactly how I planned on spending my time. These people don't even want me here. I supposed to be traveling and having adventure!"

"Look, you got this. I don't care what anyone says." She stopped me. "And this is only a slight detour. We don't have to stay here, but I really think it will be good for you to get in touch with these people. Like Kaden said, the last elite didn't see them. He didn't care about them and because of his indifference, they're living out here in one of the most dangerous places in Penumbra."

"And I can help change that." I chewed my lip. This was the real reason she agreed to Kaden's terms. She wanted me to understand the flameless.

"You can." She looked over her shoulder at the people who filed into the space and waited for me. "And if you're worried about training people, I mean, I'm not a trained fighter, but I can help."

"It's not that. I know how to fight." I shook my head. "Hell, I've spent my entire life training in twelve different styles of combat."

"Okay, if it's not that, what is it?" She asked.

"I haven't really had to fight since gaining my wings," I whispered to make sure no one overheard us. "And I've only really used them once. What if I trigger them accidentally? That won't end well for either of us."

"Oh, I hadn't thought of that." She chewed her bottom lip and considered our options. "I mean, I saw you with those rogue boys before. You held yourself together then."

"Yeah, that was different. I wasn't worried about hurting them. If I would have slipped up, well, I hate to say it but it wouldn't have mattered nearly as much."

"Your life or theirs, I get it." Ali nodded.

"Is there such a thing as accidental winging?" I joked, but was seriously worried.

"If there is, let's just try not to make it a thing here. Besides, I'll be down there with you. Like I said, I'm good, but I can be better." She mimed a few karate moves. "I want to learn to kick some major ass, too. If you feel yourself losing control, just use me as a guinea pig."

"A guinea pig?" I raised a brow. "You sure about that?"

"Yeah, whenever you need to, just call me to the front to make me show a move or something. This way, all eyes are off you and you can take a moment to cool down while I embarrass myself."

"Okay, that might work." I hugged her. "Thank you for doing this."

"Don't worry about it. Let's hope it works." She pointed to the entrance of the communal space where Kaden stood.

"Oh great, an audience," I groaned. "As if there wasn't enough pressure."

"I'm sure he is just here to make sure you know what you're doing out there. It's like a class audit." She shrugged. "Once he is sure of your abilities, he'll likely stop showing up."

"Well, let's get the audit over with." I tossed my arms over her shoulder as we marched forward.

We joined the court, where rows of hesitant eyes waited. Of course, no one there really trusted me. Like Zodiac said, trust was a thing that was earned. These people didn't even know me.

"Alright, let's get started, please take your stances," I started and was met with raised brows of confusion. "Stand about four feet apart. You're going to want some space to move around."

It took a few minutes longer than I would have liked, but they got into position. The people who stood in front of me varied in so many ways. Some were old and strong; others were young and weak. There were women and men, and one person who informed me they were nonbinary. None of that mattered to me. Only their ability to follow direction and absorb the information provided to them.

"Let's start with some simple stretches and connective breathing." I announced, then frowned when I heard snickers from the crowd.

"Breathing? I thought you were going to teach us how to fight. I already know how to breathe." The troll of a man who fought me the night before instigated a round of laughter. I'd think he'd be the last one to interrupt me, but the male ego was a powerful thing.

"Okay," challenge accepted. He'd be my example for the rest of the class. "Come to the front, please."

After a few vulgar sounds to the surrounding men, he obliged. He lumbered to the front of the space and stood beside me.

"What's your name?" I asked as I circled him, assessing yet again the massive wall of muscle. He was strong, but that didn't make him a fighter.

"Aero." His voice dripped with the same ego that landed him on his ass the day before.

"Great, Aero, nice to meet you," I paused. "Aero, I want you to hit me. With everything you have."

"You serious? I wouldn't want to mess up that pretty face of yours."

"I'm not worried about that." I winked.

As expected, he applied the same tactic he had before. He charged me time and time again, only this time I used far less effort to beat him. Without so much as lifting a foot from the spot where I stood, I dodged every blow. I let him continue his futile efforts until he stood in front of me, gasping for air.

"Are you done?" I asked calmly.

"Yeah, whatever." He waved his hand as he brushed off my false concern and returned to the lineup with the others.

"The basis of fighting is breathing. Especially for a phoenix, with or without your flame, your source of power comes from every pull of air that enters your lungs." I addressed the men and women in front of me. "My trainer believes it stems from the unpopular belief that our people and the dragons were once a single soul. Your breath is your control, it's your perception of the world around you. Control your breathing and you become a stronger fighter. So again, places, and we will start with simple stretches and connective breathing."

There were no more outbursts of questions about my ability. The men who laughed at Aero's comments quickly realized that even something as simple as breathing could be challenging, especially when combined with yoga. Only once did I feel like I was slipping over the edge, losing hold of the bird that begged to burn, but I brought myself back from it easily.

The one thing I couldn't get away from were those dark eyes that watched my every move. Standing at the back of the space, Kaden kept watch. Each breath I took, he echoed. Each new stretch I taught, e examined with great scrutiny. As I worked, I became more aware of his presence. Though he never moved, I swear I could feel his warmth on my back. Like he was standing behind me, mimicking my motions.

It's something odd about having a man watch you after being kept alone for your entire life. The only male phoenix I had any consistent interaction with was Zodiac. All the other advisers and caretakers, besides a handful of monks, were women. And there I was training a bunch of men and women who I didn't know under the watchful eye of a man who I suddenly wanted to know everything about.

The training went on for days. Each day, I arrived to find students who were more eager to learn. They weren't trolls anymore; they were people who trusted my abilities and practiced my lessons. Even Aero showed pride when I complimented his stance. As unbelievable as it sounded, there was a point where the man was actually taking notes from my lessons. And I no longer felt as if I were proving myself. I was just helping them.

I realized, as I watched them gradually improve, that's all I wanted to do. It felt good to feel needed for once in my life. I wasn't a burden, a recurring item on someone's checklist of chores for the day. And with the growing trust of my students was the lessening skepticism of Kaden. And on that fourth day, just as Ali suggested, Kaden didn't show.

"You're great out there," Kaden's voice startled me as I exited the training space. He chuckled, clearly satisfied that he'd caught me off guard. "I'm impressed."

"I'm glad you approve." I dabbed my forehead, careful to remove sweat and not foundation.

"How did you really learn all that?" Kaden repeated the questions he'd issued twice before. While he approved of my abilities, he still wondered about my history.

"I told you, I grew up in a place where education and self-defense were the only things that mattered," I repeated my answer. "There really isn't much more to tell. I'm taking them through the same sequence may trainer used for me, only a little faster since time isn't on our side here."

"Understood." The same response again. He wouldn't give up until he found out what he wanted to know. "Well, again, I'll tell you, you're doing a good job with them. I already see a strong improvement in their abilities."

"Thank you, Kaden." I smiled as he joined me on my walk to my bunker. They'd offered to move us from the visitor's section, but I requested to stay there, and Kaden agreed. It would be easier to keep my secret if I didn't have people too close by.

"Are you okay?" Kaden nodded to Aero, who jogged past us and waved.

"Why do you ask?" I nodded to the large man who I learned was much more of a sweetheart than he originally let on. Each day, he'd bring me puff pastries at dinner. Ali said he was sucking up for brownie points, but I felt it was because he was truly a nice guy who finally let his guard down.

"I see you out there sometimes. You hold back." Kaden observed. "Why?"

"I'm not a trainer," I quickly made up the excuse. "Hell, I'm still learning myself and sometimes my control can be a little off. That's why Ali steps in to help. I asked her to."

"Ah, I see. Don't want to hurt the newbies," he nodded.

"I appreciate that. We need everyone strong for what's coming."

"Didn't think it would look good on me if I came in and started harming the students." I laughed to distract from my nerves. "Besides, they have to learn to trust me and if I hurt them, they never will. This way, they can learn and build confidence. It's important for any fighter's development."

"I understand." He nodded, and his dreadlocks shifted around his face.

"Where did you learn?" I turned the questioning on him.

"I'm s-sorry?" he stuttered. I'd never asked Kaden about his history, but this was the perfect time.

"You're a fighter. I can tell by the way you handled your sword." I pointed to the weapon that hung at his side. "That's more than natural ability. Someone training you to do that."

"You're very astute, Elsfaer." He touched the hilt of the sword but said nothing else.

"You want to tell me about it?" I nudged him to keep talking.

"Not really, but since you shared, I suppose it's only fair that I do the same." He looked back at the others, still gathered outside our makeshift gym. "Take a walk with me?"

"Is that not what we're doing?" I asked, and he frowned, so I gave a simple agreement. "Yeah, sure."

Kaden led me through the barriers that protected his people out into the Darkest Forest. Whatever he wanted to share with me was enough of a secret for him to risk being caught by the creatures that lurked in the shadows. I followed him without question. Not because I didn't care about my safety, but because I wanted to know what he hid from the others.

"I learned from my father." He started when he felt we were safely out of range of any eavesdroppers.

"Your father?" That didn't sound like a big deal to me. I wondered why he wouldn't want them to know?

"Yes, he was an Elitesman, a general, actually. One of the toughest to hold the position, and his goal was to groom his son to be the same. The only problem with his plans was that he hadn't expected me to turn out this way, a flameless." He looked to the sky as if watching his history play out above us. "No one expected it. Both he and my mother were strong Blue Flames. I should have been a magnificent phoenix, yet here I am with no wings."

"Oh." I stood there looking like a moron. What more was there for me to say?

"The moment they realized I would not have wings, my family disowned me." Kaden continued, despite my dumfounded expression. "I expected it. We ostracized most of the flameless. I wasn't surprised at all, because I was the same way. After they realized my downfall, my father, the ever-proud warrior that he was, turned his back on me. He took another protégé under his wings and overnight, it was like I never existed."

"I'm sorry that happened to you." I laid my hand on his shoulder, the only offer of comfort I could give.

"We all have our tragedies out here." Kaden looked in my eyes as if searching my soul for the tragedy I hadn't shared with him.

"And no one knows yours?" I looked away from his weighted gaze.

"They have to trust me. To know that my father is a general would only cast doubt." He straightened. "Some have their suspicions, but I believe they understand my position here. We have to be one team."

"I see." I chewed my lip. One team.

"I'm glad that you're here. Ali was right about you. You've been a valuable addition to our ranks."

"Valuable addition." I smiled. Hell, if the leader could have his secrets, so could I.

"Yes." He nodded. "You bring more than combat training. There is peace here that wasn't before. Less fear."

"Good." I sighed. "Knowing you can protect yourself is comforting."

"Did I say something wrong?" Kaden frowned.

"No, not at all." Absentmindedly, I wiped a fresh layer of sweat from my brow and when I saw the makeup smeared across the back of my hand, I dropped my head. "I need to go."

"Sorry, I didn't mean to—"

"No, it's not you." I held my hand over my forehead, hoping to cover any spot that may be showing. "I just need to rest. It's been a long day of training. I haven't had days like this in a while." I lied. My days spent training the Flameless were the most relaxed ones I'd had in years. Probably because I wasn't the one getting my ass beat each time.

"Oh, right. Okay. I'll see you around," Kaden called after me as I crossed through the magical barrier to run back to my bunker.

"Absolutely," I called back to him, again thankful that they kept our bunkers isolated from the general population. *How would I explain my behavior to the others if they saw me?*

"That was great. I can't wait until tomorrow!" Ali bounced into the room moments after I started digging through my bag and noticed the worried look on my face. "What's wrong?"

"I'm running out." I tossed the bag on the floor. "What am I supposed to do?"

"The makeup?"

"Yes." I held up my stash of empty containers. "I don't have many left."

"I meant to ask, why are you using that?" She handed me a container of water. They crafted the bottles out of leaves and other materials. "Figured you were thirsty."

"Thanks, but what do you mean? Why do I use it?" I thought the answer was obvious. "I have to hide my markings."

"Yeah, but there are better ways than that human stuff. It's horrible for your skin and the environment."

"What else would I use?" I swallowed the lukewarm water in one gulp. It was better to get it over with as quickly as possible. The stuff left a horrible taste that lingered on the palette.

"Oh, that's right, you don't know our ways." She rambled in her bag. "I'm really surprised your handlers didn't tell you more about this. You'd think they'd want you to know the best ways to keep yourself safe."

"My handlers, right?" The comment hurt because it was true.

The people I grew up with were not my family. They were there to handle me. To make sure I learned what I needed and did nothing too risky. If there was anything out there that would conceal my truth, Zodiac wouldn't want me to know about it. It would have given me more reason to escape sooner.

"What's this?" I held my hand out as Ali stood with a small bottled in her hand.

"Think of it as a magical concealer. It will hide your markings a lot better than that stuff you cake onto your skin every day." She tossed a metal bottle to me. "Besides, you won't have to reapply it constantly and pray that it doesn't melt from your face in the middle of battle."

"And you're just telling me about this now?" I huffed. "This would have been convenient to have before."

"Look, I didn't want to seem too pushy." Ali held her hands up. "We barely knew each other and for all I knew, you were against this method. Besides, it's not wise to take magical potions from strangers."

"Ali," I crossed the room.

"Yes?" She braced as if I was going to punch her.

"Thank you." I hugged her again. "You've done more for me in this short time than people I've known my entire life. I don't know what I would do without you."

"So, you keep telling me." She laughed, but returned the firm embrace. "This may sound weird, but you're my family now, Elsfaer. Flames or not. And I look out for my family. I know you're still afraid of what's coming. And you have every right to be. I just want to make this time as easy as possible for you. This will help. It tastes funny, but it works."

"Thank you again."

"No problem." She turned to leave the room again, but I stopped her.

"You know we will have to leave soon, right?" I took the top from the bottle and peered at the weird shimmering liquid within. "We can't stay here forever. I need to keep moving."

"Yeah, I figured as much." She turned to me. "Just one more day?"

"Sure, I don't see how one more day would hurt." I swallowed the potion and, as the metallic taste stuck to my tongue, wished it was the odd tasting water.

CHAPTER 11

THOUGH WE AGREED ON ONE MORE DAY, THAT DAY TURNED into three. Ali was convincing when she wanted to be. Not only did she convince me to help her, but the people of the Flameless community made me feel so wanted. It was hard to walk away from that, knowing that I would be alone on the other side. Still, I worried that spending too much time in one place would only lead Zodiac to me sooner.

"It's been nice having you here," Kaden commented as we walked together again. This had become our tradition after morning training. He'd meet me at the exit, and we'd stroll for an hour or more talking about our pasts, mostly his. I was a convenient outlet for everything he'd been forced to keep to himself.

He told me of his troubled relationship with his father and how that struggle only worsened after his mother passed away. She fell ill suddenly, and because she was centuries older than his father, her flame burned out for the last time. Most thought the Phoenix people were immortal because we're reborn from our flame, but that only happens so many times, and there's no standard number of burns you got. It's different for every bird.

His father took his mourning and turned it into abuse. Kaden became his emotional punching bag. He thought that he'd be able to make up for losing his mother when he got his wings. Unfortunately, his maturing only worsened the relationship he had with his family.

"I really appreciate your sharing so much with me, Kaden." I sat on the log next to him. The fallen tree just south of the barrier wall had become our hideaway. It was far enough not to be bothered by the Flameless, but close enough that we could make it back inside without being seen if someone or something approached us.

"I should thank you for listening to it all." His shoulders relaxed. "It's been a while since I've been able to talk about any of it."

"Don't you think your friends here would talk to you about it?" I gestured back to the hidden campsite.

"Yes, but I don't want to show that side of myself here." He straightened. "They need someone who is sure to lead them. I have to give them that."

"I'm glad you could get it off your chest. It's not good to hold stuff in like that, especially when you're supposed to be leading a community of people. They depend on you to be levelheaded."

"I never thought I'd be in this position." Kaden admitted. "A warrior, yes, maybe even win a few awards to make my father proud, but then I'd have my own family.

I'd build a quiet life for myself away from the mess. This was never in the plans."

"I think we have to learn quickly when we mature that life doesn't go by a plan we design. Being here, with you, wasn't a part of my plan." I dropped my shoulders and watched the shifting treetops. "But I'm glad for it. I'm glad that I got to see how the Flameless live. There was so much kept from me where I was. I never realized how sheltered a life I'd lived until meeting you and your people. I never knew how important it was for me to feel like I belonged somewhere. But I understand that now."

"You belong somewhere, Elsfaer. You belong here with us." He turned to me and looked into my eyes. "And they aren't my people. They're our people. You are one of us now."

"I—" I almost told him everything, confessed my truth and allowed him to cast whatever judgment he deemed fitting. Almost, but then his lips pressed against mine and for a moment I forgot what my truth was.

The gentle kiss turned hot as the taste of his lips awakened something within me I hadn't realized was there. I became consumed with him. Lust rushed through my brain, pulling me closer to him. Kaden didn't hold back. He matched my passion with his own heat, unpinning the bun in my head and letting my hair flow freely down my back.

"You're breathtaking," he commented with a ravenous grin before my lips captured his again.

We'd forgotten ourselves in the moment and became lost in the growing heat between us. Everything that was

Kaden overwhelmed my senses. I knew nothing of this experience, of heat, passion, lust, but I wanted more of it.

My fingers intertwined with his dreadlocks as we kissed, and I felt the tingle dance across my spine. Thoughts of my flame entered my mind, and I pulled back, ready to give an excuse for my abrupt change in mood. My explanation wasn't required thanks to the deep growl from the shadows forced us apart.

"What was that?" I asked in a breathless whisper.

"That was our cue to head back inside." Kaden took a deep breath to calm himself as his eyes scanned the tree line.

"Do you think we can make it?" I slowly shifted my weight and stood beside him.

"Yes, if we move now." Kaden nodded, and we took off running for the entrance.

The heavy footfalls chased after us. I dared not look back to find out what was large enough to sound like a truck barreling through the forest. Horrible growls and snarling called out. Whatever it was, it was hungry, and we were nothing but tasty treats to add to the menu.

I made it through the barrier first. It was another agonizing few moments before Kaden dashed inside.

"What happened?" I asked after he nearly crashed into me.

"I had to lead it away from here." He fell to the ground as he caught his breath. "This barrier is strong, but a thing like that could easily break through."

"What the hell was that?" I stood over him looking at the barrier, but nothing came.

"We call them gnarlies, because of the sound they

make. Think if a Kynuski mated with a werewolf. Trust me, it's not something you ever want to come face to face with." He described the monster I hadn't seen.

"That sounds horrible." I frowned. What other atrocities lived out there? How could we really expect to be safe living where we were?

"It is."

"I'm glad you're okay." I offered my hand to help him from the ground. The heat was still there in our palms. And it radiated up my arm and to my chest.

"Yeah, me too." He looked at me like he wanted to take me back to that log and do other things to me. I wasn't sure I would deny him if he asked.

"Um, I think I'll go get cleaned up now." I pointed toward my bunker. "I know Ali must be wondering where I am."

"Yeah, that's smart. There are things I need to take care of as well." He swallowed the thought he didn't speak.

"Good, um," I began my retreat. "I'll see you around."

"Definitely." Kaden nodded and watched me leave.

When I entered the room, face warm and mind swimming, Ali waited inside. She laid across her cot, popping more bread into her mouth.

"Another rendezvous?" She winked.

"We have to get the hell out of here. Now," I answered.

"What? What happened?"

"Kaden happened. We're getting too close. This is dangerous." I paced the room. "Besides, I told you days ago that we would leave. Time is up. I need to move on."

"Did he hurt you?" She jumped up like she would find

him and kick his ass for whatever she imagined he'd done.

"No, he didn't." I sat on my cot. "He was wonderful. He—"

"Say no more." She sat up and put her bread to the side. "I know that look. Danger ahead. It's time to go."

———

I spent the day avoiding Kaden, and when it was time for dinner, Ali went alone and brought back food for me. It was the cowardly thing to do, but I didn't know how else to handle things. We wouldn't be able to leave until the nightfall while the others were sleeping. There were a few guards on the night shift, but they wouldn't be too difficult to dodge.

"Not even going to say goodbye. Was my kiss that bad?" Kaden called out in the darkness. "Or is it because I lost my breath after running from that gnarly? I guess I should have paid more attention to your first classes."

"No, I," I turned to him, struggling to find the words to say. How could I tell him the truth without further breaking his trust? Not that he would trust me again. I was the thing he hated most in the world. The Elite. A bird with flame.

"Where are you going?" He asked when I said nothing else.

"There are some things we need to handle." Ali stepped forward.

"I didn't ask you," he silenced her without taking his eyes off me.

"Excuse me?" she snipped.

"Every time I ask you a question, you avoid it. And if Ali is nearby, she chimes in. You're allowed your secrets. I get that, but for once, tell me the truth, Elsfaer." He looked me in the eye. "Where are you going?"

"I'm," I dropped my eyes to the ground and then back to him. "Kaden, I'm the Elite."

"Are you kidding me with this?" He stepped back, examining me with his eyes as if he would find something new.

"No, I'm not." I wanted to approach him, but decided against it. The way he looked at me, I couldn't be sure he wouldn't lash out. "I told you I was raised away from everyone else. It's because I'm different and I have been since birth. My handlers knew who I was and what I was and they knew people would want to hurt me. I know so little about Penumbra because my home was a temple on Earth."

"Get out," Kaden pointed to the barrier wall.

"What?" His response, though valid, hurt me. I expected him to be upset, but not to kick me out of his home.

"Get out before I do something we both regret." Kaden spoke through a tight jaw as he tried to manage his anger at the moment.

"Kaden," Ali interjected.

"How could you bring her here? How could you risk the lives of everyone?" Kaden's eyes were wide with his anger. He kept his voice low so as not to attract the guards.

"She isn't like the others," Ali defended me.

"Yeah right, they're all the same and you know that. She is no different. Even if they raised her away from them, the second she gets back there, she will become like the rest. She will be a danger to our people. Now we have to run again."

"You don't have to. I would never do anything to hurt anyone here," I promised.

"Save it." Kaden's anger turned on me. "I trusted you. I told you things about me I've never shared with another person and you thought so little of me that you kept this to yourself. You let me bare my soul all while you hid behind your mask. Like I said before, you are just like the rest of them."

"Kaden, please." I stepped forward, but stopped when he lifted his hand.

"I'm giving you one chance to leave before the others find out who you are." He threatened.

"I—" I didn't know what to say. There were no words that could erase the hurt in his eyes.

"Let's just go." Ali grabbed my arm, pulling me away from him.

"Yeah, um, okay." I followed her.

My last view of the inside of the Flameless haven was Kaden, shoulders slumped, and a tear falling from pain-filled eyes. I couldn't help wonder if he was right. Was I no better than the other phoenix people who'd turned their backs on him?

CHAPTER 12

"You could have stayed back there. I would have understood." I spoke to Ali. The forest moved around us, shadows came to life and creatures we couldn't see watched us from within the shifting darkness as we walked.

"Why would I stay there?" Ali hadn't said a word since we left.

"It was your chance for acceptance. I saw you there, with the others. You fit in, they loved you. You enjoyed being there. That's why you wanted to stay longer." I pointed out the obvious.

"There?" she stopped and laughed. "You can't be serious. I never wanted to be there. Hell, I'd been dodging Kaden and he crew for months. I just thought it would be good for you. If you ask me, even though it didn't end in the best way, you benefited from your time there."

"I did," I nodded. Being with the Flameless opened my

eyes to so many things that needed to be addressed. If I stood as elite, I would take care of them.

"Besides, the only reason they're interested in me is because of my fire. They claim to be so much better than the winged, but they aren't. Look how they treated you. Even though they thought you were a flameless, you had to prove yourself worthy before they would even accept you as a part of their people." Ali scoffed. "They're just as bad as the others. The only difference is that they have convinced themselves they're not, and honestly, that makes them more dangerous. At least the winged admit that they think they are better than us. They don't pretend like it's something we're all imagining."

"You're right. I'd rather my oppressor be up front about it." I agreed with her. "But I'm not sure that what they're going through is the same. They're defensive, and concerned about who they let it. As they should be."

"Still, I'd rather you look in my eye and tell me what you really think about me, so I know the truth from the start." She kept walking because we had to keep moving. There were things waiting for us to slip up. Had we taken cover before nightfall, we wouldn't have had nearly as much to worry about. "So, how are you feeling?"

"What do you mean?" I asked, but turned my eyes towards the dark void left of us where I heard an animal hiss.

"I know you felt something for Kaden. The way you two were getting all chummy." A bird called out in the distance and she listened to its song before continuing. "Those after training meetups, they weren't just to discuss

119

strategy, were they? Walking away from that couldn't have been easy."

"No, it wasn't, but I had to. Getting to know him was nice, but I'm running out of time. Either way, he would have realized who I was. Just wish I'd handled things better instead of trying to sneak out in the middle of the night like a coward."

"That's becoming a habit for you, huh?" she questioned. "I mean, isn't that how you left the temple?"

"Yeah, I guess it is." My shoulders slumped as I considered her questions. In both instances, when faced with a conflict, I ran instead of confronting them head on. How would I be an effective leader if that's how I handled things?

"Oh, don't get upset." Ali sucked her teeth. "You have that introspective look again. I'm sorry. You did what you thought was best."

"That doesn't make it right." I shook my head. "Besides, I'm not sure I did what I really felt was best. Truth is, I knew it was best to talk to Zodiac, but it was easier to run away. And that's the same thing I did with Kaden."

"True," she agreed, adding to the sting of her previous realization.

"Oh, thanks for that." I tapped her shoulder.

"Hey, I'm just being a good friend here." She stuck her tongue out, and we laughed.

Our quiet laughter was enough to bother the wildlife that rustled next to us. Ali lifted her finger to her lips, silencing the soft chuckles.

We continued through the night and found ourselves

outside of the Darkest Forest. Stepping out of the boundary brought me into the sunlight for the first time in days. With the rays of the sun warming my skin, the guilt I felt about how I handled things with Kaden eased.

We still had a few days before we would make it to Phaedrial, but Ali promised easier travels with the Kynuski's home behind us. The worst part of it was making it outside the borders of the Odious. The land of the Dark was no place for two creatures of the light.

They split Penumbra into two halves. One half, the Odious, belonged to the Dark. The other half, the Alluring, belonged to the Light. The Odious was more than just the home of beings who wielded dark magic. It hid horrible things in places that stood as the backdrop for nightmares. The Darkest Forest was just one of those locations. Our path would take us through several other territories, where creatures who fed off the dark energies of the land would take any opportunity to attack.

We made it, sticking close to the territory's borders. By the time we made it to Lake Asunder, where they said mysterious creatures dwelled within the water, we'd avoided at least five near encounters with dark beings. Two vampires, an actual ogre, and on more than one occasion, we crossed what looked like a demon, but we were never sure.

"There are new things popping up out here every day. I think it's because the balance of this place is out of whack." Ali explained after we heard another strange sound she couldn't explain. "More people lean towards the Dark each day. There is speculation that the High

Spirit chose so many new Elites because of it. Five at once! It's unheard of!"

The entire time we walked, I had a nagging feeling that we were being followed, but the evidence suggested I was paranoid, and Ali went with the evidence. Still, I was cautious of the Shadows.

I didn't tell her, but there was something else I was worried about. The Odious had more than just evil beings lurking. There were also shades. The shades were an elite group of agents recruited from all supernatural groups to police both Penumbra and Earth. Once someone became a shade, they had to leave behind all connections to their homes and cut all relationship ties. It was a lifelong commitment.

The shades were also known to work with the Elites, and their guards. Knowing that Zodiac was once an Elitesman, I worried that he might have tapped into that old relationship to put eyes on me. If a shade was following me, there was nothing I could do about it. Shades could blend seamlessly with their surroundings, only being seen when they wanted to.

"We're about half a day away from Phaedrial." Ali sat with her feet in the shallows of the lake. "We should make it there by nightfall."

"Good, I'm tired of walking." I looked out at the water, disappointed that I hadn't witnessed the monsters I read about. Ali's toes would have been the perfect temptation if there was anything stirring within.

"You could just unleash those wings of yours and fly us right out of here." Ali pointed to my back

"You know I can't do that." I looked at the sky. "I

mean, it's wonderful, flying. But the moment I do that here is the moment I am no longer me. I become the Elite, and everything changes. There are people looking for me. I'd like just one more day not to be indebted to them."

"I understand. How about when we make it there, I show you around my old stomping grounds? Introduce you to the city." Ali suggested. "Maybe once you get to know the place, you'll feel more comfortable showing them who you are."

"Is it different there?" I asked. "I mean, all I've really seen is its woods and open plains. The pictures in the textbooks don't really give a clear representation of what it looks like today."

"I hear Phaedrial is a lot closer to what Earth looks like now. Over the years, there has been a lot of technology brought in. Scouts go to Earth, learn what they can, and bring it back here to be replicated. I wouldn't be surprised if it feels more like you're there than here."

"Considering I've never been to a major city either here or on Earth, it will all feel strange to me." I laid back in the grass, bathing in the sun longer. "You think that's the problem with Phaedrial?"

"What do you mean?" She joined me in the grass.

"Kaden mentioned the change in technology, too. Like he thinks it's at the root of the problem. I mean, we're in the world of magic. That's what Penumbra is. It's a balance between light and dark, but this realm is the origin of magic. If Phaedrial is powered by technology, maybe that's what's blocking its magic. There are studies about the effects of electro-magnetic fields caused my technology. Many people think it's why things are so tumultuous on Earth. Maybe it's why there are more and more people who are now flameless."

"It's one of the better theories I've heard. But again, I don't know that much about technology except it makes everything way too bright. You can barely see the stars at night in Phaedrial now. And without wings, there isn't even the option of flying above the lights." She crossed her legs. "See, you're going to be great at being the Elite."

"I'm glad you think so."

We spent another hour lounging by the lake before we moved on. Only once did I see movement in the water. But it was nothing more than a simple eel that swam near us and that was frightened away by a strong breeze. Ali pouted when we left. She wanted to see the mysterious beast who handed out luck. Hell, so did I. I could use all the luck I could get.

CHAPTER 13

THE SUN SET MOMENTS BEFORE WE MADE IT TO PHAEDRIAL. A range of mountains surrounded the Phoenix home on three sides and on the other was the sea, making the territory one of the most difficult to enter. Most phoenixes just flew right over, but since the rise of the Flameless population, they installed magical doorways along the borders.

The barrier recognized the magic of anyone who approached. Not all magic was equal in Penumbra. Every species had a different magical signature and that could bind spells, lock curses, and unlock secret passage ways. The magic at the barrier only responded to the magic specific to the phoenix.

"Last chance to change your mind." Ali looked up at the barrier fence marked with two massive wings. The symbol seemed like a slap in the face to the people who had to use the passage. They were there because they had no wings and yet here they were hanging over their head as a reminder of how they were lesser than the others who lived there.

"No turning back. I have to face this." I straightened.

"Alright, here we go." Ali stepped up to the gate.

She reached out to the entrance and called her blue flame to dance across her hand. The gate hummed, the metal vibrating with energy as it recognized her magic. A moment later, the hinges creaked as the pathway opened to us. Just as we prepared to pass through, the gate slammed shut with an echoing bang.

"What happened?" I asked and touched the bars. They hummed the same as they had before, but they didn't open.

"I don't know. That never happened to me before." She placed her hand on one of the massive bars. Though she didn't have wings, like the other Flameless, the essence of our ancestors' magic remained inside of her. That magic was the key to opening the pathway. Unfortunately, it still wouldn't open. "It recognizes us, but it won't budge."

"Is there another entrance?" Though we were outside of the Odious, it didn't mean we were safe from harm. With the sundown, nefarious beings were out to play.

"Yea, about fifty miles away." She smacked the gate as if that alone would be enough to make it open.

"Why would this happen?" We needed to think tactically about the situation. "Are there fail safes that would stop the magic from working?"

"The only time the gates don't work is when there is dark energy near." Ali stepped back and examined the gates. She looked back at me. "Its like an emergency feature, to make sure that no one who isn't supposed to be here gets in."

"Dark energy?" I looked at my hand and removed it from the gate. Was it sensing me? Was I the dark energy that the gate warned us of?

"Yea, I—" she paused; eyes squinted in the darkness. "Fuck!"

"What is it?"

"We gotta get out of here." She grabbed my hand, pulling me away from the fence.

"What is going on, Ali?" Though confused, I followed her. If something scared her, it was for a good reason.

"Well, well, look what we have here." A short man with a cauldron for a belly fell into our path. He was a phoenix, though his wings were dark, almost ash instead of flame. "Two little birdies have lost their way."

"Leave us alone!" Ali pulled me away from him.

"Jackson, is this the one who kicked your asses?" The bearded man laughed as others appeared, some from the sky and some from the shadows. "She doesn't look all that big and bad."

"I told you she had help." The wild-haired boy appeared beside the cauldron. The same one who'd attacked me when I first landed in Penumbra.

"Two girls beat the four of you," a wild voice called out from behind us. Laughter erupted as they mocked Jackson for having let a woman challenge his manhood.

"It wasn't like that," Jackson defended himself.

"Either way," Tubby retorted. "Let's get this over with. Get 'em!"

"You remember your training?" I whispered to Ali as more of the dark figures appeared around us.

"Connective breathing," she nodded.

The first charged us, and without breaking a sweat, we sidestepped him and kicked him simultaneously in the ass, sending him flying headfirst into the large bolder behind. His body slumped against the rocks and the others gasped.

"See, I told you," Jackson muttered, and his potbellied leader ordered more attacks.

One after another, the men came for us and, for a while, we held our own. We were like the shadows themselves, fluid and untouchable. Ali defended herself with confidence, but we were outnumbered and outsized. Their smallest attacker still towered over us. After the fourth wave, Ali grew tired, and they capitalized on her exhaustion.

The rope wrapped around her chest, pinning her arms to her sides. They quickly tied another around her calves and ankle. She fell forward to the ground, nearly smacking her forehead on a large rock.

Ali became my distraction and in a mad dash to save her, I left myself vulnerable. They were on top of me within a second. Two men nearly twice my size pinned me to the ground as a third tide, my ankles together. They pulled me to my knees by my hair and forced to look up at their fat leader. I could hardly see his face over the mass that hung in front of him.

"Well, that was fun, wasn't it?" he laughed, and his stomach bounced so much it nearly smacked me in the face.

"There's something different about her." Jackson kneeled beside me.

"Yeah," Tubby waved his hand. "Whatever you say. As long as she has the markings, I don't really give a damn about how she's changed since the last time you saw her."

I knew something was off when I first ran into Jackson. The way he paused before he followed his friends away from us, he could see my markings. I didn't know how or when, but I messed up and I left myself vulnerable long before I ever became friends with Ali. I said a silent prayer as they ripped my jacket from my arms that the magic my friend provided me was still working. If they were after me because of my markings, it meant they knew I was the Elite.

"She has no markings!" The man who smelled like a cow's ass announced as he threw my jacket to the ground.

"I swear, Fado," Jackson pleaded. "Believe me. I saw them!"

"You brought us all the way to the outskirts of Phaedrial for nothing?" Fado yelled at Jackson and pushed him to the ground. "Do you know how much trouble we could get in for being here?"

"She's the one, I swear." Jackson turned on me and pulled at my shirt.

The firm hand of his leader, who backhanded him, stopped his efforts to strip my clothes away. Jackson fell to his knees and held the side of his face where the bruise appeared around his right eye.

"Yeah, well, looks like you were wrong," Fado spit at him. "Again. I don't have to tell you how much he will not like this."

"Please." Jackson begged. "Something isn't right here. You have to believe me."

"It's out of my hands, Jackson." Fado shook his head. "You know this."

"What do you want to do now, Fado?" The smelly one asked as his hand twisted in my hair. He took a deep breath, inhaling my scent. "She was with the Flameless. How could you possibly think she is the next elite?"

"She tricked them," Jackson answered. "I don't know how, but she did."

"We were told what to look for, and this ain't it." Fado leaned into me, and his foul breath filled my nostrils.

"Makeup!" Jackson shouted desperately, and pointed at my face.

"Excuse me?" Fado raised a brow.

"She's covered them with makeup." He said, as if he'd uncovered a monumental secret.

"You're really reaching now, Jackson." Fado's handler released me and two others grabbed my arms. "Just admit it, you fucked up!"

"Shut up and give me a rag or something." Jackson marched back over to me and grabbed the dirty fabric Fado pulled from his pocket.

I pulled away from him, but with my arms and legs restrained, there wasn't much I could do to stop him scrubbing my face with the disgusting material. When he pulled the rag from my skin, it left my face covered in a grime that wasn't there before.

"See, nothing." The others laughed.

Still convinced he was right; Jackson pulled the water strapped to his side and doused the rag with the water before scrubbing my face again. My cheek was raw when Fado knocked him away again.

"Give up, it's not her!" he yelled. "You're embarrassing yourself, Jackson. Just accept that you were wrong."

"I know what I saw!" Jackson cried out.

"Well, maybe you need to get your vision checked because we're not seeing it." Fado turned to the men who held us. "Take care of this mess and head back before we're spotted out here."

His ashened wings spread from his back. Before he took off, he peered at Jackson. "Find your way back, boy. And make sure you're prepared to face him when you get there."

As their chubby leader took to the sky, it gave the men he left behind free range to do whatever they wanted to us.

CHAPTER 14

Not a moment after Fado disappeared beyond the cloud did his minions start in on us. Fist pummeled my chest and back until I fell over. As they kicked me in the stomach, I fell to my side and could see the same abuse being dished out to Ali.

I could take anything they had to give me. I was strong, but Ali wasn't like me. She hadn't gone through years of brutal training to build her resistance. When the blood spilled from her lips, my vision blurred. My body grew hotter with each blow. The pain they inflicted turned into fuel for my fire.

As much as I wanted to hide my identity, it wouldn't matter if I let them kill me. Dying on the ground beneath the boots of a filthy rogue wasn't the way my story ended.

For the first time since I crossed the barrier that landed me in Penumbra, I looked within to connect to my fire. The bird burned inside of me, ready to break free, but instead of unleashing hell on my attackers, I became trapped inside myself.

Fire seared the inside of my skin as I struggled to free myself. The skin across my back sizzled from the heat of my own wings. No matter how hard I tried to pull her out, my phoenix, my fire, remained trapped beneath the surface.

"Stop it!" Jackson ran and pushed the smelly captain away from me. "You can't do this. I know you don't believe me, but she is the Elite. If you kill her, you ruin everything."

Smelly jumped back with fist ready and knocked Jackson back on his ass. I watched my attacker turned defender closely. He wasn't the same man I met in the woods. He was no longer sure of his actions and instead of fighting back he shied away from the larger man.

Instead of turning back to his project at hand, kicking my ass, Smelly locked his sights on Jackson. "Look at this. You're pathetic! Fado isn't here to protect you now. We can finally get rid of his little pet project. Hell, when you're gone, it will mean a lot less of my time being wasted on these pointless excursions."

"What are you doing?" Jackson asked as Smelly signaled the others to come to his side.

"Oh, I'm just taking care of an internal problem."

The men turned on Jackson and from where I lay on the ground, I could hear the beating they gave him. Bones broke and the smell of his blood filled the air.

"That's enough," Smelly called out. "Leave him here to rot. That's if something else doesn't get to him first."

Their footsteps were returning to us, along with the

sounds of their discussion of how they would finish the job. Smelly bragged about how they would leave no trace of us behind. Again, I reached within, hoping to pull out my fire, but only burned myself with the effort.

Smelly's hand grabbed my chin, and he lifted me to my knees. His dark eyes stared into mine as he raised his fist. "Such a pretty face, you got there. I think I can make it better."

His fist crashed into my cheek, sending a stabbing pain through my face as I fell to the ground. He lifted me again and prepared to land another blow. Instead, his eyes lifted to the sky, and he released me. Terror colored his face gray as he backed away from me.

Whatever he saw was enough to make the others run. I heard screaming, fighting, and then silence as Smelly remained frozen in front of me.

"Bring him back for questioning," the voice I thought I'd never be grateful to hear again ordered, and two men captured Smelly and pulled him from my vision.

"Elsfaer, what the hell happened?" Zodiac kneeled in front of me. He scooped his arms beneath me and lifted me from the ground.

Recognizing the grey goatee and scruff at his chin, I smiled. He spoke my name again, followed by words I couldn't understand. My heart warmed, making me feel safe again, before the fire within me burned so brightly that I lost consciousness.

My bruised ribs were still tender as I forced myself into the ceremonial robes. As if being saved by Zodiac wasn't embarrassing enough, I had to live with the physical reminder that my wings failed me. A secret I'd yet to share with anyone. As far as they knew, I hid them because I didn't want my attackers to know who I was.

Something was wrong and there was nothing I could do about it, no one I could confide in because who could help me? The only person who came to mind was Zodiac, and he was the last one I wanted to talk to.

I was grateful that he'd shown up with the others. If not, I'm sure things would have ended worse for me. I remembered little about what happened after Zodiac lifted me from the ground. There was the haze of nearby men talking, followed by the rumble of Zodiac's chest as he issued his orders. Shortly after that came the breeze across my face as he took flight, carrying me from the borders of Phaedrial into its center, where the Elite's castle stood.

They'd designed the territory of Phaedrial quite like a bird's nest itself. The surrounding mountain range and the water acted as the barrier. It presented a strong front against any intruders. But the closer you got to the center, the more life you found. I'd studied maps and images of the territory for hours on end.

What I missed from the books, what wasn't depicted in great detail, was the life of the people. And even though I'd woken up and a massive bed inside the forti- fied Castle, I could feel the life of my people outside of its walls.

When I opened my eyes, a small girl with long red hair

and eyes as wide as the skies sat by my bedside. She had a small pout and wore soft blue robes that complimented her honey skin complexion.

"Oh, you're awake. I hope I didn't startle you." She smiled and handed me a note written in Zodiac's hand, an invitation to meet with the council. Of course, with him, it was right to business.

"By the way, my name is Rose. I'm your assigned assistant, so anything you need, just say the word," she spoke in cheerful chatter as I pulled myself from the bed.

Rose showed me around the space that was apparently my room. She bounced into the closet full of robes and other dressings that would fit my body perfectly.

"You have the state of the line in here! Your shower comes equipped with a sauna, aromatherapy, and massage functionality." She gushed over the modern amenities in the bathroom. "I wish I had this set up at home."

"Well, you can use it whenever you want." I offered the luxuries to her.

"Wow, that's so nice of you." She beamed and then, as if remembering some unwritten rule about the Elite's toilet, she shook her head no. "I could never. It wouldn't be right."

Even if I was okay with it, it wouldn't look right to the others. Rose was Flameless, one of the few who secured a comfortable lifestyle in Phaedrial. One false step and she would be an outcast like all the others.

The bubbly girl would become my friend in the palace, despite rejecting my offer of comfort. They assigned her to keep me safe and comfortable for all events. After taking my meal order, she handed me my wardrobe for the day, laid out my accessories, and headed for the door.

"Do you need help to get dressed?"

"No." I looked at the attire laid out for me. "I think I can manage it on my own."

"Okay, well, I'm here if you need me." She announced before bouncing out of the room.

I dressed myself slowly because of the pain at my side. At least the fabric was soft and it fit just as perfectly as Rose said it would. When the knock sounded at the door, I assumed it was her returning with my mean, but opening the door, I came face to face with the brooding disappointment of Zodiac. I rolled my eyes and left him standing at the entrance alone.

"Elsfaer," Zodiac followed me into the space. "How are you feeling?"

"I feel just about as good as anyone who got their ass kicked by four men." I laid the robe on the bed. It was the last layer of clothing to complete my outfit, but I couldn't struggle with it while being interrogated.

"Do you think you're ever going to explain to me how that happened?" Zodiac closed the door behind him.

"How what happened?"

"I saw those men, Elsfaer. They were weak and poorly trained." He spoke of the attackers who'd nearly taken my life. "You've taken on more challenging fights. They should not have been able to defeat you, not with your training. What went wrong?"

Zodiac was right. There was no way those men, under normal circumstances, would have been able to defeat me. It wasn't the first time the numbers weren't on my side in a fight. Often Zodiac would bring in fighters, people for me to spar with. More often than not, I had to take on multiple opponents at the same time.

"You know, by the time you got there, most of them had left. The men you saw were the cleanup crew, and they were taking advantage of the situation." I explained what he hadn't seen. "Regardless of the circumstances, I don't really need you coming in here and telling me how much I sucked at protecting myself. The bruises, the pain, and the aches — they do that for me."

"You're right. This isn't the time to recount failed battle strategies." He relaxed his shoulders. "I'm just glad you're okay."

"Are you really?" I smirked. "I'm sure."

"Yes, I've been searching for you." Zodiac moved across the room, the gold and white robes flowing around him as he did. "Where were you?"

"It doesn't matter." I changed the topic. How could I tell him where I'd been without betraying the Flameless? Kaden no longer trusted me, but that didn't mean I'd break my word to him. "I'm here now, and there's work to be done. I'm supposed to meet with the council, right? That's what Rose said."

"Yes, that's why I'm here." he nodded.

"Trying to brief me on what needs to be done. How nice of you." I sat on the bed. "Lay it on me."

"Elsfaer, the council expects you to show up with a reason for your absence and give them confidence that you will be a good leader." He dropped the load on my lap. "They aren't confident in your abilities, especially after we brought you in here bloodied and beaten."

"What a surprise. They don't believe in me." I shrugged. "Can't say I blame them."

"I need you to take this seriously." He stabbed the palm of his hand with his fingers like he always did when I annoyed him.

"My life is the one that's on the line here, Zodiac." I straightened. "You think I'm not taking that seriously?"

"I just want us to put a plan together. It would be bad for you to walk out there without one."

"I can just show them my wings, my power. They will back down," I said with less confidence than an elephant on a tightrope.

"Even with your wings, there are people who are far more powerful." Zodiac looked out the large arched windows that gave a perfect view of the mountain tops. "There is still a lot we must do if we want to get you prepared for what is coming."

"Why do you keep talking like that?" I asked. Zodiac was slipping back into his puzzled language. With the pain in my chest and the throbbing in my head, the last thing I wanted was to decipher the meaning behind his words. "Just tell me what is going on."

"Elsfaer," he paused. "You should know the truth. I planned to tell you everything, but you ran away. Now there is just not enough time."

"Tell me what?" I huffed. "Dammit, just spit it out already."

"Your mother sent you away. She left you in my care,

just days after you were born." he repeated a story I'd heard a thousand times before.

"Because of my markings, I know." I tapped my forehead. "You've told me this before, Zodiac."

"It's more than that." He returned to the bedside and placed his hand on my shoulder. "Elsfaer, you were born with your wings."

"What?" I stood from the bed and winced from the pain of the quick movement. "I don't know what you've been drinking since you got here, but let me remind you, I just got my wings. Remember? Big fiery show that nearly killed Kenya!"

"No, you didn't. The magic at Kai Temple kept your wings suppressed as long as you were on the grounds, but you've had them your entire life. We used magic to block your access to them until you came of age. It's the reason we never allowed you to venture away from Kai Temple. We had to hide that from the others. If they knew about you, they would have tried to end your life immediately." Zodiac watched me carefully after he spoke.

His confession hung between us and all I could do was recount all the conversations we'd had over the years. I thought of every time I'd asked about my mother, my past, my future, and Zodiac looked me in the eye each time and lied to me. He said he hadn't known my mother at all, but he knew her. He said I would be free once I hit maturity, that I could protect myself. That was a lie, too. Instead of traveling the world, I was facing the firing squad and being forced into leadership.

"You've lied to me my entire life." I finally spoke and looked him in the eye. "How do I know this is the truth?

How do I know this isn't just another fabrication you're using to get me to act the way you want me to?"

"Your wings and your life stand as a symbol for many people." He explained his positioning. "For some, it is a symbol of hope and prosperity. For others, it is a symbol of chaos and tragedy. It is the latter that we worked to keep you hidden from."

"Instead of preparing me." I held my hand up to him so he wouldn't interrupt me. "Why wouldn't you think to tell me this sooner? Why didn't anyone consider I needed to know these things? I'm not a child, Zodiac. I haven't been for years.

"You wanted me to wait until maturity. When were you going to decide I was mature enough? Clearly, my wings had nothing to do with that because, according to you, I've had them all along. You've had twenty-five years to prepare me, but expect me to walk from complete and total ignorance into a seat of power and understanding in one month!"

"What do you think your trainings were for? Why do you think we spent countless hours teaching you ancients ways of magic and defense?" His jaw tightened as he spoke. "You are not ignorant, Elsfaer."

"Not of the history of this place but of myself, yes I am." I argued.

"We kept from you one major thing, but we taught you everything you needed to know to survive. And again, none of us knew it would happen this way. We assumed you would mature and then we could tell you everything. I thought it would be good for you to have a normal upbringing, or as close to normal as possible, before we placed the weight of the world on your shoulders."

"You keep saying that you didn't know, but you did! You all knew that I was supposed to become the Elite. That I was marked for some significant moment of power. You also knew that there was no way to determine when that change would happen. And instead of taking all the time you could have to allow me to prepare for that moment, you decided for me it was best that I not know." I pointed my finger at his chest and waited for him to debate me, but he didn't.

"You took away from me the one thing that made me special. I had my wings my entire life, and I've only ever used them twice. Two times in all the years that I could have traveled the world and really experienced life. And now I stand here, not ready to face the world but preparing for my own death. Because if that council doesn't accept me or if someone stronger tries to challenge me, my life could end."

"You don't understand, Elsfaer. That was not a message we had the right to deliver. Our prophecies have been wrong before. They could have been wrong this time as well."

"You wanted them to be wrong this time." I scoffed.

"Of course I did!" He shouted, and I flinched. "I didn't want you to have to face this. On top of being special, now you have to be right in the center of things. It's not fair to you."

"Life isn't fair, Zodiac. You taught me that, remember?" I grabbed the robe from the bed. "And our prophecies have been correct more times than they have ever been wrong. You can justify this for yourself in whatever way that makes it easier for you to sleep at night. But we both know that you made the wrong choice. That's something you're going to have to live with and something I will never forget."

"Elsfaer."

"Let's just get this over with. And, Zodiac," I turned to him.

"Yes?"

"I want to see Ali when this is over." I pulled the robe over my shoulders and did my best to keep the pain from my face. "She's my friend and I won't let any of this ruin that. I deserve at least one real friendship, even if you or that council don't believe I do."

CHAPTER 15

THE ANTICIPATION WAS SUFFOCATING. STANDING BEHIND the curtain, waiting to be introduced to a world that did not know I existed, I felt like I would faint. The anger that lingered from my conversation with Zodiac still had my blood boiling. It was unfathomable to think that he could claim to understand why his actions upset me and yet refuse to admit that his actions and decisions were wrong.

He hid so much from me, lied about the very idea of who I was. Zodiac never told me what I was, or prepared me for a life of leading a population of people who saw me as a stranger. He chose what I did and didn't need to know, and he wanted me to see that as nothing more than an omission of facts.

What he didn't seem to understand was that omissions were lies, especially when I asked direct questions. And even more so when dealing with a power as great as the one he expected me to wield.

Zodiac wanted me to accept his lies without issue. He wanted me to be okay with his decision and forgive him. Not only was I to forgive him without question, but also welcome his help with the problems I faced because of what he kept from me.

Every time I looked at him, I saw the face of a liar. How was I to trust anything else that came out of his mouth without wondering what more he was holding back? Every truth I had accepted from him was incomplete. Every experience I'd given up for him, and every bit of faith I'd given him, wasted.

As if it wasn't hard enough facing this new world, the clamoring noises from the other side of the thick curtain were telling. These people didn't know me, and without even hearing my name, they hated me. They wanted someone else, someone they knew and trusted, and that person wasn't me. What could I do about it?

I didn't know or trust any of them. For all I knew, there could have been hundreds planning to shoot me down the second I walked out into the arena. I would be defenseless against them. Again, I kept this to myself. Zodiac was ready to get on my case for losing a fight. He would have blown his lid if he knew I lost my wings.

The speaker addressed the crowd and the unsanctioned discussions quieted until the only voice heard was hers. I leaned in close so I could hear what she had to say.

"Now, I know that we all have our questions." The wholesome voice spoke. "This is unprecedented that a new elite is someone we are not familiar with. However, we will give her a chance to prove herself, just as we have everyone else."

"You should remove your makeup," Zodiac suggested behind me.

"What?" I refused to look back at him.

"Your markings are covered," he clarified, the worry coloring the deep tones of his voice. "It would be good if they could see how special you really are."

"I know." I nodded, again keeping my eyes on the curtain in front of me.

"You—" Zodiac started but I cut him off.

"It's not makeup."

"What?" He grabbed my shoulder but there was no time for further discussion. The speaker called for me to join her on stage.

"Allow me to present your new Elite, Elsfaer Ignacious!"

"Wait—" Zodiac grabbed my shoulder.

"I have to meet my people." I shook his hand off and headed for the stage.

What I thought was on the other side of the curtain was a small room. An intimate setting with maybe a hundred people. Would it have been too much for them to ease me into things? Instead of the small welcome I prepared myself for, I stepped out onto the stage of a grand stadium. There were thousands of faces, all disapproving of my arrival.

Not only were there more people physically there, but there were also cameras. They set the entire thing up like a television studio. Cameras looked at me from all angles as I crossed the stage. Hot lights blasted me in the face and impaired my vision.

I stopped at the podium, where the older woman

waited for me. Her full round face framed with frizzy gray hair, she smiled at me with pity. Green angular glasses rested on her pointed nose and her lips, painted in red, turned into a frown as I approached. Her expression validated everything I feared. That moment would be one of the worst in my life.

With my confidence officially destroyed, I nodded, shook her hand, and turned to face the waiting crowd.

"Hello, my name is Elsfaer Ignacious," I spoke, and the microphone whined and cracked. "The High Spirit chose me to be the next elite for the people of Phaedrial. While this is not a thing I have chosen, I will do my best to honor this position and make you all proud."

"Where are your wings?" Someone called from the crowd.

"Yeah, show us your wings!" Another echoed, repeating the demand, until everyone was chanting the phrase.

"I, -um—" I looked to the speaker, expecting her to step in, but she didn't. "Well, I—"

"What's the matter? Don't you have your wings?" Another man called out and again I lost any chance I had of managing the crowd.

"Yes, well I did, once. But—" I stumbled over my words. How was I supposed to explain to them what happened when I didn't even understand it myself? I'd lost my magnificent wings, the things that made me so special, and I couldn't explain why because I didn't know.

"But what?" The speaker leaned in and questioned me.

"I don't anymore," I admitted, and the room fell horribly silent for a long pause and then chaos ensued.

"How can she be the Elite if she is a Flameless?" A woman yelled out.

"I-I am not a Flameless," I stumbled over my words. The pressure of their expectations and the heat of the lights pointed in my face had my head spinning.

"Then show us your wings!" another voice called out before the chanting started.

"Show your wings! Show your wings!" They repeated while their feet stomped the floor in rhythmic demand.

"I can't," I repeated, but even with the microphone, they couldn't hear me over their own chants.

The crowd booed and yelled ugly curses. I stood proudly, waiting for them to quit, but they didn't. Instead, they started throwing things at me. They launched balls of papers, food, and other things I couldn't identify at the stage. Still, I stood there, accepting their hate until Zodiac pulled me from the angry audience.

"What was that?" he hustled me into the hall out of the line of fire.

"It was the truth," I grunted and straightened the robe around my shoulders. "I told the truth."

"What are you talking about, Elsfaer? I've seen your wings. You have them." Zodiac accused me of lying. "I don't know what you're trying to prove, but this isn't the way to do it."

"I am not lying to you, Zodiac. I don't have my wings anymore. If I had them, I would have used them to defend myself when they attacked us." I pointed out the obvious.

"How is this possible?" The speaker appeared, picking trash from her shoulder. No longer washed out by the bright lights, I could see her clearer. The soft creases near her eyes, the dewy complexion, and the reddish-brown irises peering back at me through the glasses. "It's a madhouse out there. What happened?" She checked the rest of the green peplum dress she wore for degree.

"Apparently." Zodiac's jaw tightened and his eyes darkened. "Our Elite has lost her wings."

"Along with her markings?" Jamila, who I hadn't noticed there before, asked as she peeked out the curtain barrier. She appeared sporting a new haircut, short and red. Jamila was expecting trouble. The only time she chopped her hair off was when she didn't want to have to worry about it, holding her back in a fight. "They're getting rowdy out there."

"Look, this was a mistake. We all see that now." I wanted to hide under a rock until it all blew over. Of course, that wasn't actually an option. "Can I go now?"

"We need to hide her," Jamila announced. She marched over to my side, her hand placed on the hilt of the sword hanging at her hip. "Keep her here in the palace until it's safe to move her somewhere else."

"Excuse me?" I frowned at Jamila. "You want to lock me away?"

"Like it or not, the world knows who you are now." She pointed to the curtain that hid the entrance to the crowded auditorium. "They also know that you are powerless. We cannot risk anyone finding you until we figure this out."

"She's right," Zodiac agreed, and placed his hand on my shoulder, then ushered me down the hall.

Nothing would have been better than running away from him. But as frustrated and rebellious as I felt, I understood their concern. The priority was my safety and figuring out why my wings were gone. I'd only had them for a day, I'd only lifted to the sky twice, and it looked like I never would again. One day with the freedom of my wings. That is all I got. One lousy day.

We made it back to my assigned chambers. Zodiac and Jamila stood by the desk littered with papers and discussed moving me after nightfall but decided that my current location was the best location. The Elite's chambers were the most secure in all of Phaedrial and few people would be desperate enough to attempt to break into the heavily guarded building.

Zodiac didn't think I heard him, but he worried the guards might not all be as trustworthy as we would like. The odds were, they felt the same as the members of that audience. They wouldn't want to follow someone who couldn't take to the sky and lead them in battle.

"We need to act fast. I'll make a call to Kai Temple to get Kenya here." Jamila noted and ran her hand through over her head. "She can help us protect Elsfaer until we understand what is happening."

"What if someone issues a challenge?" I asked, standing in the corner behind them. "What's the plan if that happens?"

Becoming the Elite wasn't a promise. Just because the High Spirit chose me, didn't mean my people couldn't dispute that decision. If anyone was brave enough to put their life on the line, they could issue a challenge with a blood oath.

The moment the High Spirit chose a new elite, the

altar would have appeared at the challenge grounds. On it, a golden chalice that would accept the oath of a challenger. With the binding of blood, they would promise their life for a chance to fight for the title. The problem was, only one person could come out of the challenge alive, the other would sacrifice their soul to the high spirit.

That was the reason it took thirty days for an Elite to rise. It was thirty days to prepare for the change. Thirty days to convince your people that you were worthy. And thirty days for someone to come forward and threaten to take it all away.

"What?" Jamila asked without looking at me.

"What if someone decides not to wait until you figure this out?" I clarified. "This is a prime opportunity to take me out while I'm broken."

"Elsfaer," Zodiac turned and spoke to me. "We must remain positive. No one of morals would challenge you right now. It wouldn't be an honorable fight."

"It appears not everyone cares as much about honor as you do." I lifted my hand to show the fresh tattoo that appeared on my flesh.

This was the part of being an Elite I didn't need to be told about. The marking of a challenge. It started as a small discoloration on the hand, a poisonous tattoo of markings that represented the Elite. In my case, flames. The markings would continue to spread until up my arm and to my chest. If it reached my chest before we completed the challenge, I wouldn't have to worry about someone else taking me out. The marking would do the job.

"Someone has issued a challenge." Jamila snatched my hand and pulled me over to Zodiac.

"What kind of monster would do that?" Zodiac slammed his fist into the desk beside him. "Who would want to follow such a coward?"

"Of course." Jamila paced the floor, the heals of her boots scuffed the stone floors. "We broadcasted to all of Phaedrial that her flame is gone. Do you know how many people would kill for a chance to be the Elite? Why try to bust into the palace when you can force her out? Either she shows up and fights or she stays here and dies. Either way, they have the upper hand in this."

"We need to figure out what we're going to do here." Zodiac went back to his pages on the table.

"We?" I laughed. "I'm sorry I didn't know the Elite challenge was a team event. So, you two can just jump in the ring and battle it out for me?"

"Elsfaer, this is no laughing matter." Zodiac snapped at me. "You need to take this seriously."

"Oh, save it Zodiac. You sit here and judge me. That's all you've ever done. You decided I wasn't strong enough to handle this. You judged my ability to take care of myself, but your actions handicapped me. Now you look down on me as if I am some animal that needs to be tamed, and I am tired of it!"

"I don't think there is any other choice," Jamila spoke. "She has to show up."

"There isn't. I have to fight. For my life. And without my flame, I will surely die. And that's the end of that." I pushed by the two of them and headed for the door.

"Where are you going?" Zodiac jumped in my path.

"I'm going for a walk. Now that someone's issued their challenge, no one else will dare touch me. Right?" I held my hand up, displaying the mark again, and he nodded. "I have to make it to the fighter's circle. And I will, even if I don't make it out."

CHAPTER 16

NOT ONE PERSON APPROACHED ME, JUST LIKE I THOUGHT. Zodiac also broadcasted to the city that someone had issued the challenge. After that, every firebird I saw avoided me. No one would interfere with the ritual challenge, no matter how much anyone wanted to take the title for their own.

Besides, if anyone tried to interfere after a challenger made the blood oath promise to the High Spirit, they would lose their life immediately. As odd as it was, I was the safest I'd been since the rising because no one would risk touching me.

Hidden beneath a large white hood, I walked freely through the streets, but could feel the eyes of everyone I passed on me. I left my hand uncovered for anyone who had yet to get the memo. In two days, I would walk into battle to prove myself and they would have a chance at getting the Elite they wanted. Someone powerful and with their flame, and it would be as if I never existed.

There was something strange about the city. All the textbooks I'd read depicted Phaedrial as an ethereal place. It was supposed to be full of magic and wonder and beings that lit up the sky. Instead, the place looked more like another city from Earth. They constructed buildings of metal and glass. They were no longer the natural structures that were depicted in the pictures of my books. In place of flowers and natural grounds, the paved streets carved through the city, littered with dirt and grime.

They paved over the natural plains of the ground, leaving it ugly and beaten. I passed several construction sites where the workers fought against the land. Nature was trying to reclaim its space. It was no wonder that Phaedrial was so hidden from the rest of Penumbra. This was an embarrassment.

I wanted to experience the life of my people's home before technology invaded the space. It would have been amazing to see how they lived and navigated the world. Instead of using their wings to travel, they drove in vehicles much like the cars on Earth. When did the Phoenix people lose so much of who they were?

It was after hours of walking and avoiding the people when I found the quiet garden that reminded me of the place where I grew up. The sun had just set, giving way to the moon when the comforting sight came into view. Odd to think how I would have given anything to return there. To live a life hidden from the world.

If only I hadn't been chosen for this life. If I could, I would curse the High Spirit, but if she had done this much to me, how could I put it past her not to make things so much worse?

I found the small bench that sat at the edge of a cool blue pond and finally stopped moving. The sound of the water was calming. Large colorful fish swam in front of me in synchronized dances that brought a smile to my face. They reminded me of Acai's prized Koi fish.

Sierra and Samson were her pride and joy. Unable to have children of her own, Acai imprinted those emotions on the fish. She spent hours talking to them and even invited me to join them in conversation. It wasn't long before I was visiting the fish myself. I told them all of my deepest secrets and desires, mostly focusing on my wish to leave the temple.

I became so close to Sierra and Samson that I would often jump in the pond to swim with them. Acai told me it meant I was special because Samson had a tendency to attack people. He never attacked me. In fact, he would snuggle up to me while I floated on my back, looking at the clouds.

The rustling of grass caught my attention. "Who's there?" I called out, hoping that it wasn't someone who wanted to try their luck despite the issued challenge.

"Settle down." The familiar voice of a person I thought I'd never see called out to me. "I'm not here to hurt you."

"Kaden?" I peered into the shadows, unable to see the man behind the voice.

"I thought you were the Elite." He revealed himself, stepping from behind a large tree. The moonlight bounced off his dark skin and reflected in his brown eyes.

"What are you doing here?" I hushed myself as I spoke, lowering my voice so no one else would hear me. "What if someone catches you?"

"I had to see it for myself. Your wings." Kaden leaned against the tree. "I was prepared to be blown away with awe. Little did I know, you're really a flameless after all."

"Well, sorry to make you come all the way out here for nothing." I turned away from him, focusing on the busy fish again. "And I'm not a flameless. At least I don't think I am."

"What happened?" He remained behind me, enough distance between us so he could escape if I turned on him. "If you're not one of us, why couldn't you show them your wings?"

"I don't know. I've waited my entire life to have them and now they're just gone." My shoulders slumped forward. It was hard enough to have the thoughts in my head, but saying it out loud gave the disappointment additional weight. "I would think you'd be happy about it. You wanted me to be flameless, now at least on some level, I am. Did you come here to gloat?"

"No, I didn't." I heard his footsteps as he moved closer to me. "Why would you think I'd risk being caught here just to rub salt in your wound?"

"Face it. You turned your back on me the moment you learned the truth." I accused him. "Don't get me wrong. You had every right to do it, so I don't blame you for your reaction. I should have been honest with you from the beginning. I messed up."

"I know it wasn't all your fault." Kaden joined me on the bench and watched the water. "Ali can be convincing when she wants to be. I figured she probably came up with the entire plan and because she is your friend, you went along with it."

"I just wanted to enjoy my life; you know? I wanted challenges and experiences that weren't connected to being an elite. I lived in that temple for years, just waiting for the day that I would be strong enough to leave on my own." I sighed and pointed to the sky. "Not even a day after I mature, this happens and I lost it all. No freedom, no adventure. I never wanted any of this, Kaden."

"And now you're here." He nodded.

"I am, except nothing is how I thought it would be. I'm struggling, and I don't know what to do." All of Phaedrial had expectations for me. Zodiac had already decided what my future was without even considering me. And Ali, in all the commotion, I hadn't even considered her. Where was she? "Phaedrial is so different from what they told me it would be."

"I wish I could help." He leaned back on the bench, finally looking at me and not the water.

"Why are you really here?" I looked over at him.

"I told you." He shrugged. "Wanted to be wowed like all the others. I knew you would be magnificent."

"I know what you told me, but I have a feeling that I'm not the only one who can keep secrets."

"Okay, I'll admit it. You're right. I came here in anger." The moonlight bounced off his skin and gave his face a glow I'd never seen before. That was the thing about the Darkest Forest. It hid so many wondrous things. "I don't know what I planned to do. It's not as if I'm strong enough to take on an elite."

"You wanted to fight me?" I raised a brow. That wasn't the answer I was expecting.

"I wanted to hurt you, the same way you hurt me. I

believed in you. Watching you train the others, the care and concern you had for them, it impressed me." He paused, looked at me, then back to the sky. "And I thought we had something special. I confided in you, told you things about myself I'd never shared with another person. How was I supposed to know that you wouldn't use that information against me one day?"

"I would never do that," I confessed. "Being with you all was the first time I felt like I belonged somewhere. Wings or not. I didn't want to lie to you, but I didn't think that you could ever accept me if you knew the truth. I care about every one of them and you. But I understand why you would be concerned."

"I didn't know what to believe." He lifted his hand and carefully pushed the hood back from my face so he could better see me. "I had to be sure."

"Well, your secrets are safe. They will die with me; in just a few days, it looks like." I shrugged and lifted my hand so he could see the fresh tattoo on my skin. "Someone challenged me."

"Why do you assume you will lose?" He looked disappointed in me. "Have you suddenly forgotten how to fight?"

"No, I haven't forgotten how to fight. I just know that the deck is stacked against me." I lowered my hand to my lap. "Whoever challenged me has to be powerful. Or at least someone with a flame. I can't compete against that."

"You're telling me you spent your entire life in combat training and you never once trained on fighting without your flame?" Kaden laughed. "I find that hard to believe.

Sounded to me like your trainer was a bigger hard ass than mine."

"Well, of course, I have. That's all I could do." I shrugged. "Like I said, I only had my wings for a day."

"Okay, so you're a skilled fighter and from what you taught our men in just a few short days, I know you can go out there and kick ass." He shook his head with a stern expression. "Elsfaer, you can't give up before you even step foot in the ring. That's a sure-fire way to make sure you don't come back out. Where's your confidence?"

"It's there. I think. Kaden, this is a lot to take on. In training, I knew what I was up against. Here, I don't know what to expect. We don't even know who issued the challenge." I laid out the facts. "And I gotta be honest, you're the only one who isn't making me feel like a total fuck up right now. Zodiac just treats me like a child. Jamila wants to lock me away like a porcelain doll. And I don't want to be dealing with any of this at all."

"Stop whining." He pushed my shoulder.

"Excuse me? I'm not whining." I rejected his accusation.

"Sounds like whining to me. You have time. Prepare yourself." He stood from the bench to walk away. "There are still people who want to see you succeed. Not everyone wants your life to end, regardless of the secrets you have at your disposal."

"Where are you going?" I stood wanting to follow him, but I knew it was best not to. Kaden being there was risky enough as it was.

"Back to the Odious, where I belong. Maybe you can

come to find me when you win." He winked over his shoulder.

"Wait," I called out to him.

"Yes?"

Under the rising moon, I joined him beneath the tree. With death looming and life slipping away, I needed to take advantage of every opportunity to live. I stepped as close to him as I could and looked up into his eyes. With a sharp inhale, I lifted to my toes and pressed my lips against his.

As it always did, the kiss grew with intensity and fire until I felt like my flesh was burning. His hands gripped the small of my back before his arms wrapped around me and he lifted me from the ground. When our lips parted, we were both out of breath and flushed with our desire.

He looked me in the eye with a heavy breath. "Make sure you win."

CHAPTER 17

"ALRIGHT, WHERE DO WE TRAIN?" I CALLED OUT TO Zodiac, and Jamila as I marched down the hall back towards my chambers. They stood there outside my door, waiting with the eager Rose by their side.

As much as I wanted to run away with Kaden and spend whatever remaining time I had wrapped in his arms, I knew he was right. I had to stand and face the challenge that was in front of me. It didn't matter how much the odds were against me. I couldn't give up.

I would train harder than I had ever trained before and I would prepare myself for whatever fight the challenger brought me. Because like it or not, I had to fight. And it wasn't me fighting for the people, or fighting for Zodiac's approval, or even fighting for Kaden's trust, I was fighting for me. Maybe my life wouldn't be exactly what I pictured, but it was still my life.

If I lost the fight, then at least I know I did everything

in my power to survive. And if I won, I made a promise to myself to live the life I chose. Not the life dictated to me by Zodiac or Jamila or anyone else. If I survived, I would be the Elite, I would have the power and the right to choose the way my life turned out.

"What?" Jamila looked shocked as I stomped down the hall towards them. "Well, it seems someone has changed their tune. What the hell happened on your little walk?"

"I've thought about it, and maybe a friend helped me remember who I am. I'm not going down without a fight."

"What changed your mind?" Zodiac raised a brow.

"Does it matter?" I squared my shoulders. "I'm here and I'm ready to fight. And I'm going to need both of you to help to get ready for this."

"I guess not." Zodiac looked at Jamila, who nodded her head in approval. "What do you need?"

"I need to be able to take down anything a phoenix can throw at me. According to my math, I have about thirty-six hours to get myself ready. Are you two going to help me or what?"

"Yes, of course." Zodiac nodded with pride. "I've always been by your side, Elsfaer. Nothing will ever change that. Whatever you need from me, I am here to provide."

"Right, first thing in the morning. I need sleep now." As I opened the door, I looked back at Rose, who stood there smiling and waiting for attention. "Can you get me as much information about the previous elite as possible? Whatever you have on file, I want to read over. Specifically, anything regarding the Flameless."

"Yes, right away," she beamed as I left her in the hall with Zodiac and Jamila.

I spent the night reading about the escapades of my predecessor and was shocked to find out that not only had he turned his back on a large part of our people, but in bringing in outside technology to Phaedrial, he'd messed up the very balance of the magic. It was one thing to theorize about what was harming the Phoenix people. It was another thing entirely to see it all laid out in front of me.

Rose provided me with his journals, as it was for every new elite. They handed the journals of those before them down as a piece of history. A way to get to know a person you may have never known before. It horrified me to find his notes about the developing interference with electrical fields to the source of magic. He knew what he was doing and by the time he decided to do something about his mistakes; it was too late. The people fought him on turning by the wheels to return to a home without technology.

His writings spoke of birth defects in new generations. Not only were they maturing without gaining their wings, but the last two generations of phoenix people had defects at births. It fused together the bone structure in their backs. They could never have wings. Genetic testing also showed a mutation in their chromosomes. They had no magic to pass on to their children. As the numbers grew, a small group pushed for Paereon to do something, but his loyalty to the blue flames clouded his judgement.

Greed, corruption, and a sick need to be better than their own people left everyone in Phaedrial vulnerable.

I went to bed thinking about the people that the former Elite's actions had impacted and how I would have to work to correct all that he had done wrong. The only thing was I had to survive the challenge in order to prove myself and to gain their trust.

I was up early and dressed before Rose knocked on my door.

"Come in," I called out as I tightened the belt at my waist.

"You look great." Rose beams as she carried in a tray of tea and fruit. "I picked out the workout gear. I thought the white and gold really complimented your skin. The mesh underlining makes it breathable too."

"Thank you." I looked in the mirror at myself. She was right. I looked good in the matching pants and top. "I wish I had this gear back at the temple."

"I brought you something to fuel up before you train." Rose placed the tray down. "Jamila is waiting for you in the gym. She looks like she is going to war."

"That's how she always looks." My shoulder shook with laughter. "Once she came for my birthday and she looked so serious, I spent the afternoon thinking the temple was under attack. Barely even touched the vegan cake Acai made."

"Sounds intense." Rose stood alert and looked around the room. Spotting the mess of papers, she went to tidying the desk. When she finished, she straightened the headed for the door. "I'll be around when you're done."

"Thanks, Rose." I nodded and popped a piece of orange fruit into my mouth. I could get used to room service.

My first training of the morning was with Jamila. We focused on warming up before she tested my abilities through a series of obstacle courses. The training center in the palace came equipped with customizable traps. And Jamila made use of most of them. This was her way of understanding what I was capable of before we got too far into the actual training.

Sharp spears dropped from the ceiling, and large boulders shot from the walls, all to test my reflexes. The floor fell away to drop me into a twenty-foot-deep pool filled with mechanical tethers that strapped to my legs and threatened to pull me under. This tested my strength. The longer I could keep from drowning, the stronger I was.

The physical testing went on for three hours before Jamila excused me to meet with Zodiac, who had several strategies planned out. He wanted to go over each one. We spoke of nothing else. There was tension between us. Yes, I knew I had to fight. I had a responsibility to myself and my people. No, I hadn't yet come to terms with everything he did.

We'd just covered the last fight plan when Jamila entered the room. She nodded at me before addressing my guardian.

"Zodiac, we have a problem." She spoke in a lowered tone.

"Oh goody," I clapped. "Because we needed this to get more complicated."

"Kenya is missing." Jamila announced, and my stomach dropped.

"What?" I stood from the table. "What do you mean, she's missing?"

"She hasn't been back to Kai Temple since we left." Jamila answered me, then looked at Zodiac again. "I called to have her come here to join us in helping Elsfaer prepare, but her last check-in was the night Elsfaer left."

"I saw her that night." I recalled our meeting in the sky.

"What?" Zodiac stepped forward. "When?"

"I was flying, you know, stretching my wings for the first time, and she was there in the sky." I said. "She is the one who told me all the secrets you were keeping from me."

"Of course," Zodiac rubbed his forehead, which had wrinkled with worry. "How did I miss that?"

"What?" I straightened in my seat. "What's going on?"

"You don't think?" Jamila shook her head. "She wouldn't really do something like that. Would she?"

Zodiac shook his head. "I don't know, and I won't speculate on it now."

"What are you talking about?" I was too tired to keep up with them, but I knew something was wrong.

"Nothing," Zodiac waved off my question. "You need to get back to your training. I'll work more on the strategies and we can review them again later."

"Now?" my mouth fell open. I'd planned on having a mental break after speaking with Zodiac, but that was no longer an option.

"Hey, the clock is winding down." Jamila tapped her wrist and flexed the muscles in her toned arms for emphasis. "We need to get this going. Besides, you can rest when all this is over. Or not."

"Right." I huffed. "Well, lead the way!"

"Don't overdo it," Zodiac called after us.

"Oh, we won't," Jamila promised him, but I didn't believe her.

Fighting with Jamila was a unique experience. I'd only had two training sessions with her in the past, and each time she clearly held back. Her strategy differed from Zodiac's. Jamila fought with more intuition than calculation. Zodiac focused on the opponent, learning their patterns, anticipating their next move. Jamila stressed the point of being one with the world around you. It wasn't just a choreographed dance with predetermined steps or just understanding your opponent; it was understanding yourself.

The difference with Jamila was that while she was technically advanced, she had something that Zodiac did not. She had a reason to continue fighting. For her, this wasn't just training, it wasn't just the Elite's fight. This challenge wasn't something that she took lightly. For her, this was the way of life. I knew little about her past, but what I found out through eavesdropping on her and Zodiac was dark and troubling. Somehow, she survived it.

"You know you're good at this, Elsfaer," Jamila handed me the towel to wipe the sweat from my head. "I don't think your opponent will overpower you like you're thinking. You're strong and you're sure of your actions. Now, if you could just believe in your intuition a bit more, then our shady little firebird won't stand a chance."

"Do you really think that?" I wiped the sweat from my forehead and my neck. My skin was burning up. The more we fought, the hotter I felt on the inside as if my phoenix was trying to get out, but something kept it trapped inside of me.

"Yes. Whoever issued that challenge clearly doesn't believe that they have a real chance against you at your strongest. That's why they chose now to challenge you. Think about it. They had all the time in the world to do this." Jamila handed me a bottle of water to drink. "When you were still hiding from everyone, out there doing who knows what. They could have challenged you at any point, but they didn't. They waited until they were sure that you were at a disadvantage. That tells me they are more calculated than they are prepared to fight."

"What do you mean? How can you say they aren't prepared to fight?" I scoffed. "It's not like I'm just going to go in here and lie down and let them kill me."

"If they were prepared to fight, trained with enough skill to take on anybody, the way an elite should be, they would have called you out on day one." Jamila explained her theory. "If you had come straight here and let your voice be heard with your wings blazing bright, there is no way you would have that mark on your hand right now."

"I really hope you're right." I nodded. Hell, I didn't want to fight at all, but I'd take an easy one over a tough one any time.

"I think I am, but just in case I'm not, let's get back to it!"

By the time I made it back to my room, my muscles were sore, my body was tired, and all I wanted was my bed and maybe a stiff drink. Instead, just as my head hit the pillow, just as I was about to drift away also the dreams of my happy future without my current job drama, a soft tapping on my window stole that fantasy from me.

Standing on the balcony, covered in blood, was Ali.

CHAPTER 18

"ALI, WHAT HAPPENED TO YOU?" I CARRIED HER TIRED BODY to the bed where she could rest. There was blood crusted around her mouth and nose. She wore torn dirt covered clothing and groaned when I put her on the bed.

"I'm so sorry, Elsfaer." She coughed and fresh blood spilled from her mouth.

"Why are you apologizing to me? Who did this to you?" I ran to the bathroom, returning with a warm towel to clean the blood from her face.

"I don't have much time." She stopped my hand from cleaning her and dropped her head with a sharp inhale. "I ran away to get to you as soon as I could. This wasn't supposed to happen like this, E. I didn't know it would take away your wings."

"What? My wings, what the hell you talking about, Ali?" I was too concerned about taking care of her to think about myself or consider what she was trying to confess to me.

"My sister, she told me to give you the elixir to help you." She looked at me with teary eyes. "I thought I could trust her. She was supposed to be on your side."

"You need to slow down." I grabbed her shoulders. "Who was supposed to be on my side?"

"The reason your wings are gone." She coughed, spilling more blood. "It's the magic in the potion."

"Who is your sister? What are you talking about?"

"My sister is Kenya." Ali looked me in the eye and I could hear the heartbreak in her voice.

The name fell out of her mouth and landed right in the center of my gut. *Has everything in my life been a lie?* In a moment, the person I thought was closest to me, the only friend I'd ever had, had become just another person who I couldn't trust. I confided in Ali so much. And yet there I was, staring at her like she was a stranger.

"Are you kidding me?" I moved away from her.

"I knew who you were before I met you." Ali continued her confession of betrayal. "Kenya used to tell me about how it was to be at Kai Temple with you. She sent me letters describing this amazing girl who was going to grow up to do amazing things.

"I begged for years for her to let me come visit so that I could meet you, but she told me no every time. When she asked me to do this, when she asked me to help you, there was no way I could say no. She told me to find you and to stay by your side. She said you ran away and that you wouldn't trust anyone from home. I thought she was only looking out for you."

"Why didn't you tell me the truth?" I needed to remain

calm. I couldn't let my temper get the best of me because I was already burning up on the inside from training.

"She said I shouldn't." Ali cried. "That if you knew, you would reject my help."

"Where have you been?" I asked calmly. "All this time, they said you weren't with the guards. Where were you?"

"When Zodiac saved you, he told a guard to take me. We were on our way here when Kenya caught up with us. She blindsided the guard, killed him, and took me away."

"I can't believe you lied to me." Was I supposed to feel bad for her? That the person she worked with against me had turned on her, too?

"I thought I was protecting you." Ali reached for me, but I stepped out of her reach.

"Protecting me?" I laughed. "Right, poisoning me really protected me, Ali!"

"Elsfaer." She coughed my name and again blood spilled from her mouth.

"Get out." I pointed to the window where she'd come in. "I don't know how you got up here, but I'm sure you can make your way back down."

"I want to help you." She pleaded. "Please, let me fix this."

"How do I know you aren't here doing her bidding again?" I asked her. "How do I know that this isn't an act?"

"I risked my life to come here and tell you the truth," Ali cried and cringed from the pain of moving.

"And I suppose you want a reward for it?" I laughed and clapped my hands slowly. "Yay for you Ali. Great job telling me how you stabbed me in the back!"

"I can help you."

"Help me? You're the reason I'm in this mess!" I yelled at her. "You have a lot of nerve coming here talking about helping me out of what you caused."

"Elsfaer?" Zodiac and Jamila burst through the door.

"Are you okay?" Jamila stepped between us, her hand on the sword at her side. "Who is this?"

"Someone I thought was my friend, but obviously, I was wrong."

"You weren't wrong." Ali stood from the bed forward, but stopped when Jamila held up her hand. "I am your friend. That's why I'm here."

"Do you want to explain what's going on?" Zodiac questioned me. He closed the door behind him after making sure there was no one else responding to the commotion.

"She pretended to be my friend, but all this time she was working with Kenya!" I summed up the situation to him.

"No!" Ali yelled, and more blood spilled from her lips. "I wasn't, I mean I was, but I'm not now. She lied to me about what she was doing. I'm trying to fix this!"

"Fix what?" Jamila placed her palm against Ali's chest, stopping her from taking another step.

"The potion she gave me, the stuff to hide my markings." I lifted the sleeves of my robe to show my bare skin. "It did more than that. It's the reason I can't connect to my wings anymore."

"You never mentioned a potion, Elsfaer." Jamila looked over her shoulder at me, then returned her attention to the bloodied girl in front of her. "You got it from Kenya?"

"Yes, she said it was to protect Elsfaer. That the world wouldn't understand the way she looked and that she would be too stubborn to accept help from anyone she knew. She told me that if I wanted to help protect the next elite that I would do this. How could I possibly say no?"

"How badly are you hurt?" Zodiac finally approached Ali, coming around the massive bed to examine her.

"I'll be fine. I had to escape. She had me chained in a room, in a small shack, outside of the Odious. I did everything I could to get here, and I know she is looking for me now." She looked at the window. "Luckily, I still have one friend here. He got me to your window."

"We'll discuss the security risk later." Zodiac shot a look at Jamila before continuing his questioning of Ali. "You said you wanted to help fix this. How?"

"I know the magic she used to create the potion. There is an antidote, but you have to go to the House of Trades to get it." Her face blanched as she spoke of the Dark market in the Odious. It was where the roughest of Penumbra went to buy and sell the stuff of nightmares.

"There isn't much time to do that." Jamila nodded as she considered the options. "That means Elsfaer will need to go as well."

"You want her to travel in the dead of the night to one of the most dangerous parts of Penumbra with no way to protect herself?" Zodiac scoffed. "I know we've taken risks before, but this is a big deal, Jamila."

"Yes, I think it's worth it. Besides, if she doesn't go, there is no way we can get that antidote to her in time. At least this way she has a chance of getting the cure and making it back before time is up."

"We'll be cutting it short." Jamila was right. I had to go with them. It was a risk. Anyone at the House of Trades will know about my problems. They'd be eager to offer crooked ways to solve them or take advantage of my vulnerability.

"Will you please allow me to help you?" Ali looked past Jamila to me.

"It doesn't sound like I have much of a choice in the matter." I shrugged. "But this doesn't make us okay, Ali."

"I'm sorry." Her eyes swelled with more tears.

"Save your apologies. I don't want to hear them." I turned my back on her and looked out the window. Her tears would not sway me.

"Why would Kenya do this?" Jamila asked Ali.

"I don't know." I could hear the sorrow in her voice. "My sister was never the nicest person, at least not to me, but I didn't think she would turn dark."

"Whoever is behind this is smart to have used Kenya," Zodiac offered.

"It's calculated, that's for sure," Jamila agreed with Zodiac.

"Are you seriously admiring the work of whoever this asshole is?" I flashed an angry glare at the two of them.

"Not admiring, no." Zodiac walked over to the balcony of my supposed fortified room and examined the entrance.

"We're trying to understand the way our enemy's mind works." He continued. "They used Kenya to place doubt in your mind and because of what she said to you,

you left. Things couldn't have worked more in their favor. Whatever happened while you were on your own to cause you to lose the connection to your fire only gives them a greater chance of winning."

"Kenya knows everything about you," Jamila spoke, taking over for Zodiac. "She's studied you during combat training. She knows all your habits, your hopes, your dreams. Having that kind of information about you not only makes you vulnerable, but it allows them to more accurately strategize their efforts. I only wish I knew how they got to her."

"Maybe they climbed through the window," I huffed. "I thought this place was supposed to be the safest place for me, and yet someone just dropped Ali off with no issue."

"He was a guard," Ali admitted. "An old friend who owed me a favor."

"Friend or not, he will face the consequences of risking Elsfaer's life." Zodiac walked away from the window. "I'll deal with this accordingly."

"Agreed," Jamila nodded. "For now, we have other concerns."

"You're right. Jamila, please take the girl to get cleaned up and ready for your trip," Zodiac suggested.

"Will do," her voice softened as she addressed Ali. "Let's go get you some new clothes."

"Elsfaer," Zodiac continued after they exited the room. "Are you okay?"

"No, as a matter of fact, I'm not." I threw my hands in the air and wanted to scream, but I kept the outburst suppressed. "Every time I turn around, I'm finding out that more people have lied to me. She was the first person I felt was actually my friend. She was the first person outside of that damn temple I let in and she betrayed me. How am I ever going to know who to trust, Zodiac? How do I not shut down entirely when every person I think I can count on is lying to me?"

"Everyone isn't lying." He said calmly. "These are difficult times, Elsfaer. That is all."

"Are you counting yourself in that number? Because as far as I can see it, all you've done my entire life is lie to me and hide things from me. Everyone boasts about how they're all acting in my best interest, yet no one thinks to ask me what my best interests are. As if I wouldn't know the answer."

"I'm sorry."

"Like I told her," I walked to the door and opened it for him, "save the apologies."

"Elsfaer, we need to talk about this."

"Please go." I gestured to the hallway outside the door. "I have a trip to prepare for."

CHAPTER
19

BEFORE THE SUN TOUCHED THE SKY, WE WERE LEAVING Phaedrial. This time not on foot, and I thanked the High Spirit for that small favor. Instead of walking back to the Odious, a large man named Caesar carried me. My arms wrapped around his neck as his wings took us across the border. I couldn't help but relax into him because he smelled like cedarwood and lilac.

When he picked me up before we took off, he looked at me and said, "Don't worry, little one. I got you."

I felt like a child jumping into the arms of a giant, and as odd as it was, it made me feel better. Caesar also had a tattoo that covered his necks and arms and all I could think was that this giant teddy bear also had a tough side. So while he'd carry me like precious cargo, he'd also protect me with the same care.

Ali also had a hunky ride to get to our destination. I looked over Caesar's shoulder to where she flew, carried in the arms of the man's whose name I didn't catch. This had to work. I wanted my wings back so I could take to the sky and fly away from everything without the aid of a moderately attractive man with dark eyes.

Jamila led the charge to the House of Trades. According to Ali, we would need to find a powerful sorceress who dealt in some of the ugliest magic. Apparently, she wasn't the easiest to find and going during the day would make the task that much harder, but we had to try. I likely wouldn't have another night in Penumbra without her help.

Crossing from the Alluring, where Phaedrial was, back into the Odious confused the senses. Even though it was early morning and the sun still hung in the Sky above us, the Odious was cast in shadows. The dark magic was so strong that it filtered the light to a grey cast before it reached the ground.

We touched down just outside the House of Trades and Jamila instructed the guards that escorted us to remain outside.

"If we need your help, I'll signal. It's bad enough we're here at all." She instructed. "The last thing we need is for anyone in the Odious thinking we're trying to stir up trouble. Whatever happens, we don't upset the balance of things. Got it?"

The guards all confirmed their understanding of her orders. It wasn't unlike people of the light to venture to the Dark in troubling times. As long as we kept our noses clean while we were there, there would be no issues to clean up later.

I pulled the large hood over my head, keeping my face hidden. Jamila had provided us all with the jackets equipped with massive hoods and hidden daggers should we run into any problems. As the Elite, my face would eventually be recognizable by most people. It wasn't too farfetched to think that there would be people in the House of Trades who knew who I was.

The early hour meant fewer people moving around the market. They shut most of the trading posts down, and their owners wouldn't return until just before night-fall. You would think this would make our jobs easier, but it meant fewer people to question and fewer leads to the location of the mysterious Sorceress.

The early hour meant fewer people moving around the market. They shut most of the trading posts down, and their owners wouldn't return until just before night-fall. You would think this would make our jobs easier, but it meant fewer people to question and fewer leads to the location of the mysterious sorceress.

I had all but given up hope when I saw movement behind a small hut that acted as a storefront for a gems dealer. The stones that could turn a large man into a small toad or hide an elite from peering eyes. It wasn't the first time I saw her; the woman had been following me. Not long after we entered the market, I glimpsed her tattered clothes and dirtied head. Instead of trying to outrun her, I confronted her.

An ugly woman with boils that covered her body preoccupied Jamila and Ali had stopped to question a small boy with the pointed ears of a fairy. I wouldn't do more than question the woman, the same as they were doing. If she had anything of value to give me, I would call for them.

I walked ahead, dipping behind another booth until I was sure I was out of view. I had to hurry, so I doubled back and dipped behind the tree lines to get behind her. When she walked by me, unaware of my position behind the small bush, I stepped out behind her and tapped her on the shoulder.

"Who are you, and why are you following me?" I questioned as she turned with wide eyes. She looked like she would fall over.

"I, uh—" Her dirt covered face blanched as she turned white with fear.

"You what?" I demanded. "You've been following me since I got here. Who are you working for?"

"I'm so sorry. I didn't mean to do anything wrong." She held her hands out and shrunk herself as if she thought I'd hit her. "You're new around here, and I've been here so long that I think I've seen just about anyone who would dare come here."

"You," I stared at her face closely, noticing the difference between her and the others that I'd seen in Penumbra. She was frail, her dark skin ashy and coated in dirt, and she smelled like Earth. "Wait, you're human?"

"Yes, I am." She nodded.

"What the hell are you doing here?" I stepped back and relaxed my shoulders. "This isn't a good place for your kind."

"It's a long story, but I can't get back home, so might as

well not even go over it, right?" She relaced when she realized I wouldn't hurt her. "I just make the best of it."

"Why are you following me? I can't help you get back to Earth." Once a human crossed the barrier from Earth to Penumbra, there was no going back home. That was the failsafe to keep the world safe. If humans could come and go as they pleased, they would go back and tell the others. Eventually the human governments would want access to Penumbra and it would mean devastation to the balance of our world.

"Yeah, I think I've given up all hope of going back to Earth." She spoke with sad eyes. "I've tried everything I could think of and yet, here I am."

"That doesn't answer my question. Why are you following me?"

"Well, I hear there is a better place in this world. One where there is light and sunshine. But no matter how many times I've attempted to make it there, I'm still here. I can't get out of this darkness." She gestured to the surrounding trees.

"You don't look like you're from here, and I think that's because you're not. Maybe you can help me get to the place where there's light. I've given up on any chance of going home, but I don't want to live here with these people and these nightmares."

"Why would I help you? I mean, how do I know you're not in debt to someone here?" I questioned her motives. "If I help you leave, it could mean trouble for me."

"I'm not. At least not anymore. I was when I got here and then, after I'd worked off my debt, I was told I could go home. Only when I went back to that gate it didn't open for me. It was weeks before I realized it would never open to me again."

"Oh," I imagined her standing at the gateway begging to go home and the image broke my heart. She wanted to be free, but they trapped her. I knew how that felt.

"Look, you're here for a reason, right?" She straightened and wiped away tears I hadn't noticed before. "Give me a chance to help you and if I can, then maybe you can help me in return."

"You're right, I came here for something." I nodded. "There is a powerful sorceress that I need to find, one strong enough to take the power away from a phoenix. You know where I might find her?"

"I'm pretty sure I know exactly who you're talking about." She nodded with wide eyes. "You don't really want to go there, do you?"

"I do." I nodded. "It's kind of life and death."

"You can't." She backed away from me. "That woman, she is evil. You don't want to get mixed up with that."

"I'm already mixed up with that. I just need to find her. Will you take us?"

"Us?"

"My friends and I," I pointed in the direction we'd come where I was sure Jamila and Ali were still interrogating anyone they could get their hands on.

"I can't take you all." The girl shied again. "She will know."

"Well," I looked back, wondered if I was making a mistake, but decided it didn't matter. "Can you take me alone?"

"Will you help me if I do?" She chewed her dirtied nails as she put her conditions on the table.

"Take me to her, and I'll get you out of the Odious." I nodded, making a promise to a stranger who'd likely get me killed.

CHAPTER 20

"What's your name?" We walked deeper into the trees that sat just west of the House of Trades. My guide was a foot shorter than me and walked barefoot across the rough grounds. Her clothing, pants and a tattered shirt had seen much better days. I wanted to know more about her. What pushed her to survive in such terrible conditions?

"Denise," she answered timidly. "That's the first time anyone has asked me that since I got here. What's yours?"

"Elsfaer," I nodded.

"Oh," her eyes returned to the path ahead.

"You know who I am?"

"Well, yes." She shrugged. "I've heard your name around here a lot lately."

"I'm not sure if that's a good thing or a bad thing." A small ball of fur scurried in front of us. I didn't know what the thing was, but I hoped it wasn't running from something larger.

"At first people were excited. The new phoenix Elite, I think it was, finally appeared. Not long after that, it became more of a mocking tone." She scrunched her nose. "They were saying how the people of Phaedrial should be embarrassed."

"Mocking," I grunted. Of course, the world was mocking me, the broken elite.

"You're supposed to have wings, but you don't, right?" Denise looked at me and waited for confirmation of the rumors she'd heard.

"Right." I gave a tight nod. "That's me, the wingless elite."

"It's just up ahead." She ignored my show of self-pity and pointed to the narrow path, at the end of which was a rickety shack that looked like it would fall over with the next breeze.

"She's in there?"

"Yes." Denise backed away from the path, keeping her eye on the closed door. "I did what you asked. I got you here. That's all I can do. I will go no further."

"Do you know your name?" I asked and noticed for the first time that the woman had no shoes on her feet. "Can you tell me?"

Denise gestured for me to lean into her. When I did, she lifted to her toes and whispered the name in my ear. If she were too frightened to speak it aloud, it didn't bode well for my chances with the witch.

I continued down the path alone. I wouldn't ask Denise to face this with me. Her helping me get there was enough. The closer I got to the shack, the worse I felt. The stench of onions and rotten meat lifted from the ground, and I wondered if she meant for the terrible smell to scare unwelcome visitors away. I swallowed the taste of bile and continued towards the door. It wasn't as if I could turn away after coming so far.

After the first tap of my knuckles against the old wood, the door eased open. The hinges screamed as I peeked inside. Through the small crack, I could see nothing more than a dusty table littered with glass vials.

"Hello, is anyone here?" I called out as I pushed the door open further. With more visibility of the space came the pungent odor of death.

The floors creaked beneath my weight as I entered the space. Two steps from the door, it slammed behind me and my heart dropped into my stomach, but I remained still. In the shadows there was movement, something I couldn't see, but the presence was there. The air felt heavier as I breathed, waiting to be addressed.

I knew how these things worked. The sorceress would appear when she was ready, and not a moment sooner.

"Hello young one," the low voice spoke from the shadows. "Oh, you're a powerful one, a firebird. But you cannot reach your flame."

"How did you know that?" I asked the darkness.

"I know a lot of things, dear." A low chuckle followed the statement. "But that isn't why you're here, to find out how I know the things I know."

"No, it's not." I said honestly.

"Why have you come?" The voice was in my ear, though I stood there alone.

"I need my wings back," I admitted.

"I haven't taken them," she mocked me, knowing full well what she'd done.

"No, but your magic did. A potion you made was used to block my magic. The antidote is what I need." I looked ahead, not sure where she was, but steadied myself in case she tried to attack me. I didn't know what to expect of a creature as dark as everyone said she was.

"Oh, I remember this potion." The voice took a more loving tone as it continued. "Such a beautiful creature she was. Sad soul full of envy and hatred. The best kind."

"She took my magic and now she wants to kill me." I addressed the matter at hand. "I need to defend myself and I can't do that without my wings."

"You must pay a price," the voice spoke, uninterested in my story.

"I don't have any money." I paced my hands in my pockets. It never occurred to me I would need to pay for her to fix me and that was why Jamila wanted us to face the witch together.

"Not in dollars, dear." Finally she appeared as her, her laughter ringing out around me. "Magic doesn't work with modern currency."

The minimal light offered me a brief opportunity to see her face. Her skin was a sickly gray color that hung from her face, and her green eyes sat sunken and ringed in black. Though she was frail, her presence felt imposing, nearly taking my breath away. She turned on me, still laughing, and I could see the browning teeth in her mouth.

"What do you want?" I asked, my voice shaking with fear.

"A favor." In front of her, the firepit came to life, casting a halo of light around her body.

"A favor?" Of course, I kicked myself. There was always a price when performing magic. The greater the feat, the higher the cost.

"Yes, you are powerful." The sorceress pointed her thin finger at me and I pulled away from her. "A favor from you will be worth a thousand times any amount of money you could give me." She looked back over her shoulder again, only allowing me a partial view of her face.

"Don't do it." The warning came on a wave of cool air that brushed against my face. The same as it was in the Darkest Forest.

"What?" I looked around but found no one.

"What is it, dear?" the Sorceress questioned, still with her back to me.

"Did you say something?" I asked, still scanning the space for the voice.

"I can't say that I did." she shook her head no.

"Get out of here!" It was there again, only more urgent.

"Who's there?" I looked around the small room. The fire added more light, but there were still shadowed corners. Cobwebs and dust covered every surface.

"Look girl, I have little time to spare for this." Her shoulders lifted. "Your time is even more limited than mine. What will it be?"

"I um, I don't know. Something, someone, I need a second." I looked around again, hoping to catch sight of the protestor.

"Time is ticking." A boney finger lifted in the air, mimicking the motion of the hand of a clock.

"Don't do it."

"Who is that? What do you want?" I turned, speaking again to the shadows.

"Child, have you lost your mind?" the witch frowned at me. "It may be more than that potion messing with your magic."

"No, I um—" I waited for the voice to come again, but it didn't. "I will do it. I promise you a favor."

"Excellent!" she turned to me, leaning further into the light so I could see her hollow face framed by long, stringy hair. The wide smile, yellowed and missing at least four teeth, stretched across her face.

Those boney fingers reached out and hung in front of me, waiting for my acceptance. With no other option, I reached out, expecting a simple handshake, but her fingers wrapped around my wrist, and she yanked me forward. I stumbled and lost my footing as she dragged me to the fire pit.

I felt the sting of the iron before I saw it. And I screamed as it pressed into my flesh, burning me. The woman branded me! In the palm of my hand, the skin raised from the heat. A spiral with a diagonal slice through it.

"Elsfaer?" Jamila burst through the door. "What have you done?"

The sorceress released me, and I dropped to the floor. I pulled my hand to my chest and scooted away from her. Jamila grabbed my arm, pulling me up from the floor and away from the satisfied witch.

"I–" I examined the marking in my hand.

"Please tell me you didn't promise her a favor." Jamila's mouth fell open as she witnessed the healing mark. "Elsfaer, no."

"Of course I did. How else was I supposed to give payment?" I sucked my teeth as the pain in my hand turned to a stinging sensation that shot up my arm.

"You don't know what you've done." Jamila paced. "Zodiac is going to kill me for letting this happen."

"Yeah, and we don't have time to explain it to her now." Ali stepped forward. "If she survives tonight, we'll fill her in on the horrible decision she just made. For now, we need that antidote."

"Of course, my word is bond. As is yours?" the witch produced the small vial and popped the top from it. "I'll need blood from the one without flames."

"Ali?" I asked just as she peeked her head in the door behind Jamila.

"Yes," the Sorceress pointed to Ali. "She is a blood relative of the one who requested the spell that binds you now. Her blood will be the key to undoing it."

"No," Jamila looked at Ali, who stepped through the door accepting the Sorceress' decree. "How do we know you won't do something else with that blood?"

"You don't," she smiled. "But I have no use for the blood of someone with limited magic. If you don't trust me, do it yourself. Just one drop will do."

She handed me the vial and a small knife. Without hesitation, Ali walked over to me and held out her hand. I knew she wanted to prove herself to me. She wanted to make up for what she'd done.

"Do it." She lifted a finger, allowing me to puncture it with the blade before holding it over the opening of the vial.

One drop of her blood fell into the bottleneck, and when it contacted the mixture inside, the bottle lit up.

"There, that is enough," the Sorceress announced.

I cleaned the blade of Ali's blood, wiping it against my pants leg before handing it back to her.

"So little trust from the young woman. Funny how that goes. When you're ready, simply drink it and all will be well again." That bony finger pointed to the door, a cue for us to leave her. "Good luck, young Elite."

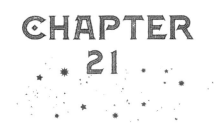

CHAPTER 21

AN HOUR LATER, WE WERE BACK IN PHAEDRIAL. JAMILA hadn't scolded me enough inside the witch's shack, so she carried me instead of the guard who had before. They charged him with transporting Denise. I promised to help her, and I meant it. Another thing I got chewed out for. It seemed I could do nothing right in the eyes of my new trainer.

The entire flight back she hammered into my head just how big a mistake it was for me to make a promise to the sorceress.

"Do you know how many people have lost their lives because of doing something so foolish?" She didn't mean for me to answer her, so I didn't. "I know you think that I'm just being overprotective here, but Elsfaer, I've lost friends to shit like this. These witches, and she isn't the only one out there, they prey on people's desperation. This is why I didn't want you to go there alone. I don't know how I'm going to tell your... I mean Zodiac about this."

I pretended to listen, but it was already done. I couldn't take it back and I wouldn't worry about it. At least not yet.

No matter how much Jamila wanted me to feel bad about my decision, I couldn't. I did what was necessary. I was the Elite and in a matter of hours they would make me to fight for my life. If there was any time to take such a high risk, it was when my life was on the line.

Yes, the Sorceress was powerful and yes, I'd promised her a favor, but in my mind any favor was a fair price to pay to better my chances of survival.

As soon as we landed on the castle grounds, I walked away from Jamila. I'd heard enough of her ranting. Besides, my absence would give her ample time to run and tell Zodiac about how badly I'd messed up.

Rose waited for me in my room with a hot meal and a bath already drawn. I settled into the large stone tub and allowed the jacuzzi jets to massage the aches and pains from my body. As I soaked, I examined the vial filled with the metallic green liquid. It no longer glowed, but shimmered beneath the light.

The instructions were simple. All I had to do was drink it and wait for it to restore me. I'd have my wings back and a fighting chance against Kenya. Jamila might be quick to underestimate my former nanny, but I wasn't. I knew what the woman was capable of, and I didn't believe she was working for someone else.

It wasn't uncommon for Kenya to take over my trainings

when Zodiac was away from the temple. She was powerful, agile, and had reflexes like a cat. There was one instance I thought of often because I just knew I had her. Her back was to the wall, and I poised my blade for a win. But as I drew back, she jumped higher into the air than I thought possible, kicked the wall and flew to the opposite side of the training room, where ample weapons waited. In less than a minute, I went from an obvious victory to an embarrassing defeat.

Kenya was calculating and strong. If nothing else, she fooled us all. She snuck under both Acai's and Zodiac's noses, and neither of them suspected her. If she could do that, there was no telling what other tricks she had up her sleeve.

Though I would have given anything to stay in that tub, there was more to be done. I popped the top of the vial and tossed back the liquid and gagged on the horrible taste. It tasted like the witch's shack smelled, onions, rotten meat, and death.

Within an hour, I'd redressed and headed to meet the others in the council room. Outside the door stood two guards, who opened it as I approached.

"How do you feel?" Zodiac stood from his seat at the large table as I entered the dark room.

Also sitting at the table were Jamila, the speaker, whose name I learned was Kiara, and two older men whose names I'd yet to commit to memory. They sat there with frowns, a symbol of their disapproval of me.

"I don't know." I nodded at the others who surrounded the table. "Still can't feel my wings. Maybe it takes time to work?"

"We're out of time," Jamila tapped her wrist.

"You're right. What am I going to do?" I crossed the room.

We had only a few hours left before I had to face Kenya. I'd done all I could, and it still wasn't enough.

"You're going to fight for your life and hope for a miracle." She stood from her seat. "There isn't any other choice."

"At least you'll be able to fight in style." Zodiac snapped his fingers, and another guard entered, carrying a leather case.

"Is that?" my eyes widened. I recognized the box. The phoenix wings scored on the front of it were the moniker of the greatest armor designers Phaedrial offered.

"Yes, your armor. Finally." Zodiac nodded.

"Perfect timing," Jamila nodded. "That will help protect you."

"How did you get it here?" I couldn't take my eyes off the box. At least I could wear it once before I die.

"Well, after we found out Kenya was behind all this, I figured I better look deeper into the whereabouts of your armor. Turns out they delivered it right on time. She'd been hiding them in her chambers back at the Kai."

"I'm surprised she didn't take them for herself." Kiara pointed to the case. "Those are hard to come by."

"That wouldn't have been wise." Zodiac smirked.

"Why not?" One of the grumpy old men straightened.

"We designed Elsfaer's armor, especially for her. It responds to her magic." Zodiac explained the method behind his madness. "The markings on her skin enhance its ability, but if anyone other than her wears it, it will kill them."

"Wait, how do we know it won't kill her now?" Jamila pushed her chair from the table. "Her markings are gone."

"Not entirely." Zodiac pointed to my face, then to the mirror that hung on the opposite wall.

I walked over to look at my reflection. Just above my cheek, a faint reappearance of the marking.

"Perhaps the potion is working." he said with hope.

"Well, let's get you into this thing." Jamila gestured to the door. "We need to see how it fits, and how it reacts to you."

Truth be told, I wanted more time away from Jamila. She treated me like dirt for accepting the potion from the sorceress, and yet here she was, excited that the cure had worked, but of course Zodiac would not accompany me into the dressing room. We made it back to my room where again Rose waited for us.

Jamila waited in the bedroom while Rose helped me into the armor. It was everything I imagined it would be, and worth the hours of standing there while the seamstress measured every inch of my body, multiple times.

The fabric snapped to my figure like a second skin, providing me with more comfort and security than anything I'd ever worn before. It was lightweight and flexible. And it made me feel stronger than I was. I needed that more than anything, considering what I was walking into.

I stood there for a while looking at myself in the mirror, appreciating the contours and the craftsmanship. But also waiting for it to turn on me. The armor was more regal than I thought it would be. The suit was white to match my flames and accented by flexible metal fittings.

It came attached with a sheer skirt that wrapped around my waist clamped on by feather adorned fasteners. The bodice was intricate and appeared soft while still strong. After accepting that it wouldn't turn on me for not being the magical creature they made it for, I faced the woman who waited for me.

I exited the dressing room to find not only Jamila, but Zodiac, who stood there looking at me like a proud father. Despite his warm acceptance, I still questioned him. If I survived, I would have to talk to him about everything that he'd kept from me. For now, I had to keep my mind focused on what was important. My survival.

CHAPTER 22

I WASN'T SURE WHAT TO EXPECT WHEN I WALKED INTO THE Fired Den. The nest shaped battle ground was where I would face my opponent. I thought I would find a crowd of angry phoenixes cheering for my opponent and waiting for my demise.

I expected to be booed and have things thrown at me, just like when they found out I'd lost my flames. But that was not the way of the firebirds when a challenge was at place. They only selected a select few to stand witness while the rest of the population watched on monitors all across Phaedrial.

A shadowed figure stood at the opposite side of the ring. Dressed head-to-toe in metal armor, my opponent was ready for a fight. I tried again to feel for my wings and only felt a faint breath of heat beneath my shoulder blades. The potion hadn't done its job, and time was officially out.

"It is time for the Elite challenge. Both the challenger and the fated Elite have arrived," Kiara announced. "As you both know, this is a fight to the death. Only one soul shall walk away from this alive."

Though the challenge grounds were silent, the spectators quiet, I could feel the energy that radiated throughout the territory. All those who anticipated the fight. There was something else, a presence that didn't belong. In the far corner of the room, a cloaked figure stood beneath a large hood.

"Is that—" I looked at Zodiac. I'd only seen the white robes depicted in pictures, but it looked the same. The robes were lighter than material and completely hid the figure beneath them.

"Yes, the Prophet. They must report back to the high spirit the outcome of the fight." He nodded.

"And they'll take the soul of the loser with them," Jamila added for impact.

"Perfect, first-class ticket to hell," I muttered as I entered the ring.

"How could you do this?" I called out to Kenya, but she ignored my question. Her only response was a smug smile.

Kiara held a long black feather above her head. As Kenya stepped into the ring, we both looked at her.

"When the feather hits the floor, the fight will begin." Kiara looked at us both for confirmation before letting the feather fall.

I held my breath as the feather danced its aerial descent to the floor. Every pair of eyes watched and waited with us. Not a second after it landed, Kenya attacked.

We started off in a familiar pacing. Kenya lunged at me, and I dodged. I took a shot, and she sidestepped me. I wanted her to feel comfortable. As far as she knew, I was still the same fighter that she met in Kai. The choreography was the same as we'd danced time and time again before. Kenya knew me. She knew how I thought and how I breathed. She understood what drove me as a fighter, my desire to live.

What she didn't know was everything I'd been through since I left the temple. She didn't know that I had new reasons for wanting to live outside of exploring the world unknown to me. She didn't know that there were people I cared about, despite their betrayals. And even though I was angry with them, I wanted to protect them.

She didn't know that there was someone out there who inspired something new in me, something I never considered during my time at Kai. I wanted every opportunity to explore the changes I felt inside me. She wouldn't take that away from me.

She also didn't know that I had trained with Jamila. In such a short time, I learned to adapt and to breathe a new life into my fighting. Just as I had her where I thought I wanted her, the same tempo, the same pacing, I switched to the style of fighting the Jamila taught.

No more was I taking part in a choreographed dance with her. Intuition took over. When she lunged, I didn't just dodge her; I breathed in the air of her motion and used her force to feed my own. Her every exertion worked to my benefit. I landed blow after blow, beating her until blood covered her face.

I thought I had her, but just as Kenya was unaware of my growth, I was not aware of hers.

She grabbed my fist just before it connected with her jaw again. "How about we switch things up?" She spit the blood from her lips.

Kenya caught on quickly and in a moment, I went once again from an obvious victory to fighting for my survival. Unlike me, Kenya had her wings, which unfolded from her back. In a fair fight, she wouldn't be able to beat me. She knew that, but her wings gave her an advantage. She took to the air and flew circles around me.

Her wings carried her faster than my feet could move me. As I spun, trying to keep my eyes on her, I became dizzy. When I tried to steady myself, she took the advantage. She flew in, punched me in the jaw, and quickly flew away again. The heat of her wings added to the dizzying effect, and I landed on my ass.

After the third consecutive blow to my jaw and Zodiac and Jamila calling out to me, something changed. My skin tingled, and the fire that struggled within me burned again. I could feel them, my wings. I reached deep within myself and begged from them to show. Though I could feel them, I still couldn't make them appear. I still couldn't use them to help me in my fight.

They would have come in handy when Kenya swooped down and grabbed me. She lifted me into the air and as I hung in her hands, she whispered in my ear, "You don't deserve the power you have. So I'm going to take it away from you."

With a wicked grin, she let me go. As I fell, waiting for the impact of the ground, I considered her words. *Did I deserve it?* My back hit the ground with such force that the surface cracked beneath me. In my blurred vision, I saw her hanging in the air above me. I could just give up, let her win, let the lost people of Phaedrial have their entitled Elite.

But then I heard it; the same voice that reached out to me inside the witch's shack: the voice of a shadow. *"Get up and fight!"*

I turned my head and searched for the source through blurred vision. When I saw nothing, I sat up, grunting through the agonizing pain. Still, there was no one. No source of the voice inside my head. When I dared to stand again, Kenya landed another blow, knocking me back to the ground. Blood spilled from my mouth as I coughed through the pain.

"This is your legacy! Stand and fight!" The voice was there, urgently pushing me to move. *"Remember who you are. Remember why you are here."*

It was like the voice reached into my soul, and jump started my desire to live. With the eerie voice came the images of my journey. The battle with the wolf, the wailing sounds of the Kynuski, the blasts of the firebombs we dodged. I saw myself fighting, being accepted by the Flameless, and training them to become stronger fighters.

I watched myself travel through the Darkest Forest, through the Odious and to my home in Phaedrial only to be attacked and nearly beaten to death. Through all of it, I persevered. Not because my life was perfect, but because it was worth living. I had done so much in such a short time and I had so much more to do! My skin burned as all the markings that the potion erased from my body reappeared and, as they stretched across my skin, the fire within returned.

The shocked gasps of the small group of witnesses were my confirmation. My wings had returned and as they lifted me from the ground, I felt the power of my flame healing my body slowly. My vision cleared just in time to see Kenya try to run away. Before she could step foot outside the ring, a circle of fire shot up around us. And it trapped inside her with me. Her eyes darted in every direction, searching for an exit strategy.

"A fight to the finish," Kiara said, repeating her earlier sentiment. "Only one may leave with their soul intact. Stand and fight."

"UGH!" Kenya yelled out then turned, accepting that she wouldn't be able to run away, and held up her hands, positioned to fight. "You think your wings will make it easier to beat me? Fine! Bring it!"

I knew then what I had to do. A combination of the fight techniques taught to me. A dance lead by intuition, by knowing and understanding my opponent. Kenya was driven by emotion, desire, and envy.

It wasn't one fight technique or the other that would give me the victory; it was both. I moved with the intuition of Jamila but was driven by the understanding of Zodiac. No longer was Kenya the ultimate opponent for me. Her fear betrayed her and revealed her weakness.

Our fight continued, but this time when Kenya took to the sky, my own wings carried me after her. I was relentless in my attack. I circled her in the air, pummeling her with my fist and feet. Giving her the same treatment she had me.

With my hands wrapped around her neck, Kenya punched at my sides, but the armor protected me from her blows. Desperate, she pulled a dagger from the holster on her calf and dragged the blade across my arm.

Where the kamular should have protected me, it didn't. The blade cut right through the material, spilling my blood in its wake. I released my hold of her neck and flew back. She smiled, holding the blade up to me.

The edge of it shined with a gold coating. I recognized it immediately as the familiar shine of fenium. It was the rarest mineral found in the Alluring and had to be mined from the mountains that surrounded Phaedrial. Through the years, they found only three of the mountains produced the mineral. It was so scarce that only the Elite or the Elitesmen had access to it.

"Remind me to thank Zodiac for the gift." She spun the dagger around her fingertip. "He thought I'd use it to protect you."

Though my cinquedeas were not coated in the material, they would do the job I needed. Kenya's armor was a standard metal. All I had to do was avoid her blade. I remembered what Jamila said about my opponent. She was more calculated than she was prepared for an actual fight.

She thought the blade would be enough to shake me and shifted her focus to taunting me with it. She lunged at me over and over, threatening to cut me and came close a few times, but I avoided her attacks while waiting for the perfect time to strike.

Still in the air, she pushed forward, blade aimed for my throat. Just as I had the times before, I dodged her. I dipped around her and pulled my own daggers out. In a crossing motion, I sliced her back from shoulder to side, creating an X across her back.

She cried out, and her wings flickered. Despite her struggle to remain in the air, they vanished. Kenya's body dropped to the ground. The sound of bones snapping in her legs was echoed by the smack of her torso.

I landed next to her and looked down at my fallen opponent. "Why?" I asked her.

"You aren't worthy of this power." Kenya coughed out. "Just because of who your mother was, and who your father is. That won't be enough."

"What are you talking about?" I leaned forward, wanting more of the information she had.

She didn't answer my question. Instead, she used my curiosity as a moment to strike a final blow. The coated blade lifted, but her injuries caused her to move slower. With one hand, I knocked the blade from her hand and with the other; I forced the cinquedea through the soft side of her chest plate and into her heart.

Kenya let out a gurgling cry as her mouth filled with blood. With the last release of the air from her lungs, the barrier of fire surrounding the challenge grounds dropped. As the silent audience watched me, I stood next to her lifeless body and felt relief wash over me. I'd done it. I'd proven myself and survived.

I waited while the people considered what they'd just witnessed. Would they accept me?

The silence lasted a beat longer than I could handle

and I nearly turned to walk out of there. But then they cheered as I stood there with my wings still burning. They cheered for me and the sound reached all across Phaedrial.

I was their new elite, and the people of Phaedrial accepted me. Finally.

CHAPTER 23

"Oh, you made it!" Ali jumped from my bed as I entered the room. "Did you get your wings back?"

"Yeah." I looked around the space for Rose, my eager helper, but she wasn't there. "What are you doing here?"

"I'm sorry. You are still mad at me. I just wanted to make sure you were alright." Her eyes dropped to the floor. "I'll go."

"No, you don't have to."

"Are you sure?" She looked back at me with hopeful eyes.

"Look, Ali, I was obviously mad at you and I won't say that I'm completely over it now. That is going to take time." I sat down on the bed and pulled my boots off. "I felt betrayed by you, but I get why you did what you did. She was your sister. You trusted her. I understand how it is to be lied to by someone whose opinion you valued. There was no way you could have known her intentions."

"Elsfaer, I—" she started, but I interrupted her.

"Look, just promise me you won't give me any other secret magical cures, and we can work on getting back to being friends again." I paused. "In time."

"I promise." She nodded. "I'd never want to hurt you."

"Good." I sighed and leaned back across the bed.

"How does it feel?" Ali asked. "To have your wings back."

"It feels amazing." I couldn't help the smile that stretched across my face. "I felt so broken and worried that I would never get them back.

"I'm glad." She whispered.

"Are you really?" I turned to her with a serious expression. "It's okay if you're not. Your sister did just die."

"I know, and I know I should feel sad about it. Maybe I will in a while, but after what she did to you, after the lies she told me. I can't help but think about how she's always been that way." Ali spoke of her sister and chewed her lip. "I think on some level I knew she was bad. She's always been kind of heartless. When we were children, she did everything in her power to make me feel weaker than her. She made my life a living hell. I should have known she was up to something when she came to me wanting to reconcile for the greater good."

"She did?"

"Like I said, she used you to get to me just as much as she used me to get to you. If it hadn't been a chance to help the Elite, I would have never agreed to work with my sister. Anyway, I just thought you should know the truth. I'm sure you have lots to get done. I'll leave you to it now."

"Ali, where are you going?" I asked as she headed for the door.

"I'm not sure." She looked back. "Zodiac said I could temporarily use a room here. Not sure when that runs out, but I'll figure things out."

"I have a lot to do." I got up from the bed. "You really think I'll be able to do it without your help?"

"You want my help?" her eyes widened. "How can I help you?"

"Yes, there are still seven days until I'm officially the Elite. I may have won this battle, but I'm not naïve enough to believe that this is the only one I'll face." I turned to the window, looking out on the city outside my room. "There are still a lot of people who don't think I'm worthy of this title. One fight didn't change that."

"They're just jealous." She brushed off my concern. "People want power. You have power. After what they saw today, no one is going to come after you."

"The thing is, I'm not sure they're wrong." I said honestly. "A few weeks ago, leading our people was the furthest thing from my mind. Now, I can say I want this, but I'm not sure that it's not only because if I lose it, I also lose my life. I don't want to die. But my desire to survive doesn't mean I'll be an influential leader for them."

"You won't die. If anyone else is dumb enough to challenge you after that display, they are nuts. You're the most amazing thing anyone has ever seen."

"Flattery."

"No, I mean it! Your wings are WHITE! I have never even heard of a phoenix with white wings before." Ali gushed. "Not only that, but you're a badass fighter. Even without your wings, you gave my evil ass sister a run for her money. You may not think you're deserving, but I think you're wrong. Sure, you may have a lot to learn about our people, but that's okay. You have Zodiac and me to teach you the ways."

"Yeah, just call it intuition, but I can tell something bad is just around the corner." I frowned. "And me being amazing doesn't address the other part of my concern. I don't want to just look good doing the job. I want to be good at it."

"Well, let's listen to your intuition and prepare for it." Ali shrugged. "Use the resources available to you. You said you read a lot about the history of Phaedrial. Now it's time to learn about its present issues."

"Elsfaer?" Rose's head followed the knock at the door as she peeked through the slight opening.

"Yes?" I addressed her, happy to see her yet again.

"The council would like to see you." She nodded to Ali and smiled when my friend winked at her.

"Now?" I huffed. "Don't I get a moment to decompress? I would like to shower and rest."

"I'm sorry, but this cannot wait." Rose grimaced.

"Okay, I'm coming." I pulled my boots back on my feet. "Wait for me here?" I asked Ali, who nodded as I left the room.

The room was full of the council members, again people whose names I couldn't remember, but the two grumps and the speaker were there. This room was unfamiliar and not our usual space. They lined one wall in monitors that provided an aerial view of Phaedrial. On the opposite side were seats paired with small writing desks.

"What's going on?" I scanned the room and the monitors on the wall.

"It seems the last elite left you a ticking time bomb." Jamila grunted and Zodiac shot her a look. "Sorry, I know I'll be quiet."

"What does that mean?" I asked. "A time bomb?"

"The Unruly are preparing a strike," Zodiac gave the explanation Jamila failed to.

"The who?" I huffed. "What's the Unruly? What do they want?"

"They are the ones who attacked you." Zodiac pointed to the wall of monitors, where the image changed to the face of a man with dark rings under his yellowed eyes. "They are a collective of dark phoenixes who stand against us."

"Is that why their wings are like that?" I recalled the wings of Fado, the fat man who led the rogue boys. "They were almost like ash."

"It is the darkness snuffing out their fire," Kiara educated me. "Once a phoenix accepts darkness into their heart, it changes the very core of their being. Their fire can no longer burn. But their wings are still theirs to claim, only now they are something different."

"Before our last Elite rose, his predecessor stirred up more trouble amongst our kind. We believe that was the reason the High Spirit replaced him." Zodiac continued, "The balance was dangerously at risk, and his interference led to the rise of the Dark Phoenixes. A group who thought it was time to shift our people to the side of the Dark. This had to be stopped."

"And it wasn't?" I inferred from his storytelling that they'd done nothing to stop the people who threatened us.

"While we pushed the groups out of Phaedrial, we did not exterminate them." Zodiac confirmed. "They held up in the Odious. But while our numbers dwindle, theirs are growing."

"And now they are coming for you," Jamila added. "They want Milo to fight you and take your place as the Elite, but considering they have cut ties with our people, they cannot simply call for an Elite challenge."

"Milo?" I raised a brow. "And that is?"

She pointed to the screen where the yellowed-eyed face was still on display. "He is their leader, and he wants you to give up your right as the Elite."

"Why would I ever do that?" I scoffed.

"They've sent this photo. Apparently, it is someone close to you?" When the screen flickered, my heart stopped. They had him bound and gagged. Bruises covered his body and his face looked swollen from the beating they gave him. Kaden.

"The threat that came with the photo was you give them what they want or he dies." Jamila reported.

Even with my own devastation, I recognized the sharp inhale of the man in the chair closest to me. He looked like Kaden. An older, darker version. I lifted a brow as I stared at him. The sickening guilt that washed over his face was the confirmation I needed.

"We can't let that happen." I refused to let Kaden suffer for me.

"You can't honestly be considering giving in to their demands." Grump number one stood from his chair, ready to protest my decision. "A dark power cannot lead the Phoenix people. It would throw off the balance of Penumbra and fracture the very foundation the High Spirit built this world on."

"He is just a flameless," Grump number two agreed with him.

"Just a flameless? Is that what we have come to? Is he not still one of our people?" I paused, taking in every face of leadership in the room, and was disappointed to see that there were others who agreed.

"You all have drawn so many lines in the sand that you no longer see which side you stand on. And you wonder why the Dark are growing while your numbers dwindle?" I scoffed. "They have something you don't. They are one people. I come here and I learn that there are Red Flames, Blue Flames, Flameless, and those who are trapped in the middle. Phaedrial is broken. The Phoenix people are broken, and you need to be focused on fixing that, not creating more ways to destroy the very fabric of our people."

"Elsfaer—" Kiara started.

"I'm not discussing this any further. I am the Elite; this is my decision to make, and I am not allowing one person under my care to be harmed by the Dark Phoenixes. And whether you believe he still deserves my protection is no concern of mine." I turned to leave the room. There was nothing more to say to them.

"What are you going to do?" Jamila followed me out of the room. I could hear the smile in her voice. She was happy I'd put the council in their place.

"I don't know, but I'm not about to stand aside and let them kill him." I looked over my shoulder at her. "He doesn't deserve that simply because he knows me."

"It's more than that." She raised a brow. "You understand that don't you?"

"What?" I stopped in my path and turned to face her. "What more could it be?"

"They didn't take him because you know him. If that were the case, they could have taken anyone." She tilted her head and looked at me like I was a dunce who needed more time to process her words. "They took him because you care about him. They know he means something to you, more than anyone else."

"He—" I couldn't rebuke what she had to say because it was true. I cared about him in a way that I hadn't cared about anyone else. I didn't know what that meant any more than I knew what it meant to care about Ali. It was just there. New and intriguing and I didn't want to lose it.

"I can help you. I want to." She smiled. "It's about time someone fixed what is broken here. I'm so proud of you for seeing that."

"Hopefully, I can actually make a difference here." I took a deep breath. "I've been reading the journals of the old elites and it's so much worse than I could have ever imagined it would be."

"You will figure it out." Jamila nodded. "You have us by your side to help you."

We started back on our path down the hall but skid to

a halt when we heard the enormous explosion. It was in the distance but still too close for comfort. I looked at Jamila with terrified eyes. Before she could speak, there was a second one. It was close enough that the floor shook. We ran to the closest window just in time to see a third ball of fire cutting through the air, headed for the castle.

Phaedrial was under attack.

CHAPTER 24

"Looks like they aren't waiting for that attack." Zodiac ran into the hall, where Jamila and I stood by the window.

"Wasn't there a timeline on that threat?" I asked as I watched the guards running down the hall.

"If there was, it doesn't matter." Jamila took off after the guards. She would join them in the defense of our city.

"We need to act now," Zodiac urged.

"Where are the guards?" I peered out of the window, looking at the grounds and the sky. Besides the ones in the hall, I saw no one. "Why aren't they fighting back?"

"They have no orders."

"They need orders to protect the damn city? Shouldn't that be the protocol? Someone attacks, you fight back!" I looked at Zodiac incredulously. "Who gives the orders?"

"Whoever you appoint." he responded.

"Fine, I appoint you! Get them off their asses!" I called

my wings; with a powerful flap of the white flames, I shot a burst of energy that shattered the glass and flew out of the window.

As I reached the sky outside the Castle, the fourth ball of fire was streaking through the air. With another burst of energy, I flapped my wings and sent a blast of hot air that pushed the ball in the opposite direction, landing back on the attacker's ground. Without waiting for a backup, I pushed forward. This was not a time to be subtle. I had to send a message.

Again, they shot another ball of fire, and again I directed it back towards them, this time landing on the catapult that sent it to us. It was a minor victory, considering they still had two others fully intact and loaded.

I was the only one in the air, and I waited for their shadowed wings to lift them from the ground. They never did, instead they continued their assault with the fireballs. After I knocked another to the ground, Zodiac and the Elitesmen appeared. Led by Zodiac, they charge forward, dropping from the sky onto our enemy. I watched from above as the brief battle ensued.

Our men were powerful, properly trained, and ready for a fight. That was encouraging to see. They rushed through the opposing force. Those that could be captured were, and the others escaped through the trees. In the distance, we could see their dark wings lift from the ground as they escaped.

"That was unimpressive." I commented as I land back on the grounds outside the Castle. "I expected more from them."

"That was a test," Zodiac commented, dropping

beside me.

"A test?" I glanced at the others who landed beside him.

"Yes, they wanted to see if you would put up a fight, and how strong you are. No doubt they have insiders reporting that you succeeded in your battle with Kenya. This way, they got to see you in action without actually having to battle you head on."

"That was smart." Jamila approached. "The captives are being taken to holding. We can question them and find out what the plans were."

"Yeah, it was. Do you think they would know anything other than what they were told to do today?" I doubted their leader was dumb enough to share all their plans. These men were pawns in a much larger game.

"No, not really, but it won't hurt to try." Jamila shrugged. "Any information we get is more than we have now."

"So, what now?" I looked at Zodiac. "What do we do? Are there people hurt?"

"I've dispatched a team to go out and help anyone who needs it." Zodiac reported.

"Now, we try to figure out a way to get to them before they get to us." The regretful councilman, and the man I suspected was Kaden's father, approached us. He wore his battle gear, having joined the Elitesmen in their fight. "They want a fight; I say we give them one."

"You?" I eyed him. "You want to fight with us?"

"I know you know who he is," he spoke with fading pride.

"Yes." Zodiac and Jamila left us as I addressed him.

"Councilman Knight, Kaden is your son."

"Look, I have regretted every moment since sending him away. I was foolish, high on pride, and not much else. I wish I could take it back, but I cannot. But I refuse to sit aside and let them use my son like this."

"He'll be happy to know you care." I smiled, but wondered if that was true.

"I always have." His gaze rose to the castle top. "Things were hard for a while, after his mother died. I thought I could handle it all, but I was wrong. Instead of being there for my son, I became lost in my work until that was the only thing that mattered. I shouldn't have done that. He deserved better."

"I'm not the one you need to convince that you care." I interjected. "Tell it to your son when we get him back."

"I'm sorry to interrupt," Kiara joined us, breathing like she'd just run a marathon. "There is the matter of the public. People are panicking now that we've been attacked."

"And I suppose I need to address them publicly?" I looked at her for guidance because I honestly didn't know what the protocol was.

"Yes. That would be best." She placed her hand on her large chest and took several deep breaths.

"Can it wait until morning?" I asked because I needed rest and time to gather my thoughts. What was I supposed to say to them?

"Well, I-" she started in a judgmental tone.

"Absolutely it can," Zodiac reappeared and answered for the snooty woman. "Elsfaer, you need the rest. Please go."

"She should address them now." Kiara pushed. "We need to calm the people's concerns."

"This has been brewing since the last elite. It is not her doing." Zodiac responded on my behalf. "It's best if she waits until the morning to address the people. With a fresh mind."

"I agree," Councilman Knight cosigned Zodiac's argument. "Give her some time before she makes her first public address."

"I wish it were under better circumstances," I muttered.

"One day it will be," Zodiac placed his hand on my shoulder and ushered me away from the disapproving speaker.

"You won't be able to coddle her forever!" Kiara called after us.

Hot lights baked my skin as I waited for the cue to begin my address. I stood behind the podium in an empty auditorium. The only ones there were the camera crew, the speaker and Zodiac. My night was anything but restful. I tossed and turned, thinking of how I could convey a positive and inspiring message to people who were worried about their safety.

Kiara stood next to the camera, a clipboard held at the ready, and counted down on her fingers. When she pointed to me, that was my sign to start the address.

"People of Phaedrial," I began. "I stand before you as

your new Elite, and I realized that I have a lot to prove to you. This is not a title I campaigned for. It was one that was put on my shoulders, but I've chosen to carry it with pride. Already my position was challenged and even without the full strength of my fire, I won that battle.

"Now I am here, speaking to you all, because there was a recent threat in our home. One that apparently is not new at all. There has been a divide between our people. And we cannot continue in this way.

"None of you know who I am, none of you trust me, and I understand that. Trust is something that is earned. And I intend to earn the trust of each and every one of you. But right now, I need you to understand this. The Phoenix people have lost their way.

"I've read about it in the notes of our former elite. The choices he made left us relying much more on technology, an advent of the human world, than we do on our own magic that flows through our veins. Is there any wonder that more and more of our people are born immature and never reach their flame?

"The balance of our people is already thrown off. This isn't a matter of trying to stop it from happening. This is a matter of trying to correct what is already waning. There is darkness in this technology. We have paved over our homelands with concrete, forgetting that our connection to the Earth beneath our feet. We've blocked our skies with radio waves, forgetting that we need the air to fuel our fire. These things must be repaired, or we as a people will cease to exist.

"What these dark phoenixes want, if I am honest, is exactly what I want. I want to return to a world where we are connected. I want our people to believe in magic again, to rely on what is naturally within us and to burn brighter than we have ever burned before.

"The thing about it is that they will kill every one of you that has turned your backs on our ways to do it. That is not my way. We will work back to what we were. We will build again the world in which we thrived. Because it is not only our people who rely on it. It is all of Penumbra and we will not let them down."

Kiara signaled for the cameras to cut and the lights shut off, and I stood there with my skin tingling from the nerves I'd swallowed before we began. I wondered what everyone who listened to me felt. Did they believe in me? Did they think I'd gone too far with my assessment of the situation? Had I reassured them that they would be okay?

"Elsfaer, we need to speak." The moment the cameras and the lights shut off; Zodiac pulled me to the side. Kiara frowned and turned to leave the room. Clearly, she had something to say, but didn't want him around to hear it.

"Yes?" I followed him. "Was that okay? What's wrong?"

"Privately please." He nodded to the small office that sat behind the auditorium wall.

I walked ahead of him, nodding at the camera crew, who gave approving smiles. Maybe I had done something right.

"First, before I say anything else, I want to tell you that was an amazing speech." Zodiac closed the door behind us. "And I have always believed that you were capable of what you just did. While you will face resistance, I can tell you they want the same thing you do. You're an outsider. That will not change overnight."

"Thanks for that. I didn't know what I was going to say until I got up there. Then I just went with what felt right." I leaned against the small wooden desk. "Paereon's notes were disturbing. He knew what would happen and he still did it. I'm not sure how long it will take to correct. There is so much work we need to do, Zodiac."

"You're right." Zodiac beamed with pride again. "There is a lot that needs to be done, and we will do the work."

"Well, what did you want?" I questioned. "If you approve of my message, I'm assuming there is another reason you wanted to speak to me privately."

"Please tell me you didn't promise a favor to a sorceress." He lowered his voice as if someone outside the doors might still hear him.

"Great job, Jamila. Rat me out." I rolled my eyes.

"He needed to know." Jamila stepped from the coat closet.

"What the hell were you doing in there?" my eyes darted between them. "You two are ambushing me now with your disapproval?"

"As the Elite, your promise comes with a much larger price tag than you could ever imagine." Zodiac ignored my question. "You might have put all of Phaedrial on the line, Elsfaer. Don't you realize that?"

"A sorceress' favor is rarely something small," Jamila added on. "It's going to be a big thing. Likely world changing, big."

"I didn't think of that." I sat on the small desk as the weight of understanding landed on my shoulders. "Dammit, I only wanted to fix everything. I wanted to get my wings back so I could survive. You saw what happened out there. There was no way I was going to defeat Kenya without my fire."

"Fix it, you did," Jamila ridiculed.

"That's not helping," Zodiac warned her. "We're here to make this right, not to belittle her for her choices."

"What can we do now?" I asked. "There is too much going on. I don't want this to interfere in stopping the dark phoenixes from hurting anyone else."

"Unfortunately, all we can do is wait for the old grungy witch to call in her favor and tell us what she wants." Jamila crossed her arms over her chest. "No telling how long that will take."

"You know, you could pick a stance." I snapped at her, tired of her switching her moods like she did her underwear. "Either you're on my side or you're not, but you can't be both!"

"Of course I'm on your side." Jamila looked hurt by my words. "I've been by your side."

"Maybe you need to remind yourself of that. Because all the snippy comments aren't helpful and make me question you."

"There is something else we could do," Zodiac whispered when Jamila said nothing.

"What is it?"

"Don't worry about it. If I'm right, this won't be an issue anymore." He placed his hand on my shoulder. "Just promise me, no more giving out favors to potentially evil people."

"I promise." I nodded. "Not like I have a list of them waiting for me to need my life saved again."

CHAPTER 25

"You know I never thought that I would be friends with an Elite." Ali stepped out of my closet, sporting an airy dress that hung from her shoulders. "Let alone be allowed to be inside of their chambers. Now, if only I had the boobs to support your wardrobe!" She smacked her hand against her small chest and laughed.

"Yeah, I never thought I would be the Elite or have a friend to talk about any of this with." I squinted at her. "Maybe some padding would help?"

"Oh ha, ha, ha." She stuck her tongue out at me.

"I'm really glad you're here, Ali. Despite the almost getting me killed thing, that I'm still trying to get over."

"Well, that was loaded, but so am I." She danced over to the vanity and lifted a small gold medallion from the jewelry box on my stand. The thing had been locked until Ali started playing dress up. "Just look at all the amazing things you have at your disposal. I mean a cloaking medallion! Do you know how rare these are to get?"

"A cloaking medallion?" I perked up, taking my attention away from the book in my lap.

"Yeah, you know you wear this and it hides you from the world. Only those who you wish to see you can." She showed how the medallion worked by pulling the chain over her head. As the medallion rested against her chest, she winked at me, closed her eyes, and vanished.

"Okay," I moved to the place where she just stood and waved my hand in the air. She wasn't there. "That is pretty cool."

"Isn't it?" She answered behind me. I turned to see her sitting on the bed, the medallion still hanging from her neck.

"How did you do that?"

"You just have to focus on what you want. If you want to be seen, you will be. If you don't, then it hides you from view." She pulled the medallion off and handed it to me.

"That's amazing." I looked over the. piece and ran my finger across the spiraling etches along the surface.

"You know, there are stories that one of the former Elites was a pervert who totally used this to peek in on women as they were dressing. Men have a way of making even the coolest things creepy."

"Ugh, of course he did." I rolled my eyes. "How could someone like that ever get the approval to be an elite?"

Ali removed the medallion and handed it to me. "Maybe you can use it to get a good look at the menfolk. Not that there is all that much to see."

"I think I'll pass on that one." I shuddered to think of what I would see if I were degenerate enough to do something like that. "Let's leave the perversions to the men. Besides, I have to get ready for dinner."

"Dinner." She raised a brow. "Is this a special dinner?"

"Yes, my first official meal since I got here. Rose has delivered every meal to my bedroom since I got here, but Zodiac insists we sit down for an actual meal tonight."

"I suppose I'm not invited?" She poked out her lips in a forced pout. "No worries. I'll find some bread to nibble on."

"Don't be so dramatic." I laughed at her pathetic expression. "Of course you're invited. You don't think I'm going through this alone, do you?"

"They will not want me there, Elsfaer." She shook her head. "I appreciate it, but they haven't forgiven what I did. Hell, you haven't even fully forgiven me. It's probably for the best that I don't go."

"Well, one of the perks of being the Elite is I can invite whoever I want to dinner, and the rest of these uppity birds can kiss my ass if they don't agree." I placed the medallion back in the box where she found it. "I have a lot of people to forgive. But that's not going to happen by avoiding everyone. We need to talk and be honest about everything."

"Are you sure?"

"I'm sure you better find something in that closet to wear, oh and while you're at it, find me something as well."

"What about Rose?" Maggie headed for the closet. "Isn't she supposed to be at your beck and call? Not that I mind, of course."

"I gave her the evening off to spend time with her

family." I walked over to the window to look out onto the city again.

"You did?" Maggie called out.

"Yes, I think we should all be with the people we care about right now. Like it or not, there is a war brewing. I only wish I could run home to my family." I answered. "Which is another reason you have to come to dinner. I care about you and I want you there."

"I understand." Ali disappeared into the closet but popped her head out for a moment to address me. "But you know, it may not be a perfect one, but you are with family."

"Yeah, I know." I returned my attention to the sky. She was right. They were the only family I was ever going to get, so I needed to make the best of it.

Dinner wasn't what I thought it would be. The massive dining hall felt awkward to be in because there were only four of us at the long table. I'd expected the entire council to be there, but it relieved me to see that Zodiac meant for it to be an intimate event.

My jaw nearly hit the floor when Jamila joined us. She wasn't in her usual gear, ready for combat, with her sword hanging at her side. Instead, she wore a peach dress that hung from her shoulders in loose waves. It was simple and soft, and it gave her a motherly look I hadn't expected of her.

She smiled at Ali and invited her in for a hug before complimenting the white dress she'd picked out for me. There was something there between them I didn't understand, but it was good for both of them. Jamila softened, and Ali brightened whenever they were around each other.

"You look great." I told Jamila. "I don't think I've ever seen you in anything but pants."

"Yeah, well, you've never seen me off duty before."

"Even at my birthday parties?"

"Even then. But I wanted to be there." She winked at me.

"Ladies, shall we?" Zodiac entered the room, wearing his version of off duty attire. A black suit with a gold tie and handkerchief. Very relaxed.

We sat down and they served our meal we spoke of everything from childhood pastimes to recent events. As the night went on, and our plates we cleared our plates, I realized just how true Ali's words were. We were a family, a dysfunctional one, but a family, nonetheless.

It was when the conversation turned to recent events that we lost Zodiac. His focus was on the timepiece chained to his jacket. Jamila told us how lucky I was to not have encountered The Darken, a wandering body of water in the Odious.

"It appears in different areas throughout the Dark territories and they say it's inhabited by a siren who would call you to your death." She looked at Zodiac as if expecting him to add to her story, but he didn't. "Anyway, I've heard stories of people who thought they got away from her only to be suffer painful and mysterious deaths later."

"That sounds terrifying." I pushed my plate away. "And it can just appear anywhere?"

"Yeah," Jamila nodded. "I'm not even sure it's always

present here. I think it crosses realms. Goes to other worlds to torture new souls before returning to Penumbra."

"That's insane." Ali balked, and the two entered a debate about the limitations of the moving lake.

I tried my best to stay focused on the conversation, but Zodiac was up to something. Unfortunately, I couldn't outright ask him about it. I didn't want to ruin the evening, but my intuition told me that whatever it was, I needed to know about it. I didn't want to be consumed by paranoia, but Zodiac had already lied to me about so much. It wasn't too farfetched to think he'd be hiding more from me.

Dinner ended, and we agreed that the best thing to do was rest. Tomorrow, we would need to plan for our confrontation with the Dark Phoenixes. Though, while everyone else slept, I couldn't settle. As Ali snored softly in my bed, I stood by the window, rubbing the cloaking medallion in my hand and wondering what it would feel like to hide from the world.

I wanted nothing more than to disappear, if only for a day. There was still so much I wanted to do, experiences that seemed just out of reach. As I thought about vanishing, I caught sight of wings taking to the sky. They exited the window of Zodiac's chambers.

I thought about minding my business. I considered letting him go on his way to handle whatever it was he had to without my interference. That lasted about five seconds. Zodiac was hiding something. I was right. And maybe I didn't have the right to know all of his secrets, but something told me that this one, like many of the others he kept, affected me.

As I placed the chain of the medallion around my neck, I could feel the magic working and hiding me from the eyes of the world. I peeked at the mirror to confirm that it worked before calling my wings and left out of the window. Ali still slept soundly as I left.

I caught up to him quickly and remained high above the clouds. I didn't know if he could hear or see my wings with the cloaking, but I wanted to make sure that he thought he was alone. It was hard to see him through some of the thicker cumulus clouds, but the flames of his wings made it easier to keep up.

He finally returned to the ground, landing in a discolored patch of land near the border between the two territories. Trees stood around him, casting shadows in every direction. I landed far enough from him so he wouldn't hear my footfall. It meant I had to walk a few minutes before I found him again, but when I did, he stood alone.

Zodiac was still. He stared out into the shadows, completely silent. For a moment, I thought I'd wasted my time following him. Maybe he just wanted some time alone. Maybe this was the place he went to clear his head, and I'd intruded on that. As I turned to leave him with his solace, he spoke.

"Thank you for coming. I know I said I wouldn't come here again, and I meant that when I said it." His deep voice filled the night air as he spoke into the darkness. "But she is at risk."

I thought he might have gone crazy standing in the dark talking to no one at all, but then I heard it. It was the same whispered echo I thought I heard before. The one that came to me in the witch's shack, and the one that motivated me to continue fighting through my Elites challenge. That shadowed voice answered him.

"I know." It spoke softly and its tone was full of sorrow. "I tried to help her. I tried to stop her from making that promise, but she wouldn't listen to me."

"You were there when it happened?" Zodiac asked.

"Of course I was. I've been with her since she stepped foot in Penumbra." The voice returned as if it were obviously their position. "I've been watching over her, trying to keep her safe without interfering. How could you let this happen?"

"This is not my fault." Zodiac defended himself. "I've done everything you asked me to do and more."

"Your job was to protect her. You were supposed to keep her safe from this." The voice spoke, this time with a tinge of anger. "And yet here she is in the middle of chaos and you stand here and say it's not your fault?"

"There will come a time when she has to learn to protect herself. We both knew this. I've done everything I can to prepare her." Zodiac huffed. "She is the Elite now. I can't watch over every movement she makes. Not anymore."

"If the sorceress gets what she wants, Elsfaer won't be able to protect herself, or anyone else, for that matter." The voice spoke, but this time I hear movement in the shadows. Whoever this was, they were getting antsy. "We have to do more."

"I won't let that happen." Zodiac proclaimed. "She will get through this. She has to."

"She is our daughter, Zodiac. We have to protect her."

I heard nothing after that. Zodiac stood there hosting his conversation with the unknown person, and I just watched the last words float around the space like a child's lost balloons. *She is our daughter.* It wasn't like I could pretend the conversation wasn't about me. They'd said my name outright. She was me. I was their daughter. Zodiac was my father, and this mysterious person he snuck out to see in the middle of the night was my mother.

My mother, who Zodiac told me all my life that he hadn't known. My mother, who I'd only recently discovered that he had known. That intuition that told me to fly after him was right. Here was another lie, uncovered. Not only did he know my mother, he was with her. Intimately enough to make a damn baby he would spend over twenty years lying to!

The fire burned inside of me, growing until my skin felt hot and I could feel the tingles of the magical tattoos lighting up all over my body. "I'm your what?" I stepped out from behind the tree where I hid. No longer wanting to be invisible, the magic of the medallion allowed him to see me.

"Elsfaer? What are you doing here?" Zodiac turned to me and, as he did, the shadow behind him flickered.

"Who are you talking to?" I squinted, trying to pinpoint the source of the voice, but there was nothing but darkness.

"You shouldn't be here," he avoided my question.

"I'm your daughter?" I looked at him and he didn't respond. "So many lies. How many are there? Every time

I feel like I can forgive you, move on and take steps towards healing, there is more. More lies, and now this?"

"This isn't the way I wanted you to find out about this." Zodiac stepped forward, holding his hands out like he was approaching a bull who was ready to charge.

"Right, because you didn't want me to find out at all. Like all the other secrets you've kept from me!"

"Elsfaer—" Zodiac said my name, but I didn't want to hear anything else he had to say.

"Who are you talking to?" I peered around him into the darkness and again found nothing more than shadows.

"I—" Again he spoke, but I couldn't deal with hearing his voice. Every word only added to the pain in my chest.

"You know what, just save it. I don't have time for any more of your lies." I called my wings and leapt into the sky, leaving the man who was apparently my father behind.

The anger I felt only grew the further I traveled. If I thought I had any chance of winning, I would have turned around and flew back to him. I would have screamed, kicked, and fought my way to the truth, but even then, I wouldn't trust that I'd gotten it. How could someone spend so much time telling blatant lies to a person they claim to care for?

How could my own father allow me to believe I was an orphan my entire life?

CHAPTER 26

FOR HOURS I FLEW AROUND THE ALLURING, TOO ANGRY TO return to Phaedrial. Zodiac would be there waiting for me, but it was too soon to face him again. I would go back, because I had to, but I'd do it on my time. Not his.

I still had a job to do, even if that meant working alongside people who I didn't trust. My focus was getting through the last days of my rising without losing my life. I would have to deal with the rest of the family drama later. I made it back just as the sun rose in the sky and the city of Phaedrial came to life.

"Where were you last night?" Ali yawned as she sat up on the bed. "Man, I haven't slept that good in a long time."

"What?" I took my eyes from the page I'd been doodling on. I sat at the desk, intending to write out everything I felt about what happened, but the second I pulled out the page, my mind went blank.

"I woke up, and you weren't here. Are you okay? What happened?" She scooted across the bed, her voice holding more worry. "I thought maybe you just went to the bath-room, but I waited up and it was hours before you returned, or at least I think so. I fell asleep before you got back."

"Yeah, I just wanted to take a flight. Break in the wings," I lied. "You know how much I've missed them and it's not like I got to use them all that much to begin with."

"Ah, you wanted to see your land?" She climbed from the bed. "Take in all that is yours!"

"My land?" I raised a brow and laughed. "What are you talking about?"

"Yeah, I mean as the Elite, Phaedrial is pretty much yours." She jumped from the bed and headed to the large windows. "Imagine, this city is yours to command."

"Command?" That didn't feel right. I didn't want to command Phaedrial or its people. Lead them, yes, but I had no desire to become a dictator.

"What's wrong?" She turned with another stretch. The second yawn reminded me I hadn't slept at all the night before.

"I'm still not convinced that I'm the one for the job." I balled up the scribbled notes and tossed it in the trash can beneath the desk. "There is so much about this world that I don't understand."

"You realized you have the answer to that, right?"

"What?"

"You're the Elite. Inside your head are all the answers you need. Every Elite is connected in spirit to the previous elites. I'm surprised the voices haven't been driving you insane." Ali moved to the table where a pitcher of water and two cups sat, no doubt provided by

Rose. "That's what they say it's like for a new Phoenix Elite. Your head becomes flooded with the thoughts and feelings of those who came before you."

"I hear nothing, or at least I haven't, not since this began." I frowned. There was the rush of voices just after the High Spirit chose me, but I had heard nothing since. The only voice in my head was my own, and that was more than enough.

"Hmm," she scratched her chin. "That seems odd."

"Do you think something is wrong?"

"I think you should probably mention this to Zodiac and the others." Ali agreed. "Even if you're not from here, in your position, you should know more about our history and people than anyone else. I know you have those journals, but they don't have everything in them and most have been edited, anyway."

"Edited?" I picked up one of the books she spoke of. "You think someone changed the journals?"

"You don't think the historians, or whoever keeps those books safe, have left them untouched, do you? I mean, just think about what you've read so far, and how shocking it was. Imagine what they took out." Ali returned to the bed and sat down. "I mean, there are people here who need to cover their asses. Just because the last Elite let them get away with dirt, doesn't mean the next one will."

"Dammit, I need to speak to Zodiac." I grunted.

"Is there a problem between you two?" She crossed the room again to sit on the edge of the desk, her butt covering the blank pages and stopping my pen from creating any new drawings.

"The only problem we have is the way he constantly lies to me." I leaned back in my chair and tossed the pen to the table. "I swear since this began, I've found out more secrets about him than I care to count."

"I'm sure he had his reasons for the secrecy." Ali tried to soothe my concerns. "We all have secrets, even you."

"I would never keep a secret from someone if I knew it would change their life." I rejected her attempt at rationalizing his actions. People were allowed their secrets, but not the kind he kept. "Zodiac knew all these things about me, and yet he kept them to himself. He made choices for me, decisions that should have been mine, and I don't know that I can get past that. Every time I think I am ready to forgive him, I find out more."

"I'm sorry." She said simply and sipped her water. "What are you going to do? You'll have to face this issue with him. I suggest sooner rather than later."

"It's fine. I'll deal with my problems with him when this is all over. I have to keep my mind clear."

"You're right. So, what's next?"

"What's next is we try to figure out why I don't have access to this unlimited well of knowledge that should be available to me. If I'm going to defend Phaedrial and save Kaden, I need to know everything there is to know about our people." I pushed my chair back from the table to stand. "It's obvious that my education provided at the temple was lacking. Can you please find Jamila and ask her to arrange a meeting? I'll get freshened up."

"On it." Ali smiled and headed for the door.

"Don't you think you ought to get dressed first?" I called after her and laughed when she did the quick ninety-degree angle, adjusting her path from the exit to the bathroom. Ten minutes later, she appeared freshly dressed in black pants and a ruffled top that was too big for her and danced out the door.

I sent Ali ahead because I wanted time to clear my head. I needed to get myself together before facing Zodiac again. *My father.* The thought simultaneously warmed my heart and set my soul on fire. *How could he not tell me?*

My entire life, I thought I had no family. No mother or father. I was an orphan. Now I find out that not only was that a lie, like so many things, but I'd spent my life with my father. How could he think that wouldn't be a good thing to tell me? All I could think about were the moments we missed out on. The conversations I wanted to have with him but didn't, because I didn't know who he was.

What potential benefit did it produce to let me think my parents didn't want me? That's what it felt like. I was told that my parents sent me to Kai for my own good, but as a child, I wondered why they hadn't come with me. Why hadn't anyone checked on me? Every explanation given was only a brush off, so I told myself it was because they didn't care. They didn't want me, and I thought Zodiac was protecting me from the pain of finding that out.

I took my time bathing and dressing. I styled my hair into a long braid that fell down my back, and tied at the end with a single white ribbon. This was my first official day as the rising Elite. The first time the people in that room would look at me with the expectation of a new direction of our people, and I had to tell them I was lacking. That the knowledge I should have wasn't there. How was I supposed to face them?

I examined my reflection in the mirror when Ali returned to the room with Rose in tow.

"Rose," I smiled at my returning aide. "I hope you enjoyed your time with your family."

Rose nodded with a small smile before taking to her chores. Within minutes, she'd straightened the bedding and picked up the pile of clothing Ali left thrown over the floor after her fashion montage.

"They're ready for you," Ali returned to the room, popping a piece of fruit into her mouth.

"What are you so happy about?" my stomach growled as I watched her finish her sweet snack.

"I'm just excited to be a part of all this." She shook her head. "I never thought I would see the inside of this place, let alone be an official aide to the Elite."

"An aide?" I raised a brow. I didn't remember anyone telling me they had made Ali an aide.

"Yes, sorry if I overstepped, but when you asked me to arrange the meeting for you I—" She dropped her eyes. "I just assumed that you wanted me to be around to help."

"No, I like it." I smiled. "You're one of the few people here who understands what I'm going through. Still working on rebuilding that trust, but I need you by my side right now."

"I'm here as long as you want me to be." Ali beamed. "Whatever you need, I'm on it."

"You know a good aide would have brought me some fruit as well." I laughed.

"Oh, sorry," she frowned. "I can go get you more."

"I was joking, Ali." I threw my arm around her shoulder to reassure her.

"You know when we're in front of people, they won't like it if you touch me, let alone hug me." Ali looked at Rose, who still moved around the room. Rose nodded, agreeing with Ali.

"Oh?" I frowned. "That's ridiculous."

"It may be, but an elite would never be seen touching an aide," Rose chimed in. "Especially one who is a Half-flame."

"Ali," I paused. "I have a feeling I will not be the type of elite they want me to be, regardless of what I do. So, I'll hug whoever I want. I'll lead however I want, and they can just learn to deal with it."

"I like that in you!" she laughed as we headed out the door, leaving a smiling Rose standing in the room alone.

At least that was two people I'd pleased. Just had to work on the rest of the population.

We entered the chamber, the same room where they told me about our pending attack, and as the doors opened, they all stood. They replaced the individual seating with a long table which was already fully occupied with men and women I had met, and some I hadn't. As I rounded the room, heading for my seat at the head of them, I noted those who were indifferent to my presence. Not to say that I trusted any of them in the room, but clearly there were ones I'd need to keep a closer eye on.

"Thank you all for coming here today. I mentioned in my address to the people, I want to lead an alternative path for Phaedrial. There is a lot of work for us to do, but the first and most important effort will be to address the Dark Phoenixes." I began with confidence. "Now, I have my ideas of how we can overcome this, but I will depend on you and your knowledge of this situation to help address the issue. I hope to reunite those who we can with our people, but make no mistake, anyone who stands as a threat against Phaedrial and the balance of our world will fall."

"How do you plan to do that?" A short woman wearing a dark grey dress and with eyes like the midnight sky spoke from her position at the table. "Make them fall?"

"Together." I answered plainly.

"Together?" A tall man wearing a black hat and blue suit scoffed from the corner. "That's a weak response."

"Look around our home and tell me what you see." I paused. "Our people are divided, and it's because you, the leaders who sit in this room, allowed it to happen. You sat aside and watched as the color of flames dictated who deserved to be at peace. You watched the rising number of the flameless and did nothing to find a solution to that problem. That is why the Dark Phoenixes are after you now. That is why they attacked. They know that the people of Phaedrial are no longer one. And if we're going to survive, we must come together."

"And you think you can make that happen?" The short woman spoke again.

"What is your name?" I asked her.

"Lixa." She pushed her shoulders back as she spoke the name with pride.

"Lixa, when was the last time you sat across the table from a flameless and shared a meal? What about a hug?" I asked.

"I-" she stuttered, her blue lips pursing as she thought about her answer.

"Exactly, you haven't. Again, this isn't just on my shoulders to fix. I just got here, as I'm sure many of you want me to remember. You are the ones you allowed for this mess, so as much as I will lead, you will help me fix it." I looked around the room and waited for more rebuttal, but it didn't come. "We will start by getting out there and talking to people. Inviting the flameless back into our fold. And we will clarify that we aren't just doing this to save our asses. This is a permanent change. We are one people and I expect everyone to act accordingly."

Just then, as the other mumbled about what I said, I realized there was one person missing from the room, Zodiac. I looked at Jamila with a raised brow and she tightly shook her head no.

Now was not the time to address his absence. Instead, I acted as if I knew why he wasn't there and went about familiarizing myself with the members' plans. Or at least I tried to. The speaker, Kiara, made it her point to take up as much of the time as possible. She rambled on about her ideas for getting everyone together, which ranged from candlelight vigils to full out ballroom dances.

After she finished her list of party plans, Kiara spoke of the former elite and his plans to foster a bridge between the Dark Phoenix and the light. The more she spoke, the more it sounded as if this bridge was her own idea, and it would not deal with the imbalance that was being created. It would give the Dark Phoenix more access to the power of the light.

Instead of debating the flaws of her proposed tactic with her in front of the others, I listened. I had to appear as an elite, willing to consider every option put before her. By the time Kiara finished speaking, the others seemed uninterested in telling their ideas. Jamila instead proposed that we find another time to meet. She made excuses for other appointments that Zodiac had set up. Once again squashing any concern about his absence.

"What's wrong? Where is Zodiac?" I asked her as the Kiara exited the room. She lingered behind the others and when Jamila gave her the side eye, she finally left us alone.

"He had an urgent matter to tend to." Jamila answered in a quiet tone. "What was this really about?"

"What?" I pushed my hair out of my face and looked over the papers Kiara left behind that highlighted Paereon's supposed plans.

"Ali said you had something you needed to discuss, and while that speech was inspiring, I don't think it's what you really wanted to talk about."

"You're right." I nodded. "But it didn't seem right to do so without Zodiac here."

"So, what's the issue?" Jamila asked. "I'm no Zodiac, but I'm resourceful when I need to be."

"Something is blocking my access to the ancestral knowledge." I lowered my voice.

"What?" She leaned in. "What do you mean? Are you sick?"

"No, I mean I feel fine. Ali said I should have access to the knowledge of the Elites before me. She said we're spiritually connected, but I have nothing. Not since that initial moment in Kai." I explained. "I had all these voices in my mind, but something changed. When everything went dark, I lost them."

"That's bad." Jamila sat in the seat next to me.

"Tell me about it." I slumped in my seat. "What do we do?"

"Only one thing I can think of." Jamila sucked her teeth and turned her nose up.

"And that is?"

"Something that Zodiac is probably going to be furious at me for doing, but he isn't here to debate me on it, so who cares?" She stood up and held her hand out to me. "Elsfaer, it's time for you to go home."

CHAPTER 27

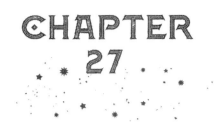

Returning to Kai wasn't something I ever thought I'd look forward to, but as we flew across the lands and I felt the beacon calling me home for the first time, I couldn't help but to be excited. Kai stood as a symbol for so much more than I had ever appreciated before.

Growing up, it was my prison. It was a thing that kept me away from everything I wanted. Its walls caged me in and refused to let me free. For a long time, I blamed the temple, not the people inside it, for my inability to live the life I wanted. It was the safest place for me, so I couldn't go anywhere else.

I wondered how Kai would have felt to me if I had known the truth. Would I have appreciated its legacy more? Would have I respected what it stood for? Or maybe I would have hated it more, knowing it limited my abilities and refused me the only thing I wanted. Freedom. Speculations of what ifs about the past were a waste of time. I needed to look to the future.

As we touched down on the temple ground, Acai met us. She stood alone with a wide smile on her face, abandoning her usual generalized disdain. Of course, she'd been expecting us.

"Well, what a wonderful day it is! The Elite visits me." She opened her arms and embraced me. "What do I owe this honor?"

"I wish I could say I was here for better circumstances." I hugged Acai and smiled as I inhaled the scent of lilacs. "But something is wrong, Acai. I need your help to make sense of things."

"Well, young firebird, you know you can always come to me for help." She looked over my shoulder at Ali. "I see you've brought a guest and a flameless, no less."

"You know that I'm Flameless?" Ali asked as she approached Acai.

"I know a lot of things. I also know that you are a lot more powerful than even you know." Acai examined Ali in the way she did everyone she met. It was as if she could see through their physical self into the very core of their soul. "Perhaps one day you'll figure that out."

"I hope you're right." Ali smiled.

"Yes, well, I wish we had time to sort out everyone's inner power, but we really need to focus on Elsfaer," Jamila interjected. "

"Yes, yes, let's get to business." Acai turned and headed into the temple.

"Go ahead. I want to set up a perimeter check with the guards here. I'll meet you there." Jamila nodded to us and took off with the four Elitesmen who'd accompanied us to Kai.

Acai led us through the quiet halls of the temple. As we walked, memories of my life flooded my head. I could hear the echoes of my childhood, my laughter, conversations with the monks, and even my cries as I begged to be let out into the world. It was all there, etched in the walls, and I could never escape it.

A cool breeze swept through the space as we turned down the hall that led to the Sanctuary. The same space where they held me when I became the Elite. A knot formed in my chest as Acai pushed the doors open.

They'd repaired the interior of the space. The last time I was there, the ceiling shatter and glass shards covered the floors, but that was no longer the case. It looked as if disaster had never touched before it. As if my power hadn't broken not only its structure but left scars on the people trapped there with me.

"I don't have to get on that table again, do I?" I pointed to the place where they tied me up. "I mean, we can do this without restraints, right?"

"No," Acai chuckled. "This is just a safe space to have this discussion."

"You know what's wrong already, don't you?" Though I hadn't told her why we'd come, Acai moved as if she'd already prepared everything we'd need.

"I do." She smiled. "You know me, always ready for what's coming."

"What is it?" Ali asked. "What's wrong with her?"

"As you already know, there is a disconnect between Elsfaer and the for phoenix elites." Acai touched my forehead. "We've expected this might be the case. This is not a mistake or something you can easily fix. It was also a part of the prophecy."

"Of course it was." I took a deep breath to control the resentment I felt. "And of course, no one told me about it."

"How could we? You left without our knowledge." Acai tapped my forehead. "Not every secret was held with malicious intent, Elsfaer. Some were because we just didn't know if they were necessary to tell."

"Right." I rolled my eyes. "So, what do we have to do?"

"Live, learn, and it will come to you." She said calmly before stepping away to the tea that was set up nearby. She poured a cup for herself and watched as I considered her words.

"You want to be more specific?" I asked her. Living and allowing things to fix themselves wasn't really an option.

"The High Spirit has blocked your connection to your predecessors so that you may lead you people without bias. You need to see them through fresh eyes. You've already recognized some troubling things and spoken about them. In that alone, you are serving your purpose."

"I'll never have the knowledge." My shoulders slumped. "I'm supposed to do this alone?"

"That, I do not know. What I know is that for now, you must lead without it."

"What did I miss?" Jamila entered the room.

"Elsfaer must lead without the knowledge of the prior Elites." Ali provided the recap. "Apparently. That's the way the High Spirit wants it."

"This is going to make her job tougher, but she needs to heal the divide among the Phoenix people. If she cannot, Phaedrial will fall and the Phoenix power will go dark, which will destroy the balance of Penumbra," Acai added.

"Great, no pressure there." I sat down on an empty pew.

"So, this attack is more than a play for power. They aren't just trying to take over Phaedrial, they want to take over Penumbra," Jamila speculated.

"There is a lot more at stake here." Acai nodded with worried eyes.

"How do you mean?" Jamila asked.

"The balance of Penumbra affects the balance of Earth as well." She moved towards the window that looked out over the mountains. "Should things fall out of balance there, it would lead to turmoil here on Earth. That is why we are here. Places like the Kai Temple exist around the world. We do more than harbor orphan beings. We protect the balance on this side of the gate as the Elite does on the other side. The people of the temples work with you to maintain that balance."

"So, all of Penumbra and all of Earth are depending on me to not fuck things up, even though I don't have access to the knowledge that would help me navigate all this."

"Pretty much." Her shoulders lifted with a small laugh. "Funny how the spirits choose to do things, isn't it?"

"Great." Jamila clapped her hands. "This couldn't be any easier, could it?"

"What do we need to do?" I rolled my eyes. Jamila spoke as if she was the one responsible for solving a centuries old mess before it tore the realms apart.

"I cannot tell you that. You are the Elite. It is your decisions that will lead us forward." Acai answered. "I believe the High Spirit thinks you see things like no other. Don't observe things from the perspective of those who are around you or those who came before you. Focus on the matter at hand from your own eyes."

"I feel so lost right now." I dropped my head to look at the newly repaired ceiling.

"Good." Acai left the window to sit next to me.

"How can that be good?" I found her eyes. Aged with wonder and wisdom. I missed her, and in that moment, it weighed heavier on my heart than it had before.

"It is when we feel lost we get the most creative." She smiled. "You want to find yourself? You better get moving."

"I need a moment alone with Acai," I announced, and without a word, Ali and Jamila gave us the privacy I requested.

"How can I help you, child?" She sipped the tea she had offered none of us.

"Zodiac." I looked her in the eye. "You knew, didn't you? All this time."

"Yes." Of course she knew. The woman was a psychic. She never confirmed my suspicion, but how else could she be privy to so much that was unspoken?

"Why didn't you tell me he was my father?" I spoke in low tones, still trying to protect the secret I wasn't sure I was ready to face.

"That wasn't my place." She answered.

"How can I ever forgive him?" My vision blurred as I spoke the question that I'd asked myself countless times before. I wanted to, but I didn't think I had it in me to move past everything he'd kept from me.

"What do you need to forgive him for?" Acai sat next to me, still holding her cup.

"He lied to me." I looked her in the eye.

"When did he do that?" She asked and sipped the tea.

"He never told me he was my father." I huffed. "He kept that secret from me."

"He never told you he wasn't either." She sipped her tea again. "Did you ever ask?"

"No, but I—" I stumbled to explain myself.

"A better question. Did Zodiac ever tell you anything about your father, either good or bad?" She asked and again sipped from her cup.

"No, I guess not." I thought back and couldn't remember one time Zodiac spoke of my father in any direct terms. "He only ever spoke of my mother."

"Because he didn't want to lie to you, but he needed to protect you. And not only you, but he also needed to protect her."

"Her?" I raised a brow. "Who else could he have wanted to protect?"

"Your mother." She tapped my knee. "Not everything is about you, child. I know that may be hard to believe with the weight of the world on your shoulders."

"Why would he need to protect her?" I frowned.

"Your birth is special for more than just how you turned out." She placed the cup on the seat next to her and took my hand in hers. "Your existence alone is something that shouldn't have been possible, simply because of who your mother was."

"Who was she?"

"A shade."

"That can't be." The word hung between us.

"It is true. Your mother was a shade. But somehow fell in love with your father and sparked a forbidden love affair that resulted in your life." She shook her shoulders, excited to spill tea that wasn't from her cup. "Now that's a story I'd love to read. How the two of them got together, I'd love to know. Had anyone found out, it would have meant trouble for not only you, but your mother and your father."

"The Elitesman." I sighed with understanding.

"Yes, it was why he left. Zodiac felt terrible about breaking his code. But he loved your mother, and he loved you. He walked away from the life he built for himself so he could protect you all. Telling you, a talkative little girl, that he was your father would have raised suspicion."

"Well, I feel like shit now." I chewed my lip and pulled my hands from hers.

"Why is that?" She asked and returned to her cup.

"With every secret revealed to me, I grew more and more angry with him. I blamed him for so much and never stopped to see it from his side." I admitted. "Hell, I didn't care about his side of it. Just that I was hurt, and lost, and afraid and the one person I would turn to when I felt like that, I couldn't. Because he was the one who caused it."

"Sounds like there may be a lesson in that. But don't invalidate your own feelings while trying to understand his. You have every right to be upset. This is your life, and you should have been able to decide for yourself." Acai calmed my growing angst. "Parents often forget what it was like to be a child. Now that you are an adult, speak with your father, make amends, and move forward. There is a lot ahead of you and you won't be able to face it alone."

"I'll need him by my side."

"Yes, although with this amazing new armor, I don't think you need him that much." Acai complimented my attire.

"It is nice, isn't it?" I beamed and stood up to turn so she could see the full armor. "I forget I'm wearing it. It's amazing how they do that. It's like a second skin!"

"Well, strut your stuff, girl. If only a second skin looked that good on this old body." Acai stood and posed like she was a mannequin in a storefront. Our brief laughter echoed in the surrounding room, only to be cut off when Jamila ran into the room.

"We have to go now." Her face was red and serious.

"What's going on?" I turned to her. "What happened?"

"It's Zodiac. He's hurt."

CHAPTER 28

IT DISAPPOINTED ACAI THAT WE HAD TO CUT OUR VISIT short, but Jamila's news left us no choice. She had little information, only that Zodiac was hurt, and we needed to get back to Phaedrial as quickly as possible. I hadn't seen him since our encounter in the shadows, so of course my mind immediately wondered if his injuries were my fault.

He might have been looking for me, chasing me down in the night, and hurt himself in the process. I could only hope that it wasn't life threatening.

As we landed outside the gateway to Penumbra, the sounds of wolves howling rang out just before a massive fur covered body jumped from its hiding spot behind the trees. It landed on the back of one of the Elitesmen, who fell to his knees but flipped the wolf forward. It slid, hitting its back on a large boulder.

The beast whimpered as it struggled to return to its feet.

"Fuck, we need to move before the rest of them get

here." I stepped to the portal to speak the words to take us to Penumbra.

"The rest of them?" Ali asked. "There are more?"

"Yeah, wolves run in packs, you know." After reciting the spell, the gate opened, and we quickly jumped through. Just as it closed, we saw the wolves approaching.

"What the hell was that about?" Jamila questioned as the gate sealed and we lost sight of the threatening pack.

"I may have had a run in with one of their mates before." I shrugged, calling my wings to emerge. "No big deal."

"You make enemies everywhere you go, don't you?" Ali laughed as she wrapped her arms around the Elitesman who'd become her official carrier. Neither seemed too bothered by the arrangement.

"Apparently." I winked and called my wings to show.

Traveling to Phaedrial with wings was another experience entirely. Though we were in a hurry, I still couldn't ignore the beauty of Penumbra. There were many things that trouble the world and Penumbra had more than its share of issues to be fixed, but it was also pure magic. Everything from the ground we walked on to the trees we flew above had a life like no other. As my wings carried me forward, I became overwhelmed with the sense of responsibility to protect my new home.

There was no time to waste. As soon as we landed at the castle, we ran to find Zodiac. Rose waited by the door for me and pointed me toward the healers. They were magical beings who were descendants of some of the oldest spell workers in Penumbra. Their kind had nearly gone extinct until they fostered an alliance with the Phoenix.

The healers were voiceless beings who we called Sykals. We had no other name for them. As long as we protected them, they healed our wounds. Sykals were so rare that those who remained in Penumbra lived in the Elite's castle.

I stepped inside the room to lay my eyes for the first time on the Sykals, and my heart stopped. The books had done them no justice. They were ghostly figures that looked like a rainbow haze. Never touching the ground, they floated about the room as they worked their magic. Their movement caused a constant static noise in the air and if you touched them without their permission, an intense electric pulse would shock you.

"What the hell happened?" Jamila asked for a report from the guard who remained in the room with Zodiac.

"We don't know. They found him dumped out on the front steps like this." she answered. "We're not even sure how he got there. No one saw him fly in and we've watched the skies closely since you left for Kai Temple."

"Those lacerations, I know them." Ali cringed as she watched the Sykal work.

"You do?" I stepped forward to get a closer view.

"Yes." Ali pointed to the openings that spread across Zodiac's arms and chest.

"What is it?" I focused on getting answers and not the dread about how I wouldn't be able to talk to him about everything if he died.

"The Sorceress," she winced. "That is her work. She uses dark magic that eats away at the flesh."

"Are you sure?" Jamila turned Ali from the view of the Sykal. "You've seen this before?"

"He must have gone there to fix things for me." I shook my head and turned my back to the table where he lay. "That's why he wasn't here."

"She did this to him?" Jamila asked for confirmation again. "Ali, are you sure about that?"

"They're nasty people." Ali nodded. "A sorceress will do whatever it takes to get what she wants. This one, she is mean. I've seen her in action before."

"How?" Jamila asked with more urgency. "When have you been around this woman?"

"Need I remind you who my sister was?" Ali lifted her shoulders. "Kenya got mixed up with a lot of shifty people over the years. I wish I could say the sorceress was the worst of them."

"I need to fix this." I moved turned back to the table, but Jamila grabbed my arm, stopping me.

"How do you plan to fix this, Elsfaer? You can't stand against a sorceress." Jamila nodded to the door for us to leave the healers alone.

"I don't know what I'm going to do." We stood in the hall outside the doors and heard a small groan from Zodiac. I winced at the sound. "This is my fault. I can't just let him suffer and not try to fix this. You said it yourself. She won't stop until she gets what she wants."

"Yes, but we don't know what she wants," Ali pointed out. "Hell, she may not even know what she wants, Elsfaer."

"Can we agree to wait until Zodiac is awake?" Jamila pleaded with me to take a logical route with my response to the situation. "We can speak to him about all this and deal with it then. I don't think it's wise for you to go running in there again without a plan."

"Yeah, okay, maybe you're right," I caved. I wanted to find the Sorceress and make her pay, but they were right. If I had listened to them the first time, Zodiac wouldn't have gotten hurt trying to fix my mistake.

"Thank you," Jamila sighed. "I need to rest, and so do you. I'll make sure they notify you as soon as he is awake. Okay?"

"Okay." I looked back at the door and thought about returning to the room with Zodiac to rest.

"Make sure she rests, please." Jamila looked at Ali, who agreed with her.

"I will." Ali placed her hand on my arm. "Elsfaer, come on."

Ali did as Jamila asked. She ushered me back to my room and forced me to get into the bed. Considering the lack of sleep I got before our trip to Kai Temple, my body welcomed the warm hug of the mattress. Ali stayed with me until I fell asleep, then went to her new bedroom.

Jamila set her up with sleeping quarters in the castle, now that she was officially a part of my team. Besides, I wouldn't have been able to rest if they left her outside the castle walls where the Dark Phoenixes could get to her.

I slept until Rose awakened me with a gentle tap on my shoulder.

"Elsfaer," she whispered my name.

"Yes?" I rolled over and blinked until my vision cleared.

"Zodiac is awake," she said with a small smile. "He is asking for you."

"Where is he?" I sat up and reached for my robe.

"He's back in his chambers now." Rose answered. "They just moved him there."

"Thank you."

I dressed quickly and headed straight for Zodiac's room.

"Zodiac?" I knocked on the door and waited for his response. After a minute, he called out for me to enter.

"Elsfaer, I thought you would be resting now." He smiled as I stepped around the corner. "I hope they didn't wake you."

"Yes, I was." I closed the door behind me. "And I told them to wake me when you were up. I just wanted to check in on you and see that you were alright."

"I'm fine, as usual." He sat in his bed; chest wrapped in bandages covering the wounds we'd seen before. "I'm a little banged up, but I will be okay."

"Why did you go there?" I crossed the room so I could stand by his bedside. "Ali said the Sorceress did this to you."

"Doing my job, protecting the Elite." He groaned again as he adjusted himself on the bed. "It's my position, after all."

"The Elite," there it was. I was the Elite, nothing more.

"And my daughter." He added, contradicting my thought.

"I am, aren't I?" I looked into his eyes. "I'm your daughter."

"Yes, you are." he nodded. "Feels good to admit it to you now."

"I wish I'd known." I gently lowered my weight on the edge of the bed as not to aggravate his wounds. "It would have been nice to interact with you as my father and not just my trainer."

"So do I."

"My mother, she was—"

"Shh," he lifted a finger to his lips. "Some things don't need to be spoken, Elsfaer."

"Oh, right." I took a deep breath. Of course, we still couldn't talk about her. We couldn't allow anyone to find out about who she was.

"We did our best. We didn't expect you, didn't even know it was possible. But you happened, and we were thrilled and yet terrified all at the same time." Zodiac explained what happened. "Neither of us knew what it meant, and then you were born. This special little being that took our breath away. What happened between us happened because it was meant to be. You were meant for this world and we knew you would do amazing things. But knowing how special you were terrified us. All we could think about was what the world would do if anyone found out about you. The biggest risk I ever took was leaving Penumbra with you."

"How did you manage it? All these years, balancing this life and that one?" I wanted to know more. "I mean, keeping her a secret and then me. How did you keep it together?"

"I found people I could trust, like Jamila." he smiled. "There aren't many friends as loyal as her."

"She knows?" I looked back at the door as if the woman would come marching through the doorway. "Everything?"

"Yes, she figured it out the moment she looked into your eyes." He laughed. "Even as an infant, you had my eyes. They've changed over the years, as you became more yourself and as the magic spread over your body."

"Did she know about my mom?" I asked.

"Yes," he nodded. "She warned me against it, then told me to be safe."

"Sounds like her."

"She is amazing." He smiled. "We've been through so much together over the years. Even before you were born. Your mother was happy to know that she would be a part of your life. I only wish I had pushed for her to be more present."

"Are you going to be okay?" I asked, as a deep breath brought pain to his face.

"Yes, I've had uglier battle wounds than this one." he grunted. "You need to focus on the matter at hand. You have a city full of to protect, and time is running out."

"How am I supposed to do that when my commander is out of commission?" I placed my hand on his leg. "I'm worried, Zodiac. There is so much at stake."

"I've given that post to Jamila, awaiting your approval, of course." He nodded. "Temporarily, of course. I will act as a consultant until I am healed again. That's about as much as I could get her to agree with."

"I think that makes sense." Jamila was the smart choice. I hadn't had time to become acquainted with any of the other elitesmen. I didn't yet know who I could trust, and clearly there were some traitors in our midst.

"Jamila told me about your problem." Zodiac steered to conversation to my disconnection from the other Elites.

"Oh, right, that." I stood from the bed and moved towards the window. There was a small candle lit. It was a sign to the others that he was okay. If it went out, they would know he'd died. I stared at the flame, wondering how I would feel if it no longer burned. "I wish that for once something about all this would go as it should. But I guess my existence alone isn't exactly the status quo. I'm just so afraid of not being able to do this, of not being able to protect our people and save the balance of Penumbra."

"You can do this. With or without that connection. You're smart and brave, and you've always been able to find solutions where others see none." Zodiac encouraged me.

"I hope you're right," I returned to him. "I have to make another address tomorrow. One that I don't think everyone is going to like."

"Why is that?" He leaned back against the pillows.

"It's time for Phaedrial to come together." I spoke. "Not just the Red Flames and the Blue Flames, but all of us."

"I agree with you." he nodded. "It's long overdue."

"You do?" I smiled because it meant a lot that he agreed with me.

"Absolutely." He chuckled, then frowned at the pain it

caused him. "You're going to have a difficult time convincing Kiara of that."

"Kiara, and a lot of the others, too." I nodded. "I already told them what I think we need to do and I could see there were some who were resisting to my idea."

"Well, that's the power of the Elite. Fostering unity and paving the way for our people. Even if it means knocking other people off their pedestals."

"Yeah, right?" I headed for the door. "I'll leave you alone. You need more rest, and I need to do some planning."

"Elsfaer," he called after me.

"Yes,"

"I'm proud of you, how you've handled all of this. Even when I wished you would have done things my way. I'm so proud of the woman and the leader you're becoming."

"Thanks." I paused with my hand on the doorknob. "Dad."

I didn't look back to see it, but I could feel the smile spread across his face.

CHAPTER 29

WE SPENT THE NEXT TWO DAYS PLANNING AND convincing the reluctant members of the council to at least hear my plans to begin the healing of our people. After deliberating with Jamila and consulting with Zodiac, I'd come up with a three-phase strategy to address the problems. The first and most difficult would be to convince the people to eliminate the divide.

I took the time to walk through the city, and really see what was there. The segregation was far more significant than they described to me. They marked every establishment with either a Red Flame, a Blue Flame, or a smoke signal. I learned the signs meant it was safest for those who the sign represented, but they assured me the signs didn't specifically mean that others couldn't enter.

How long would it be, however, before those signs meant the spaces were not safe if they didn't belong to you? How long before the Red Flames and the Blue Flames turned on each other like they so clearly had the

Flameless? There were fewer than ten prominently displayed smoke signals in the city's center.

Outside of the inner city, they separated the homes. The Blue Flames to the west, Red Flames to the east, and the Flameless were the furthest from the city center. Though they had no wings to carry them, yet they had the furthest to travel to get the things they required.

After my assessment, it was time to address the people, and not just the council members, but the population of Phaedrial. They were just as much to blame as the ones who led them. They accepted the separation readily. How many ever stood up to call out the issues they faced? How many sat by silently in the privilege of their Blue Flames, unmotivated to speak because they benefited from the inequities?

I stood outside the auditorium, the same one where they'd rejected me for having no fire, the same one where I told them we had to heal. People filed in and as I watched them from my place behind the curtain, I felt justified in what I had to say. The Red Flames took to the right, the blue to the left. The Flameless weren't represented.

Kiara took to the podium as the crowd quieted and the lights came up. The cameras turned on, broadcasting the space to everyone who couldn't be there, and she introduced me.

As I walked out from behind the curtain, they still met me with indifference, but there was something new there. Respect. I took the stage and not one person spoke. There were no boos or murmurs. They waited for me to speak. That was progress.

"Thank you all for being here," I started. "My last address to the people was not the first I wanted to make, but it was necessary. Not only was it necessary, but the events also brought light to some issues that our people are facing. Issues that we need to address. That is the reason I call you here today. Not just the leaders, but the people of Phaedrial. It is time to recognize the problems and come together for the greater good or perish." I paused, waiting for my words to sink in before continuing with my message.

"Blue flames and Red Flames once were one and there is no reason they shouldn't be now. I walked through the city, I flew across the lands, and what I saw was division. You've branded buildings with symbols that stand as territorial markings. You've isolated one another and made it so that not all feel welcome in their home. The tension bleeds out on the streets. Since when are we better than our own brothers and sisters simply because of how our flames present?"

"Now is the time for change. We will not continue like this. And that change calls not only for the reuniting of those of us with flames but also those without."

With those words, the doors to the auditorium opened. And as the Flameless filed into the room, the people erupted in hushed discussions.

"What are they doing here?" Kiara questioned, giving a focal voice to the concerns of the people.

"We are all one, including those who don't fit your standards of perfection," I answered her directly and then returned to my address of the people. "The Flameless, as you call them, and I really don't find that name fitting, are

269

just as impacted by the struggles of our people as anyone else here. If Milo leads the Dark Phoenixes here and they win, all of us are at stake. Not just those who burn red or blue. The flameless are trained fighters and will be respected. If we want to win against the Dark Phoenixes, we need to be on the same side. One side, united."

"I will not stand with them," a tall man on the side of the Blue Flames stood and announced his disapproval.

"Neither will I," a short woman on the side of the Red Flame did the same. I was sure she was the same who disapproved of me before.

"Look, we came here because you invited us," Aero, the large man who'd become my reluctant friend and best student during my time with the Flameless, spoke. "Elsfaer, we respect you, and we believe in your vision. We also want to save Kaden, but we don't have to stand here for this."

He gave the signal to the others, who turned and headed for the door. They had every right to want to leave. Here they were, hoping to bring peace and aid to the Phaedrial and yet their bravery in coming was being mocked.

"Wait!" I called out to them. "I can't believe that you all are so set in your divisions that you would risk your own lives to protect it. The Flameless are here. They will fight with us and you all will suck it up and get over yourselves. Either you get past indifferences or the balance of Penumbra will suffer. Humans of Earth will find out about this world and just like their ancestors did those of us who dared to be seen on Earth, they will come here and hunt us down! Is that what you want? How will you justify your actions, then?"

"We will stand together," Councilman Knight, Kaden's father, was the third to announce his alliance with me. "We have lived like this for far too long. If we continue this, I fear what it will bring for our people."

"You would stand with her?" Gyes, the grumpy councilmen whose name I'd had recently committed to memory, questioned his fellow councilman.

"I will," Councilman Knight answered. "And if you could look beyond your biases, you would do the same. Like me, you have lost family and friends because of the divide, have you not?"

"Yes, I have." Gyes groaned. "My daughter." I would learn later that Gyes' daughter, Jane, was also flameless. She unfortunately was captured by the Dark Phoenixes and lost her life because she refused to betray her father.

"It's time to change this. How many more will we lose? How many will we turn our backs on?" Councilman Knight looked at the other councilmen.

"No more." Gyes stood from his seat.

"No more." Victor, his companion and apparent yes-man, also stood. I'd prefer my council had more spine, but at that moment I took what I could get.

With his approval, the energy in the room changed. The people of Phaedrial respected his opinion. And as they settled, he nodded to me. They would cooperate even if they didn't agree with my vision. This would be a temporary concord.

"Thank you," I expressed my gratitude for their backing. "We need to prepare. We are going to battle people. Not just for us, for all of Penumbra."

"What do we do?" Kiara challenged me. "You bring everyone here, present us an impressive speech, but do you actually have a course of action?"

"Of course, I do. We train, we fight, and we get ready to take this battle to them. I am not about to wait until they decide to come to us." I turned to the people. "Make no mistake. There are traitors among us. They will know we are coming. They will expect us. But we will be smarter, stronger, and bring more force than they could ever imagine. They don't think we can do this. They doubt our ability to come together and do what is right. We will prove them wrong, work together, and protect our home."

"How do we know where to go?" Gyes asked. "We've never located where they are."

"We have someone here to help us with that." Jamila took her cue and stepped out on the stage with a cuffed Jackson in tow. "I think this one here is ready to talk."

"You." I turned from the podium to address the still bruised man.

"I'm sorry, I was just doing my job," he pleaded with me. "I had no choice."

"What are you doing here?" Kiara asked him with an odd familiarity.

"They kicked me out." he dropped his head. "They thought I was helping the Elite. Didn't understand how she got away after how they left us."

"Cut the cameras." I instructed, and Kiara cued the

men to comply. As the lights powered down, I turned back to Jackson. "How could they think that?"

"All I know is that they are coming for you." He looked out into the crowd. "They're coming for all of you. And they're using Kaden as bait."

"Is he still alive?" Councilman Knight asked what I couldn't.

"I don't know for sure, but I imagine he is. It's the way Milo operates. He'll have him up somewhere for you to find. Try to get in your head."

"When?" Jamila asked, and he said nothing. "When are they going to strike?"

"Answer the question," I demanded.

"Four days," he admitted, and the worried whispers rushed through the room.

"That gives us three days to get our shit together and take the fight to them." Councilman Knight stepped up. "That's more than enough time. Our men are ready."

"Okay, turn the cameras back on."

"Are you sure?" Kiara asked.

"Yes." I nodded and took my place again at the podium. When the lights turned on, I spoke. "People of Phaedrial, the time now is to prepare. The Elitesmen will deliver important information to you all, information that we cannot broadcast over the airwaves. Remember, now is the time for us to come together, to stand and fight together. Not just for the Phoenix, not just for Phaedrial, but for all of Penumbra!"

The audience clapped as I finished my speech and the cameras shut off for the final time. I left the stage with Jamila and Councilman Knight. Kiara attempted to follow us, but the guards cut her off as instructed by Jamila.

"I don't trust that woman," Jamila smirked as Kiara struggled with the blockade.

"Me neither. Did you see the way she looked at Jackson? It was like she recognized him. Had she seen him before?" I marched forward.

"No," Jamila confirmed. "He's been in lock up since we found him. The only ones to see him were the guards and myself when I questioned him."

"I caught that as well," the councilman confirmed. "What are your orders, Elite?"

"Ali will work with the Flameless to get them ready for battle. Jamila will work with the elitesman and any other fighters we can get. We do not tell anyone when we plan to strike until we are ready to move. There are clearly people in this city that cannot be trusted. They're expecting us in three days, we move in two. Are there any questions?"

"Not a one," the Councilman saluted me before taking off down the hall.

His action caught me off guard. The salute, a single fist across the chest, was a customary show of respect in Phaedrial, but not one person had done it, not even Zodiac.

"Good, let's get to it." Jamila, taking a note from the Councilman, also saluted me before she led four other guards in the opposite direction.

"You were amazing out there." Ali tapped my shoulder. She'd remained silent until the others left. "Just in case no one else tells you."

"Thanks, it felt good." I pointed to the group that had just left us. "You saw that, right? They saluted me. That's never happened before."

"The council has accepted you." Ali stepped to my side. "Everyone always talks about the High Spirit choosing the Elite, but really, it's the Councilmen and the people. Zodiac and Jamila, though they are on your side, are driven by tradition just as much as everyone else. With the council's acknowledgement of your right as the Elite, comes a different level of respect and acceptance. It's a good thing."

"Its crazy to think how much there is still I don't understand here." I placed my hand on her shoulder, ignoring her no touching in public rule. "I'm glad you're here."

"I bet," she whispered. "So, do you think we stand a chance?"

"Yes, I do, if everyone cooperates." I answered honestly. Our survival depended on the people coming together.

"What do you think the odds of that happening are?" Ali asked.

"I choose not to comment on that at this time." I winked at her.

"Oh, how diplomatic of you!" She laughed and led the way back to my chambers.

CHAPTER 30

IT WASN'T LONG BEFORE THE REPORTS OF TENSIONS CAME. The Flameless were cooperative, even the Red Flames were playing their part, but the Blue Flames, the ones who'd spent most of their lives pampered, were the troubled children. The smallest in numbers, but the greatest pain in my ass.

"Zodiac." I entered his room, where he sat by the open window.

"Elsfaer, it's good to see you." Zodiac looked from the window at me. He held a small cup in his hands.

"How are you feeling?" I crossed the room and could smell the mint coming from his cup. "It's good to see you out of bed."

"I'm healing. A few more days and I'll be as good as new." He gestured to the seat directly across from him. "Join me."

"I'm glad to hear that," I accepted his offer.

"What brings you to visit me?" He gestured to the kettle to offer me some tea, but I refused.

"The Blue Flames are becoming a problem." I informed him. "While everyone else work together, they act as if they are too good to do the work. And of course, everyone else is upset about it."

"Ah, I expected as much. They never were ones to want to do hard labor." He chuckled. "I'm surprised they even pretended to be willing to get their hands dirty."

"Their lives are on the line just as much as anyone. How could they be so against doing what is necessary to save their own asses?" I huffed. "It makes no sense, Zodiac."

"Put yourself in their shoes. They've been spoon-fed everything since they were born. Most of them are the offspring of Blue Flames and therefore were treated special simply because of who their parents were, and when they got their own flames, that special treatment only multiplied. They have the nicest jobs, the easiest existences of anyone in Phaedrial. And now here you come, asking them to fight, get dirty, and even risk injury."

"Well, they're going to have to get over themselves." I tapped the table with my fingers. "No one wants to fight. We all want to sit back and relax, but this has to be done."

"You're going to have to inspire them to want to." Zodiac advised, as he adjusted the black robe he wore. I could see the bandages still covering his chest.

"So, what you're saying is that you won't give me the answer." I slouched in my chair.

"No, I won't." He smiled as the door opened and a

small man entered with a tray carrying a fresh tea set up. "But I will offer you a cup of tea. I bet you could use something to ease your mind."

"You're right," I accepted his second offer and spent another hour talking to Zodiac, mostly about logistics and how he shouldn't join us in battle. He didn't want to sit on the sidelines, but he was already hurt, and we couldn't risk worsening his injuries.

After two more meetings with Councilman Knight and Jamila, a strategic session with the Elitesman, and a flight around Phaedrial to check on the progress our people were making, I returned to my room. We had one more day until we needed to strike, and we'd yet to inform the people when we were leaving.

Jamila would be the one to issue the order. That is all they knew. The Elitesmen would light up the sky and our people would move. The issue was the Flameless. How would we transport them? As much as I was against the modern technology that was brought to Phaedrial, it was going to come in handy. An invention that mixed technology and magic would carry them at a rate only minutes slower than we could fly.

I spent the last hour of my day looking over the schematics of the contraption and staring at the prototypes in awe. We had to protect our world. If the human realm found out what we were capable of, it would mean a war between the worlds. After a quick tour of the vehicle that could carry three hundred passengers, I returned to my chambers.

I intended to do more research and spend my night in bed with my notes, as I had the nights prior. Just as I picked up the stack of papers I'd left on the desk, I felt the shift in the air. I was no longer alone.

At first, I ignored it, hoped that whoever my unexpected visitor was would announce themselves, but they didn't. Instead, they watched me from the shadows, lingering in my space until I couldn't avoid addressing them anymore.

"Who are you?" I waited, but received no response. "I know you're there. Either you answer me now or this becomes a problematic visit for both of us." I lifted my hand, calling white flames to dance across my flesh.

"I'm a friend," the whispered voice called out from the darkest corner of the room just opposite the door.

"A friend who just sneaks in my room in the middle of the night?" I question. "A friend who remains hidden in the shadows, too afraid to show their face. What kind of friend is that?"

"A friend who is here to tell you that your mother is in trouble." The curvy woman stepped forward; her form was still hazy as she moved. She was a shade, never settled. Her body looked like static.

"My mother?" I stood from my seat. "You know my mother?"

"Yes, the one no one is supposed to know you have." She took another step forward, bringing her form to a constant state. She looked at me with piercing gray eyes. Dark hair fell around her full face as she addressed me. "I shouldn't be here, but I couldn't let her do this without your knowing about it."

"What happened?" I put the pages in my hand back on the table. "What did she do?"

JESSICA CAGE

"She went to make a deal to save your soul." The shade announced.

"The Sorceress." Of course, she would try to make a deal. Zodiac had done the same. With everything going on, I never considered that she would.

"Yes, and now her life is on the line."

"But Zodiac," I turned to her.

"Failed," she sucked her teeth. "He gave a valiant effort, but it wasn't enough."

"You were there?" I tilted my head. "How do you know?"

"Yes," she exhaled. "That's our job, in the shadows, always watching. If only your mother had accepted that, we wouldn't be in this mess. Again."

"I can't let her suffer for my mistake." I shook my head. "How can I help?"

"She is suffering because of her own mistakes, not yours." the woman corrected me.

"You think having me was a mistake?" I asked, offended by her statement.

"No, but I think her decision to hide you was. I think lying to you for years and not teaching you everything you should have known was an even bigger one. If they had done right by you, you wouldn't have been foolish enough to make such a deal with a sorceress."

"What is your name?" I asked of the shadowed woman. I still didn't trust that she was there with good intentions, and I needed to learn as much about her as I could. If nothing else, I could go to Zodiac with a name and find out if she was being truthful.

"Olivia." she answered as I turned to grab my jacket from the chair where it rested.

"Olivia, it's nice to meet you." I pulled the jacket on and turned, hoping to question her further, but she was gone.

"Your mother needs you; this may be your only chance." Her voice called out to me from the shadows before I felt her presence melt away.

I stood in the dark room, the only light from the lamp on my desk, and contemplated the message given to me. Should I trust her? Would I be walking into a trap? I returned to the desk where the papers waited for me and found something that hadn't been before. A small emerald box.

I picked up the container and examined it. Intricate etchings covered the surface and shimmered under the light. I'd never seen the symbols before, but the longer I held the box in my hands, the more attached I felt to it.

"*Open it,*" the shadowed voice, the echo I'd heard so many times before instructed, and I did as told.

The release of the latch emitted a small hiss, followed by green smoke that escaped the box and filled my nostrils. As I inhaled the vapor, my vision blurred. When it cleared, I looked through eyes that were not my own.

I could smell the rain, feel the moisture on my skin and even taste the seasons changing. The small wails of a baby sounded off and my heart swelled with love and something else, pain.

"Are you sure you want to do this?" His voice was the same, youthful, less colored by experience, but I recognized it. When I turned, he stood there with a lot more hair and fewer wrinkles around his eyes.

"Yes, it is the right thing to do." The voice was not mine, but the words crossed my lips. "We have to protect her; we must do what is right."

I turned, picking up a bundle, a child wrapped tightly, hidden from the world. Cradling the baby in my arms, I removed the covering from her face and there she was, wide eyes, and face covered in tattoos of light. She was me.

"We can find another way to do this." Zodiac, my father, spoke in a pleading tone.

"Maybe, but none as safe as this." I felt the moisture leave my eyes and saw the tear that dropped on the baby's forehead. "I love her so much."

"She loves you, too," Zodiac reached out, and I kissed the child's forehead before handing her over to him.

"Keep her safe, always."

"I promise." He smiled, eyes full of pride and love.

My head flooded with images, flashes of a life I didn't live. A woman fighting a war that wasn't her own. Tears on a pillow that belonged to a child she would never hold again. A friend, curvy and strong, holding her while she expressed her anger and hurt over the child she couldn't be with. It continued with a dizzying effect until I stood again with Zodiac. Only this time in a dark field cast in shadows.

"Thank you for coming. I know I said I wouldn't come here again, and I meant that when I said it." His deep voice filled the night air as he spoke into the darkness. "But she is at risk."

"I know." It spoke softly and its tone was full of sorrow. "I tried to help her. I tried to stop her from making that promise, but she wouldn't listen to me."

"You were there when it happened?" Zodiac asked.

"Of course I was. I've been with her since she stepped foot in Penumbra." The voice returned as if it were obviously their position. "I've been watching over her, trying to keep her safe without interfering. How could you let this happen?"

"This is not my fault." Zodiac defended himself. "I've done everything you asked me to do and more."

"Your job was to protect her. You were supposed to keep her safe from this." The voice spoke, this time with a tinge of anger. "And yet here she is in the middle of chaos and you stand here and say it's not your fault?"

"There will come a time when she has to learn to protect herself. We both knew this. I've done everything I can to prepare her." Zodiac huffed. "She is the Elite now. I can't watch over every movement she makes. Not anymore."

"If the sorceress gets what she wants, Elsfaer won't be able to protect herself, or anyone else, for that matter." The voice spoke, but this time I hear movement in the shadows. Whoever this was, they were getting antsy. "We have to do more."

"I won't let that happen." Zodiac proclaimed. "She will get through this. She has to."

"She is our daughter, Zodiac. We have to protect her."

"I'm your what?" Behind Zodiac, I saw me. It was me from just a few days prior and with her shock at seeing the daughter she'd given away, my head flashed again. Again, I was taken from that moment to another.

Standing outside a familiar door, the dreaded doorway to the shack of the Sorceress. I looked over my shoulder at the friend who watched me with sorrow filled eyes, Olivia. And stepped into the darkness.

Tears soaked my face when I returned to myself. The emerald box still clutched in my hands. There was no doubt about what I had to do.

I wrote two notes for Rose to deliver. One to Jamila and the other to Ali. They would have to move ahead with the plans without me. I instructed when to leave Phaedrial and promised that I would meet them in the Darkest Forest. I didn't tell them of my plans to save my mother. Jamila would scold me; Ali would want to come with me. Neither option was one I wanted to deal with.

Finding my companion for my trip proved difficult to do while letting no one know my intentions. They had given the human wo

CHAPTER 31

man safe housing in the Flameless territories. It was the safest place for her in our world. She could work and blend in with the others.

When I knocked on her door, she was happy to see me, of course, until I told her what I wanted. While she was hesitant to return to the Odious, she agreed. I promised her that all I needed was her guidance to the Sorceress, nothing more. I would bring her back to Phaedrial safely when we were done.

When we touched down outside the House of Trades I walked ahead of her. She called after me to stop me.

"I don't mean to be disrespectful, but do you know where you're going?" She frowned. "Isn't that why I'm here?"

"I vaguely remember the way." I shrugged.

"Well, I suggest you follow me. We don't have time for your vague memory of this place getting us lost."

"Lead the way." I gestured for her to show me the way.

"Hide yourself." She looked over her shoulder at the market entrance. "This is a busy hour for the market. I don't know a lot about this world, but you're an elite. From what I've gathered, if the wrong person sees you in there, it may cause more trouble than it's worth."

"You're right." I touched the medallion, focusing my intention and activating it to only allow Denise to see me. "This will cloak me. Only you can see me now."

"Are you sure?" She pointed to an approaching figure to the east of us.

"Let's try it out." I smiled and ran over to the ogre. I danced around him, waving my hands in his face, but my foolishness garnered no reaction.

"I guess it works." Denise wore a nervous smile as she approached me. "We better get moving."

Walking through the market at night was a unique experience, one that I wasn't sure that I would ever have. During the day, it was vacant. Only a few people moved through the space and those who were there were weak. They were the ones meant to watch over the spots for their masters. The marketplace awarded the best deals to those who secured the prime locations. Often there were fights over someone sneaking in early to still another seller's position.

Desperate people came there hoping to get their hands on something rare, something powerful, something that could change their lives. And on the other side of those deals were evil, greedy, and deceitful beings who would use their victim's anguish in their favor.

As much as I wanted to intervene and tell those people to go back to their homes and find a better way, I couldn't. Denise was right. As an Elite I didn't belong inside the marketplace. What happened there was legal on those grounds, regardless of how I felt about it. As long as the dirty dealings didn't happen outside the market's barriers, I had no say in it. I kept my head focused on my goals. I had to find the Sorceress, find my mother, and stop her from ruining her life to fix my mistake.

Before long we were standing outside the Sorceress' shack. The same rancid smells of death and decay filled my nostrils. I lowered the cloak at Denise's suggestion. To appear there hidden from view would only make the Sorceress think I was up to no good. I didn't want to make matters worse.

"This is where we part," Denise announced, stepping no further than she had the first time.

"Thank you for doing this." I shook her hand. "I really appreciate it."

"Of course, just make sure you come out of there alive." She scanned the surrounding trees. "I'd like to make it back home in one piece."

Just as I had my first time visiting the home of the Sorceress, I left Denise waiting for me. This time, instead of an edging fear, I felt anger. Anger that I was there again, trying to undo what dark magic created. The door to the beaten down home opened slowly as I approached, giving me access to the inside.

I stepped across the barrier to find myself somewhere entirely new. Instead of the shadowed space covered in dust and cobwebs, it transported me to the lavish interior of what looked like a room in a palace.

Bright rays of sunshine filled the room, coming from a source obviously not from the Odious. I did not know where I was, but I knew for sure that I was no longer in Penumbra. There wasn't the feel of magic floating in the air, light or dark.

The room was large, and the walls draped in sheer fabrics layered in a variety of colors. The air smelled of flowers and pastries. This was not the home of the dark sorceress. At least it wasn't the one they initially introduced me to. I kept in mind that time was of the essence and went to work trying to find my mother. Examining the space, I found two doors. To the left of me was a black door, and to the right, a gold one.

The gold door called to me. It beckoned me to enter and find out what wonders waited on the other side. The black door left me with a sickening feeling in my stomach, and every time I considered nearing it, I felt as though I would vomit. As much as I wanted to go to the gold door, I knew I had to choose black.

I walked to the door, holding back bile, and pressed my hand on the doorknob. The cool metal was like ice to the touch. The chill traveled from my palm up into my shoulder as I twisted the knob and pushed the heavy barrier. On the other side of the door was something much more expected of the dark sorceress.

Chains hung from the ceiling in the space void of color. The only source of light came from the candles that lined the walls. The smell of decay, death, and torture returned as the door closed behind me.

In the center of the room stood a cage, and in the cage was a shadowed figure.

"Mom?" I approached the enclosure. "Are you okay?"

"Elsfaer? What are you doing here?" Her voice was the whispered echo that I'd heard so many times before. It was her guiding me, pushing me forward. "No, don't!"

Her warning came too late because my hands grabbed the bars of the cage. The moment I made contact; my palms seared with red hot fire. I pulled back to see blisters already forming.

"Fuck!" I cried out.

"Are you okay?" Her figure remained shadowed, unstable between the bars.

"Yes, I'll be fine." I cradled my hands to my chest. "How are we going to get you out of here?"

"Elsfaer—"

"Mom, we gotta get you out of here before she gets back." I cut her off because I knew what she wanted to say. She wanted me to leave her there.

"You can't." She spoke. "I cannot leave here."

"What do you mean I can't? That's why I'm here. You're not going to stay here and suffer for my mistakes." I looked around the room for any way I could get her out. "I don't know how, but I'll make this right on my own. Just let me help you get out of here."

"You don't understand," her voice shook with sadness. "I can't get out of here. What's done is done."

"What do you mean?" I looked back at her, squinting to see her clearly. "What did you do?"

"She made a deal," the wicked voice of the sorceress called out, echoed by her hollow cackles. In the back corner of the room, she materialized out of gray smoke. "Everyone who comes to me comes with a deal in mind. And this still was one I could not turn down."

"What did you promise her?" I asked my mother, who was still a blur of herself.

"The only thing that would get you off the hook. The only thing I had to offer," my mother answered me.

"And that was?"

"Oh, young naïve Elite. You have so much to learn," the sorceress said from her corner. "In exchange for your virtue, your mother promised me her life."

"Why would you do that?" I asked my mother. "How could you make that deal?"

"I had to; I couldn't let you be indebted to her." My mother responded. "Your life is much more important."

"It's not worth it. Nothing is worth this." I turned to the Sorceress. "Don't do this. I'll grant you the favor, just don't do this!"

"As tempting as that is," she pondered, "a promise of a favor is only as good as the one who grants it. As it is, I still have a long way to go before your favor would ever do me any good. And as much as I hate to admit it, this girl is getting old. Her life, however," she pointed to my mother, "the essence of a shade. Now that's a power I can use now!"

"I won't let you do this!" I called my flames to me. If she wanted a fight, I would give her one.

"You don't want to do this, trust me!" the sorceress

warned me. "I'm playing nice now, but you attack me in my home and I'll get real mean."

"You're out of your mind if you think I'm going to stand aside and do nothing."

"Baby girl, I'm just so glad to see you once. Even if you save me from this, my life is over. They know now. The other shades. They know what I've done." My mother spoke, pulling my attention from the sorceress, who looked less than impressed by my bravado. "I've broken so many rules. There's only one punishment fitting. I don't want you fighting now, not to save a life that is already on the chopping block. I'd rather my last moments be the way I decide. Let me do this. Let me protect you the way I couldn't all those years ago."

"I don't want to let you go. I only just found you, I've never even," I choked up. "There is so much that I want to say to you. I don't even know what you look like. How can I possibly walk away from you now?"

"I know, but you have to. You have greater responsibilities now. There are people who need you. They depend on you."

The door to the cage swung open. I turned my head to the sorceress, who'd calmed down. She waved her hand with indifference at the touching moment that played out in front of her.

"Go ahead, have your moment. But she stays here." The same smoke she appeared in wrapped around her and she vanished.

My mother's shadowed figure exited the cage, and when she materialized my heart broke, healed, and broke again. It was like looking in a mirror, one that had a fuller figure, but she and I were the same. Her eyes were mine, her skin tone, even the slight tilt of her lips.

"Elsfaer," she smiled and pulled me into her arms.

I never thought that I would feel my mother's embrace, but I had imagined it more times than I could remember. It was exactly like I dreamed it would be. In that moment, when she placed her lips against my forehead, I felt it all. Decades of missed hugs, kisses, and love.

"You're just as beautiful as I knew you'd be," she spoke, and her voice was no longer the shadowed echo but the warmth of love. "All these years I wonder what you look like, but I never saw you. I made Zodiac promise me not even a picture because it would be too difficult not to come find you if I ever saw your face."

"That must have been hard for you," I spoke into her chest.

"It was, and it still is. I wish we had the time together. There are so many lessons that I wanted to teach you, so many secrets to share. But at this moment, all I want you to know is that I love you and I'm so proud of the woman you've become. There are great things in store for you, Elsfaer, amazing wonders like nothing you can imagine. And I'll be there watching over you."

"How am I supposed to say goodbye to you when I don't even know your name?" It was another secret kept from me. One that I hadn't found the strength to ask to be revealed.

"My name is Xenira. And please don't be mad at your father for never telling you." She kissed my forehead again. "It was another thing that I asked him not to do. If you ever knew my name, because of who you were, and who you were meant to be, simply speaking my name would have been too much. As an elite you can call any shade to you and as my child, I feared you would have been able to do the same even before you were called to rise. Had I ever heard you call out for me, there was no way I would have been able to deny you."

"Xenira," I spoke my mother's name for the first time as tears flooded my eyes. "Why did everything have to be so complicated? Why couldn't we have had a simple life? How is it fair that I will never really know you?"

"I've learned that the best lives, and the most amazing journeys, they all come with complications. The complexities make it worthwhile. Trust me, an uncomplicated life is a life that's not worth living."

"I don't want to let you go. I don't want to walk away from here knowing I will never see you again."

"And I don't want you to go either. But we both know that you have to. I know that there are things developing out there, things that you have to stop from happening and you can't do that from here. It's time for you to leave, my beautiful daughter." She paused, lowering her voice. "Olivia has something for you. I cannot be there, but it will help you with what you need to do."

"What?" I asked but she pressed her finger against my lips.

"Just find her when you leave here." She looked me in the eye until I nodded in understanding.

"I love you." I wrapped my arms around her, hugging her as tightly as I could, trying to make up for all the years lost in one moment.

"I love you more than you could ever know. Now,

baby girl, it's time for you to go." She released me from her arms and pointed to the exit.

The door was ten times heavier to open on my way out. And when they closed behind me, I was standing back in the woods, under the cast of shadows, outside the Sorceress's shack where Denise waited for me.

"How did it go?" Denise stepped out of hiding; she took cover behind an overgrown hedge that left scratches on her arms. Better that than to be snatched up by something more sinister.

"Not as great as I hoped." I looked back at the structure, hoping it would collapse. "I couldn't save her."

"Will you be okay?" she asked, but I could tell by her eyes she knew I wouldn't be.

"Yes, I will," I lied. "I have no other choice."

"What now?" she asked.

I looked to the sky where the light of the sun struggled to get through the darkness of the Odious. The palm of my hand tingled, and I looked just in time to see the last of the branding fade. It was done. I was no longer indebted to the Sorceress.

"Now I try to save my people and make sure that my mother didn't give her life up for nothing."

CHAPTER 32

We flew back to Phaedrial where I dropped Denise off at her new home before heading to the castle. As I flew over the city, I saw the people leaving. The last were the Flameless, carried by the motor-powered vehicles towards the Odious. I would join them soon, but there was something I needed to do first.

I landed through the open window where the flame of the candle still flickered. Zodiac sat just beyond the candle, looking out over the city.

"I have to find her," I announced as my feet touched the floor.

"Who are you trying to find?" He looked up from the cup of tea cradled in his hands.

"The shade that came to me." I recoiled my wings.

"Of course, she came to you." He stood from his chair. "I should have expected this. And you went?"

"I did, and I'm not surprised that you know." I

laughed. "You know everything, don't you? Is Acai the psychic, or are you?"

"I'm not psychic. Olivia visited me last night as well." He placed the cup on the table. "She told me her intentions, and I asked her not to do that."

"You wanted to keep another secret from me? Have there not been enough or do you miss having things to hold for me?"

"It's not that, Elsfaer." He stopped me before I could really go off on him. "I wanted to be the one to let you know. Your mother came to me and told me her intentions. I didn't know that she shared it with Olivia as well."

"We can talk about your obsession with deciding things for me later, but I need to find Olivia now."

"Elsfaer, do you want to talk about what happened to your mother?" He asked.

"What's there to talk about? She sacrificed herself for me." My heart pounded in my chest as I paced the floor. "I couldn't save her, Zodiac. I wanted, but I wasn't strong enough. And she didn't want me to. She promised her life to the sorceress in exchange for my freedom from a promise I never should have made. That is something I would have to live with for the rest of my life knowing that had I just been less hardheaded, she might still be here. I may have had time to get to know her."

"Elsfaer." He started, then wore an expression of conflict. "I'm not sure what to say now."

"I know. You don't have to say it. I fucked up."

"That's not what I was going to say." He stood. "I'm so sorry."

"What?" That wasn't what I expected from him. I

thought he would tell me that my focus should have been on leading the people. That I should have headed to the Odious instead of returning to look for shades.

"You just lost your mother." He opened his arms to me, inviting a hug. "That is a difficult thing, no matter the complexities of the relationship."

"Yeah, well, I lost her a long time ago." I refused his embrace.

"You—" His arms dropped to his side.

"Just tell me how to find her, please." I reminded him of my original goal, which wasn't to bond over the loss of my mother.

"Yes, of course." he nodded.

"I don't have a lot of time here. My mom said Olivia has something that can help me." I told him.

"You can call her." he returned to his seat.

"I can call her? Just like that?" I frowned. "Any other instructions?"

"I'm not sure how it works. All I know is as an elite, you can call an audience with any shade."

"How am I supposed to figure that out?"

"Don't make it more complicated than it needs to be." Zodiac spoke calmly. "Simply call to her. Ask for her audience."

"Right, okay." I took a deep breath, not sure what was really required, and thought of the curvy woman who appeared in my room. "Olivia, I need you."

We waited, searching the corners for the woman to appear. Minutes passed and just as I'd given up on it working, I felt the presence join us.

"You called?" She appeared as a shadow briefly before her image stabilized.

"Yes, it actually worked." I celebrated. "Olivia, thank you for coming."

"How can I help you?" she waved at Zodiac who returned the gesture but said nothing.

"My mother, she said that you have something that I'll need." I explained my reasoning.

"Yes." she gave a slight smile.

"A weapon?" I asked, because I wasn't sure.

"A powerful one, yes." Olivia reached her hand into the shadowed corner behind her and pulled out a long black case.

"What is this?" I took the case from her.

"This is your mother's most prized possession, outside of you, of course." She winked as I released the clasps that kept the case securely closed. "It's the jade sword. Handed down through your family for generations. Your mother was the last to receive it and with her, it left the family. Because of our rules, she could never return it to them, but now that you're here, and she has so clearly broken every rule or the shades, well, it can return to its rightful place."

"This is beautiful." I ran my hand along the length of the sword. They reinforced the green mineral formed into the blade with something more powerful. Fenium. "Wait, how is it that this has fenium? I didn't know that shades had access to this material."

"Zodiac? You want to explain that one?" She stepped aside.

"Elsfaer, there is more that makes you special besides

the obvious list. They fortified the blade that way because of its original owner." Zodiac stood again, straightened his shoulders and lifted his head with pride as he continued. "You are the descendant of Sileish, the former Phoenix Elite."

"I am?" I looked between the two of them. "Is this true?"

"It's in your bloodline. Making you more unique than ever because you're the first Phoenix Elite to have any familial relationship with another. When we say that something destined you for this, we mean it. The High Spirit chose you and I believe everything that has happened was orchestrated, not by us, but by a greater power to make sure that to put you in the position you are in now."

"This blade is amazing and so powerful." I stared at the weapon and wondered about the hands that crafted it. From the sleek form of the blade to the kamular wrapped hilt, it was a product of patience and skill.

"Beautiful and deadly, just like its owner." Olivia touched my hand. "Look, I know your mother. I have for a long time. She knew what she was doing when she went in there. It was a sacrifice meant to save your life. And that is what she did."

"If I hadn't been so dumb." I dropped my head.

"Well, you wouldn't have been if your mother had listened to me," Olivia grumbled.

"What?" I closed the case, sealing the sword inside again.

"I told her it was a bad idea to send you away. And when they told me how they were keeping you in the dark on so much, it felt so wrong, but what was I to say? I was just the friend of the shade who broke all the rules. And she swore me to secrecy. They should have told you everything." She looked at Zodiac. "They should have prepared you for this life."

"That's a drum I've beat to death." I laid the case on the table next to Zodiac's cup. "What's done is done. I need to move on."

"If it's any consolation and I know it won't be much, your mother really loved you. She sacrificed so much and put her own life on the line to have you." Olivia offered the comforting words. "If any of the shades ever found out about you, it would have meant her life. But the love she felt for you was without measure."

"I just wish I could have known her, and that I knew more about her now. I met her and moments later she was gone." The tear fell from my eye as I spoke.

"Well, now you have me. And I'm not much, but I swear she used me as a diary most days." Olivia winked. "I believe that the vow of best friend secrecy is okay with me telling the daughter her mother's deepest secrets. I mean, I'm basically your aunt." The full smile stretched across her face.

"My aunt, the shade." I chuckled and wiped my face.

"Yeah. I like the sound of that." She put her hands on her wide hips and puffed her chest out like a superhero.

"Wait, you're not supposed to have family ties." I said. "Won't you get in trouble if the others find out?"

"I think I can make an exception for the Elite." She nodded. "Besides, I didn't give birth to you."

"Well, aunt, the shade, I have to go off to war." I picked

up the open case again and looked down at the sword it held.

"First week as the Elite and already a war?" She frowned. "How is that possible?"

"The Dark Phoenixes are out there, and they are planning to take down the light. We have to protect the balance." I turned to the window. "Our people are already on their way."

"Would you like a little help in that department?" Olivia offered.

"You would help?" I glanced at Zodiac who silently watched our interaction.

"I'm a shade. That's kind of my job. Defending and protecting the balance of our world. If they mess things up over here, they mess things up everywhere."

"Well then, yes, we could use your help." I frowned. "Why didn't you know about this before?"

"We've had some issues lately, but we can talk about that at another time. Just call me when you're ready and I'll bring some friends along." She touched the case with her fingertips, then looked to wink at Zodiac before she dematerialized and left us alone.

I lifted the blade from its cradle. Inside was also a holster, which I strapped around my waist before securing the blade within the sheathe.

"I better get going," I announced as I headed for the window.

"I'm going with you." Zodiac stood behind me and headed for his closet. When he emerged, he was strapping on his own armor.

"What do you think you're doing? You're hurt!"

"I'm fine. I've rested and what minor aches I still have won't hold me back." He secured his sword around his waist. "Besides, there is work to be done. Asses to kick and a world to save."

"Are you sure?" I watched him carefully secure the protective gear around his chest and wince.

"Elsfaer, I have sworn to protect my people, but above that, I have sworn to protect my daughter. I will do that."

"Thank you." I nodded.

"For what?" He asked.

"Being here, for always being here. I can't say that I'm past it all, but I'm working to understand it."

"Thank you for trying to." Zodiac pulled me into a hug, and this time, I didn't resist him. "Now, let's go win this battle."

CHAPTER 33

WE FLEW SIDE BY SIDE ACROSS THE TERRITORIES FROM THE Alluring to the Odious until we reached the Darkest Forest where the Dark Phoenixes were. Jackson had all but given us their battle plans. Jamila's interrogation was effective enough to uncover that Milo was Jackson's father. It was why he wanted so much to impress the leader. Jackson was the Flameless son of the leader of the Dark Phoenixes. Talk about the pressure to perform!

We made it to the edge of the forest, on the opposite side of Kaden's hideout, just as Jamila moved the Red Flames into position for the first attack. Councilmen Knight stood with the Blue Flames watching the others move ahead.

"Councilman," I addressed him, folding my wings into my back.

"Elite, you made it." He turned and shook Zodiac's hand. "Didn't expect to see you here."

"A minor wound can't keep me down." Zodiac puffed out his chest. "They make Elitesmen tougher than that."

"What's the status?" I examined the members of the Blue Flames who lined up behind Councilman Knight.

"Everything's going according to plan. The Flameless are in place at the territory's edge. They will only engage when necessary." He pointed to the sky where the Red Flames lifted above the trees. "You're just in time for the first wave."

"What about the Blue Flames?" I scanned the group that remained grounded.

"It's been a challenge, but I doubt we will have many issues for now." The councilman spoke with surety. "They will fight. We've all lost someone to this. They are no different."

"And what about after this battle?" Zodiac asked.

"That's a problem for the Elite to deal with." He lowered his voice. "Look, I can't speak about what they'll do when this is over, but through a lot of persuading, and a few well-placed threats, I've convinced them to work with us. They're the last wave for a reason."

"That'll have to do, I guess." I wished I were more confident in the pampered group, but time wasn't on our side. There was only so much that we could accomplish in a few days. I had to trust that the councilman could keep them to their word.

"It will all work out. Now, I have to get to my post." He saluted before leaving me alone with Zodiac.

"You know I was happy when he first saluted me," I spoke to Zodiac, "but now I'm second guessing that."

"It's still a good thing," Zodiac placed his hand on my shoulder. "In time, they will all get on board."

"I'm glad you're so sure. I need to find Jamila." Looking at the sky, I didn't see her. "Will you stay here?"

"Stay here?"

"I know you want to help, but you're still hurting. I only want you to get involved in this fight when it's absolutely necessary."

"You're asking me to stay on the sidelines?" Zodiac chuckled.

"No, not really." I pointed to the group ahead of us. "I mean, I'm sure Councilman Knight could use some help with the Blue Flames."

"Right, of course. Well, you're the Elite," he placed his fist over his chest. "I'll fight only if it's crucial to our side."

"Thank you." We exchanged the salute before I took off.

I reached the head of our group just as Jamila returned to the sky. Her face was a mask of worry.

"Jamila." I stopped next to her.

"You made it." She placed her fist over her chest. "Just in time."

"Of course." I looked down at the campgrounds. "What's going on? Why are the Flameless down there?"

"They aren't here." She searched the horizon. "We've searched everywhere."

"They aren't?"

She pointed to the ground where the Flameless searched the abandoned homes of our enemies. "Not a single one there. They knew we were coming. And from the looks of things, they recently left."

"How is this possible?"

"Someone must have given them the heads up. Someone who was with us just a few hours ago."

Familiar wailing of a beast I'd only heard once before interrupted our speculation and drew our attention back to the ground. It was the Kynuski. The beast broke through the tree line just south of the Flameless. The chains hanging from its tentacles evidence some had trapped it and released the monster just in time to spoil our plans. Jamila was right. Someone had betrayed us.

The massive tentacle wrapped around Aero's waist, lifted him into the air and slammed him back on the ground. The impact knocked him unconscious, leaving him defenseless against the monster as the others tried to defend against it.

As the Flameless fought on the ground, a siren sounded and suddenly we were surrounded. The ashen wings of the Dark Phoenixes rose around us. And leading their ranks was the person Jamila suspected, Kiara.

"That bitch," Jamila pointed to the traitor. "I knew she was sleeping with the enemy."

Kiara flashed a cocky smile before she signaled her men to strike.

"Can you handle this?" I looked down at the Kynuski, whose enormous mouth opened with intent to swallow its unconscious victim.

"Yes, do what you need to do." Jamila looked to the ground where the Flameless struggled.

I dropped to the ground to help the Flameless with the Kynuski. The thing was massive and just as ugly as Ali had described. Purplish skin with a sticky texture, large orange eyes, a mouth fitted with seven rows of teeth, and twelve tentacles fit with suction cups that made it impossible to escape.

As I dove to the ground, I lifted my sword above my head and aimed for the tentacle that captured Aero. My momentum aided the force, and the blade cut through the thick flesh. The monster cried out as its appendage hit the ground and the Aero, who'd he captured, rolled free.

It took a moment, but he regained consciousness and, with the help of another flameless, returned to his feet. With a quick nod, he thanked me before pulling out his own sword. Even after the blow he took, Aero was still ready to fight, and a few minutes later, he removed another arm. With the help of the Flameless, those who I helped train, we made quick work of the Kynuski. But before we could celebrate, the howling alarm of the gnarlies sounded.

The heavy footfalls pounded, the beasts weren't far off, and the Flameless prepared for impact, creating a strong wall against the enemy. Above my head, Kiara and Jamila locked in battle, the traitor speaker fought well, but from what I could see, Jamila would have no problem taking her down.

I hesitated, trying to determine where they needed me most, but as I thought to rejoin the battle in the sky, I saw the calvary, the Blue Flames lifted behind the blackened wings and surrounded our adversaries. With Jamila and Councilman Knight leading them, they would be okay.

I returned to the Flameless, moving to join the line of defense. Something heavy slammed against the ground behind me. I couldn't make out the lump of fabric at first.

But the bound figure moved, and I saw his bloodied face. *Kaden.*

I ran towards him, but before I could make it to his side, two arrows pierced the ground, forming a standing X between us. I looked up to find three Dark Phoenixes flying above me. Two with arrows and the third, I recognized from the image on the screens of the council room. The leader of the Dark Phoenixes and my greatest enemy, for all intents and purposes, Milo.

They poised the arrows for Kaden. The threat was obvious. If I tried to free him, they would kill him.

"The Elite is here!" Milo lowered to the ground. The tall man wore attire that made him look like the superheroes of Earth. Leather from head to toe, large shoulder pads and a cape that touched the ground. "How lovely of you to visit."

"I wouldn't exactly call this a visit." I retorted. He spoke as if I were an old friend coming over for tea.

"Well, whatever you call it, I'm happy you're here." He pointed at Kaden. "I know I'm not the only one."

"What do you want?" I asked.

"Nothing too complicated," he waved his hand. "Just your head on a platter. How motivating it would be for my men to see that."

"I'm sorry to have to disappoint you, but that won't be happening." I tightened my hold on my sword.

"Oh," he drew the blade from his side. "I think it might."

The Flameless still defended against the gnarlies, and the war still went on above our heads. This was something I'd have to face on my own. I waited, watching him carefully as he decided what his next move would be. A moment later, Milo charged me, his weapon ready for a kill, and our dance began.

I thought we would have a fair fight as our blades met. Milo was older, stronger, and a skilled fighter. He reminded me of Zodiac in the way he moved. The evil man was sure of his actions, and as hard as I looked for his tell, I couldn't find one. He had no discernable pattern to his actions, no favored side of his body.

Each time, our blades connected. I learned more about him. Though I couldn't find any weaknesses, I knew his strengths. He was powerful, but using his strength took a lot of space. If I could limit his movements, I could handicap him. I changed my course of direction, luring him between two of the tepees that were constructed as housing for the Dark Phoenixes.

In the small space, his strikes were weaker, and his motion hindered. He lifted his sword to strike me down, and I took the opportunity afforded to me. As his blade came down, I stepped to the right, and quickly slid between him and the wood fashioned structure. I pulled the cinquedea from my hip, the better choice for the close encounter, and sliced into his calf.

While his attire was fashionable, it wasn't functional. It left him vulnerable to attack. He fell forward and, as he did, I managed two quick stabs to the left side of his torso.

Milo rolled through the fall, and off behind the tepee to my right. I stalked him as he returned to the open space where the lifeless body parts of the Kynuski covered the ground.

I fixated on my goal; I hurt Milo. Blood leaked from his side and leg, and it gave me the perfect opportunity to take him out. I stalked his limping form, awaiting the chance to strike. It wouldn't be long.

The arrow whistled as it cut through the air before the meaty thud of the tip punctured his flesh. Kaden cried out from the shot. His pain was the exact distraction they hoped for. I turned from Milo for just a moment to find Kaden laying on the ground with the arrow sticking out of his side.

One moment of lost concentration, and the odds turned against me. Milo's fist connected with my cheek right beneath my eye, sending me stumbling backwards. Despite his injured leg and the open wound on his side, he came at me with force. I lifted my sword intending to defend myself but tripped when my foot landed on uneven ground and fell, losing hold of the hilt.

I scrambled to retrieve my weapon, but just as my fingers touched the handle, his foot kicked it away. I flipped to my back to meet the tip of his sword pointed in my face. When I reached to pull the cinquedea from its holster, he stepped on my hand, crushing my fingers beneath his uneven weight. I punched him in the leg where I'd cut him before. He screamed, then swung his sword, cutting my arm open. My armor had yet to be repaired from my fight with Kenya, and the opening gave him clean access to my flesh. When I cried out, he rejoiced.

"Isn't this just wonderful?" he placed his hand against his side where the blood still spilled. "Ending the life of the Elite, taking down an empire. It's a beautiful thing.

Don't be sad, with your death will come a great change, the betterment of our people. Phaedrial will return to its roots, to power, and magic. I will make our home true again, and when I'm done there, I'll take on the rest of this pathetic world."

"You want to destroy Penumbra?" I asked, horrified.

"Destroy it? Not at all. I want to fix it!" He pushed his blade closer to my face. "Look around, dear heart, there is much that is wrong with the world. The balance of power is uneven and has been for far too long. There is time for a new age. A new understanding of power. I will bring that new age in. I will usher in the rising of the Phoenix people. Penumbra will bow to us and thank us for saving it."

"You're delusional," I choked out, trying to keep my mind from the pain of my wounds.

"Perhaps," he laughed. "But that is of no concern to you. You won't be around to see any of it."

He lifted the blade, and despite my effort to reach my weapons, I couldn't. The jade sword was too far from my reach and with my hand still under his foot, I couldn't get the cinquedea. The best I could do was lift my already bleeding arm to defend myself.

Just as his sword was about to cut down, another entered its path. The loud clang of the two blades echoed over the sounds of battles waging on. Fire still lit the sky, while the Flameless took on the last of the monsters of the Darkest Forest. And Zodiac stood above me.

"Well, well, my brother. I thought I'd never see you again." Milo grunted as he leaned into his sword, trying to push Zodiac's blade into me.

"Looks like we're having a family reunion here." Zodiac lifted his sword, forcing Milo back. He stepped between us.

"Brother?" I reached for my sword.

"Unfortunately," Zodiac kept his eyes trained on Milo.

"Man, this is one messed up family." The weight of the sword felt uncomfortable in my hands, but I held it, ready to fight.

"Tell me about it!" Milo grinned and whistled. On cue, the men above us started shooting their arrows at us.

"I got it." My wings emerged, and I took the fight to the sky. I danced in the air while they shot their arrows, missing time and time again. The first one I took out with my blade, first knocking the arrow from her hands and then removing her wings. She fell to the ground as the other attacked.

Out of ammo, he chose an aerial fist fight, but I didn't have the time or patience to deal with him. I smack him with one of my wings before calling my fire into my hand. I threw a ball of fire into his chest, setting him ablaze. Engulfed by white flames, he hung in the air until there was nothing left of him but ash.

I looked to the ground just in time to see Zodiac as he took a nasty hit that cut into his side and, as Milo moved to finish the job, my vision turned red. I never burned as hot as I did at that moment. My wings were white, feverish light that blocked out everything around me. As my vision struggled, I saw a shadow moving, watching me closely, and then it was gone.

With every bit of force that I could muster, I clapped my wings, sending a blast so powerful it didn't just knock out Milo but everyone around us. The trees bent beneath the force of air. The firebirds, both light and dark, fell from the sky and the remaining gnarlies took off running.

I aimed my sword for Milo and dropped from the sky just as his dark wings unfolded from his back. The jade sword cut straight through his wing, leaving him with one that flapped wildly, trying to carry his weight. He reached to his back, howling from the pain.

I waited until he turned back to me. The sword was still in his hand, ready to fight, but losing his wing weakened him. Unable to accept his obvious defeat, Milo lifted his weapon and, with a desperate battle cry, he ran towards me.

I dropped beneath his blade, kicking him in the open wound, and dropped him to the ground. Before his knees contacted dirt, blood coated jade. With his head rolling across the ground, the sounds of battle continued.

It was naïve, but I assumed it would end there. Their leader taken out, they would stop their fight, but the Dark Phoenixes fought for more than Milo. He was the figurehead, someone to drive their agenda, nothing more. If I wanted this to end, I would have to send a message. I took to the sky where and looked down on the disaster.

"This ends now!" My voice amplified by the power that coursed through me, I called the attention of everyone on the ground.

"We are one people. A people of light!" I stared down at them, all struggling to look at me, hands covering their eyes. "Anyone who isn't on board with that will be dealt with. This isn't an option. The entire world of Penumbra depends on it!"

"I will not bow down to you!" I heard her voice before I saw her dark wings lift her above the tree line. Kiara held a long sword in her hand, prepared to fight. "You're an outsider! You don't get to decide what's right for our people!"

"I am the Elite, and it is the opinion of the High Spirit that I do." I corrected her.

"Well, it is *my* opinion that the High Spirit doesn't know what's best for us." She lifted her weapon, ready to attack, and her wings pushed her forward.

I didn't hesitate. If she wanted to stand as an example for the others, I wouldn't deny her the right. I folded my wings in front of me and opened them with such force that projectiles of fire lifted from my wings. They flew into her chest, setting her ablaze. Fire consumed her body before she turned to ash.

The sword she intended to use to end my life fell to the ground and with that, our battle ended.

Though they stopped fighting, I knew we still had a long way to go with the dark ones.

CHAPTER 34

I**T TOOK A WHILE TO CLEAN UP THE MESS THAT WE MADE IN** the Darkest Forest, but we would not leave the disaster area behind. There was still the matter of respecting the Odious and if anyone thought the phoenix people had stepped out of line, it would mean more battles that I wasn't ready to face.

Jamila and Councilman Knight worked together to gather the Blue flames, the Red flames, and the Flameless and directed them back to Phaedrial. I watched as two men carried Kaden back to the vehicle that would drive him home. With his injuries, it was too risky to fly him out.

"Are you okay?" The aged voice of my mentor and trainer asked.

"No, do you really think that I can be after all of this?" I looked at Zodiac who stayed behind the others to monitor me. He looked around and frowned at the pieces of the Kynuski's that littered the ground.

"No one ever really is after a battle, I guess." He kicked away a piece of thick flesh.

"Milo was your brother." I recalled the information. "I just killed my uncle. This was more than just a battle."

"Yes, you're right. It was." Zodiac agreed. "This was a turning point for everyone involved."

"What happened to him to make him turn and accept darkness the way he did?" I asked.

"Milo was like everyone else. He wanted to be special. And when his wings appeared they were red, not blue, like the coveted color everyone wants. He wasn't a powerful fighter and, honestly, there wasn't much else that made him stand out. That was like the last thing he thought would get him status in our world. And when it didn't, he broke down. I no longer knew the man I grew up with. He was no longer my brother, and he looked at me like I betrayed him."

"Why?" I picked up an arrow. "What did you do to him?"

"I did nothing to him. He was upset because I left. Not only was I an Elitesmen, but I walked away from it all for you."

"Did he know about me?"

"No, he didn't. By the time you came along, my brother was already showing signs of horrible doings. Even though he hadn't gone completely dark, I knew I couldn't trust him, not with something like this. It wouldn't have been safe for you."

"I'm sorry."

"Why are you apologizing to me?" Zodiac groaned and placed his hand against his side.

"You know I've been so angry with you about everything that you kept from me." I wiped the sweat from my forehead and sighed. "I wanted to hold on to the anger because I couldn't let go of the hurt I felt about not knowing my mother when I could have. And I didn't know you, not really, and being angry was easier. I've learned about a lot of lies Zodiac, I have, but I've also learned about everything that you gave up protecting me. Everything that you did to keep me safe. I don't know that I can ever forget what was done, but I forgive you."

"I'm glad that you do, Elsfaer." He looked around as the last of the fight with cleared away and grunted. "Maybe now we can move forward and get to know each other as father and daughter."

"I'd really like that." I stepped closer to him and put my arm around his waist in a half hug. He grunted when I touched his side. "I'm sorry."

"No, it's okay." He looked down at me. "This is nice."

We stayed there for another half hour. I needed time away from everything for a moment to breathe and reflect on everything that happened and Zodiac, though he was in pain, remained by my side. Later, we flew back to Phaedrial to be with the others. When I landed on the steps outside of the castle, my people were there. The Blue flames, the Red flames, and the Flameless stood around the castle steps and as my wings folded into my back, they cheered.

"This is amazing." Ali said as she stepped to my side.

"It really is. I think maybe I've actually done something right this time." I put my arm around her shoulder. "Are you okay?"

She nodded and smiled. "Of course, you did good. You're the badass elite."

"There's still so much to do," I looked at her.

"Well, you have us by your side," she looked over her shoulder at Jamila, Councilman Knight and Zodiac who stood behind us. "We're not going anywhere."

"You had us waiting and didn't even call us." Olivia stepped from the shadows. "Glad to see that you survived without us."

"Yeah, I'm sorry. In the heat of the battle, I just didn't think to call you." I apologized. "I hope I didn't cause you any trouble."

"Don't worry about it. You fought your first battle without the help of the shades. The other elites will hear about this and they will respect you more for it. But next time don't keep me on the sideline. I like a good fight." she winked at me.

"Thank you," I nodded at her, waved to the people who watched us, and then turn to face Councilman knight. "Where is he?"

"He's with the healers." he answered me. "I've just come from looking in on him."

"Is he gonna be okay?"

"Yes, I think so." he responded. "Most of his injuries look to be superficial."

"Good."

"Do you want me to take you to him?" Ali asked.

"Yes, please." I acknowledge Jamila, whispering my thanks for her help with everything, then followed Ali away from the crowd.

Ali waited outside the door as I entered the room

where Kaden was by himself. The healers were gone, bandages covered his wounds, and he slept. His shallow breaths were the only sound in the room.

I thought about leaving him alone to rest. I could have stood there and watch him, but somehow that fell inappropriate. Just as I turned to leave, he spoke.

"Where are you going?" His eyes opened and the corners of his lips lifted into a slight smile.

"You're awake." I stepped back toward him.

"Yeah. It's hard to sleep with people coming in and out of here." He looked at the door.

"Someone else was here?" I wondered who could have possibly been there and worried about his security.

"My father." He nodded.

"Oh. Right." I remembered then that his father said he'd just come from checking in on him. "How did that go?"

"Better than I could have imagined." He coughed. "It's almost like he loves me or something."

"Well, that is good." I smiled. "And how are you feeling? Are you okay?"

"No, I'm not okay, but I will be soon enough. I'm a tough bird with or without my wings."

"Yes, you are." I nodded. "I see where you get it from. Your dad is pretty tough, too."

"Did you come here to talk about my dad, or is there another reason you come to visit me?"

His question caught me off guard, and I hesitated to respond.

"I wanted to make sure you were alright." I finally spoke.

"Is at all?" He set up on the bed and winced from the pain of his injuries.

"You need to lie down." I huffed. "What's wrong with you men? Relax."

"What I need is for you to tell me why you really came here." He ignored my concern.

"I told you I just wanted to see that you were good." I admitted, then admitted more of how I felt. "Hated the idea of them doing anything to you because I knew I cared about you."

"You care about me?" He smirked.

"Yes, of course I do." I rolled my eyes. "But you knew that already."

He held his hand out to me, then I crossed the room to take it.

"I care about you, too. When I was there being tortured, I didn't think about my father. I didn't think about the other flameless. I thought about you." He caressed the back of my hand with his thumb. "They didn't have to tell me what they wanted. I knew why they had me there and I didn't want you to come, not if it meant that you got hurt. I tried to get out, don't get me wrong, but when I couldn't, I accepted losing my life if it meant keeping you safe. That was enough."

"How can you say that?" I shook my head. "How could you ever be okay with losing your life to save me?"

"The same way you care for me, Elsfaer, I care for you. Neither one of us planned for this, I know. Hell, I never thought I would even find love. But you walked into my life pretending not to have your fire and somehow reignited mine. And I know we have a lot to learn about each other and to say that I love you may feel heavy right now, but I'm not going anywhere."

"Is that a promise you're gonna keep to me, Kaden?"

"I make no promises I don't intend to keep." He leaned forward and kissed me.

When I left Kaden to rest, I returned to my room and looked out over the city. I told Rose that I wanted to be alone because it was necessary. She would make sure no one disturbed me. I took a quick shower to wash the battle from my skin and nursed my wounds. Sitting in the gigantic bed, beneath the warm comforter, I reflected on everything that I had lost and on everything I gained and for the first time; I understood the weight of it all. The High Spirit chose me to be the change that my people needed. And I wouldn't let them down.

EPILOGUE

IT HAD BEEN A YEAR SINCE MILO FELL BENEATH THE JADE sword. And while Phaedrial was healing, there was still a long way to go. On the anniversary of the date, I stood ready to announce the plans to cut ties with technology. While we wouldn't be able to eliminate it entirely, we could limit it. I expected some push back, but it was nothing I wasn't used to.

"They're ready for you." The deep voice spoke from the doorway.

"Thank you." I looked up to find Kaden leaning against the frame.

"My pleasure." He entered the small office, tucked behind the auditorium stage, and closed the door behind him.

"What are you doing?" I raised a brow as he crossed the room with a devious grin.

"Taking a moment to show my appreciation to our

Elite." He held his hand out, helping me from my seat, and pulled me into his arms.

"Appreciation?"

"You have done wonderful things in your first year, and I know you have so many more in store. We are not a healed society, but because of you, we are on our way. And I cannot express my full gratitude to you for doing that."

"There is still so much that needs to be done." I lifted my arms around his neck to complete the embrace.

"I'll be here, if you'll have me."

"Of course, I will." I lifted to my toes and pressed my lips against his for a quick kiss. "Now I have to go address our people."

"Of course," he released me, straightened his collar, and went to open the door for me.

Rose stood by the door with blush colored cheeks. She obviously overheard us. As always, she offered me a glass of water. I took a sip, refreshing my throat before my speech, and handed it back to her.

"I still think something is suspicious about her," Kayden pointed to her as she retreated.

"Stop it," I warned with a smile.

As they pulled the curtain back, I walked out onto the stage, where my trusted councilmen, Zodiac, Jamila, and Ali, sat waiting. I smiled as I passed them and headed for the podium.

The sound of the remaining electricity hummed as the cameras captured my image and sent it out on a live stream to the public.

"People of Phaedrial," I started. "There is work to be done, and together, we will continue to heal."

The End

THE RISE OF THE ELITES
COLLECTION

Reign of the White Phoenix

USA Today Bestselling Author Jessica Cage

House of the Blue Flame

Delizhia Jenkins

Order of the Shadow Dynasty

USA Today Bestselling Author Jennifer Laslie

Ascension of the Blood Throne

USA Today Bestselling Author Mikel Wilson

Trials of the Black Throne

E.M. Lacey

Fellowship of the Last Fallen

Kish Knight

Riseoftheelites.com

ABOUT THE AUTHOR

Jessica Cage is an International Award Winning, and USA Today Best Selling Author. Born and raised in Chicago, IL, writing has always been a passion for her. As a girl, Jessica enjoyed reading tales of fantasy and mystery, but she always hoped to find characters that looked like her. Those characters came few and far in between. When they did appear, they often played a minor role and were background figures. This is the inspiration for her writing today and the reason why she focuses on writing Characters of Color in Fantasy. Representation matters in all mediums and Jessica is determined to give the young girl who looks like her, a story full of characters that she can relate to.

You can also sign up for Jessica's general newsletter here:

https://www.jessicacage.com/nlsignup

Join Jessica Online: www.JessicaCage.com
Tiktok: https://www.tiktok.com/@jcageauthor

READ MORE OF JESSICA'S BOOKS

The Djinn Rebellion Series
The Siren Series
The High Arc Vampires Series
The Alphas Series
The Scorned by The Gods Series
No Love for the Wicked
Fairy Tales of the FYP

Made in the USA
Columbia, SC
11 April 2023

15148364R00185